BLACK CAT BLACK DOG

A JACK VALENTINE THRILLER

by the same author

THE SIRIUS CROSSING

THE DAY OF THE DEAD

JOHN CREED

BLACK CAT BLACK DOG

A JACK VALENTINE THRILLER

First published in 2006
by Faber and Faber Limited
3 Queen Square London WC1N 3AU
This paperback edition published in 2007

Typeset by Faber and Faber Limited
Printed and bound in England by Bookmarque Ltd, Croydon

A CIP record for this book
is available from the British Library

ISBN 978-0-571-22789-1

2 4 6 8 10 9 7 5 3 1

BLACK CAT BLACK DOG

He had lain there for more than four decades. Sunk in the ooze and cold and darkness of the north Irish Sea. The flesh had slipped away many years before, but the cold and the mud had preserved the bones. His clothing had rotted away as well, leaving only the metal buckle of his belt, the heavy clasp of his coat and the tarnished dog tag still clasped in the bony dead fingers, as he had clasped it in his dying moments, turning as he fell to see the ship that had already died, bodies strewn on its decks, the mate face down on a hatch cover, the captain lying out of the wheelhouse window, his fingers pointing downwards as if he was in the act of issuing a ghastly order to his crew of dead men.

The man's body lay in a shallow depression at the edge of the Beaufort Dyke – the deep channel between Ireland and Scotland – but it was not alone. In the darkness around it lay hundreds of metal canisters. Sometimes when a great storm swept the surface, or an ocean current surged through the deep, the canisters would stir and clank against each other as if the movement of the water granted them momentary life, and then they would cease and lie still again. This time it was different. Something had happened in the water above, and a great tremor shook the seabed, and the mud fell away a little so that the man's skull was exposed, the empty eye sockets staring upwards into the dark as if to bear witness to what had taken place.

There was a silence. A long silence, ominous in a place where all seems ominous. Then something fell from above. The seabed shuddered as tons of metal crashed into it, sending great clouds of silt upwards. The canisters on the seabed were flung upwards and swept along by the deep-sea current, but the impact was not enough to loose the dead man's grip on the dog tag. Not yet. Several days later there was another impact, a little closer, controlled this time, as a giant metal leg settled on the sea floor, scattering the remaining canisters. It was then that the dead man released his grip on the chain he had held for over forty years. As one of the canisters was propelled along the sea bed the corroded valve on top caught the chain of the dog tag and the chain looped around it and was caught in the valve mechanism. As it did so the dead man's hand seemed to open gently. As if he had been waiting for this moment. As if he knew the time had come to send out a summons, that the truth of his death and those of his crewmates would be known so that they could rest in peace.

ONE

It was a blustery October day, the last of the leaves falling from the wind-stunted trees around the cottage. The forecast was promising gales and I had spent the day at the small dock below the cottage making sure that my converted trawler, the *Castledawn*, was securely tied up, with the decks clear and her fenders in good order. I was looking forward to getting a fire lit and settling down for the evening with an Angus steak and a good bottle of Bordeaux. As I walked up to the cottage the wind rattled the fuchsia bushes that sheltered the path and I felt the first cold drops of rain and quickened my pace.

I closed the gate, locked it and crossed the small open area in front of the house – and then slowed. I didn't know what had alerted me, but it seemed that as my body slowed with age, the survival instinct quickened. I stopped just in front of the door and made myself think. If whoever was in the house meant harm, it would have been easier to waylay me on the path or down at the dock. I lifted a heavy stick from the stack of logs against the wall and pushed the door open.

It was dark inside, but not too dark to make out the shape of my neighbour sitting at the kitchen table. I didn't see that much of Jimmy Kerr, although he would keep an eye on the house when I was away, nipping away at my stock of Irish whiskey as a reward for his vigilance. But he wasn't given to letting himself in when I was at home. I saw the Redbreast bottle was open on the table in front of him. He didn't look round. I crossed the room to the table and looked down at him. He looked up at me. His eyes were wet. He had a letter in his hand. I sat down across the table from him. I lifted an empty glass from the draining board and poured myself a Redbreast. I thought about it, then I filled his glass.

'What is it?' I said as gently as I could. There was almost no light in the room, the gloom outside filling it in a way that, perversely, I liked. More than anything else, autumn gave me a sense of the natural order of things. It also seemed the right atmosphere for what I sensed in the room. Terrible regret, and the feeling someone gets when they near the end of their life, the feeling that they can no longer change the future, but that there might be time to put right a wrong done in the past.

Wordlessly he pushed the letter across the table to me. I read it in the half-light. It was from the State Solicitor's office in Belfast. It was to inform him that a set of dog tags had been washed up on the beach in County Antrim on 20 January. The dog tags belonged to Seaman Robert Kerr reported lost at sea, presumed dead, on 14 October 1952. There was an apology for the delay in contacting Jimmy. The letter went on to say that an inquest into the death of Seaman Kerr was to take place in Belfast Coroner's Court on 30 November.

'Your brother?' I asked. He nodded.

'His ship sank off the coast of Scotland in 1952. All hands lost. I never even got to the memorial service. I was in Kenya with the forces. The ma and da was dead by then. There was only the two of us.'

It occurred to me that I knew very little about my elderly neighbour, even though I saw him at least once a week when I was at home. He seemed to delight in leaning over my hedge and commenting on the likely fate of the vegetables in my small patch, pronouncing slow and prolonged demise on my crop of peas and potatoes and raspberries through various blights and mildews and pests. He was invariably right as well, although if I was away for more than a week at a time he would tidy the garden up with the hoe.

I knew that he had spent time in the services, then more years working in the peripheral tasks that passed for industry in marginal coastal areas: fishing, farming, grouse beating for rich Londoners. I knew that he was good with his hands and built models which were occasionally displayed in maritime heritage centres along the coast. But apart from that I knew nothing. I pulled my chair close to the table. I had a feeling I would learn more.

It was a long night of halting reminiscence. A simple enough childhood, though poor. Then his older brother going to war, serving on the Atlantic convoys, and a child's jealousy of what seemed like adventure, though we both knew that the experience of the convoys was bleak enough to freeze the soul, and Jimmy said that when Robert came home, he never spoke about it. The picture got a bit murky after that, I thought. The whiskey may have had something to do with it, but I didn't think so. It seemed that Jimmy had come home from Kenya on leave and that the two brothers had fought about something. Jimmy had gone back to Kenya without resolving the row, and then Robert had died at sea, so there was never a chance for them to make up. An old story. I probed gently to see if he would tell me what they fought about, but he was evasive and I let it go. I had the impression of the older brother as a principled but unforgiving man, and perhaps not aware of the way a younger brother can look up to an older man.

We finished off the bottle of Redbreast and started another. Jimmy was feeling the pace and things were getting incoherent. In the end he was mumbling, and I got him up from the table and helped him lie down on the sofa. I went into the bedroom to get a blanket for him, and by the time I came back he was snoring gently. I put the blanket over him and went back into the kitchen and poured myself a last Redbreast. He had asked me to go over to Belfast for the inquest. I thought it a simple enough request, and had agreed to it, although if I had known what was going to happen I would have taken the *Castledawn* out of the little harbour and sailed at top speed in the opposite direction. But as it happened the boat needed a little work done, which was usually carried out at Kilkeel on the County Down coast. It would be a last long trip before the winter, and a chance to catch up on old friends. And one part of me thought, slightly patronisingly, that the old man would be grateful for my support, and I felt the warm glow experienced by those dispensing charity at little cost to themselves. It was a sense of indulgence that I would pay for over and over again.

TWO

Four weeks later I found myself sitting in a small courtroom in Newcastle, County Down, the small resort town dominated by the imposing bulk of Slieve Donard. Outside, an autumn storm was pounding the small harbour, and a few late holidaymakers were battling their way down the promenade, but inside there was a sleepy, small-town feel to the proceedings. Lots of paper shuffling and people going to and fro. The coroner was a small man in his sixties with a relaxed manner, although I thought that the eyes behind the gold-framed glasses were piercing and shrewd. Jimmy sat beside me. He wasn't saying much, but he had the dog tag in his hands and he was turning it over and over. The novelty of an inquest after fifty years had drawn a reporter from the local paper, a girl of about nineteen with blonde hair pinned back and a serious face, and an air of impatience about her which suggested that she didn't want to spend the rest of her life reporting on inquests in dingy provincial courthouses.

There was one man there, however, who interested me. The one person in the courthouse who didn't look as if he belonged there. He was a man of average height with black hair greying at the temples, wearing a black pinstripe suit.

There was nothing exceptional about him, yet he projected the authority that only comes from being a member of one of the central pillars of the London Establishment, one of the quality law chambers for instance. The coroner had noticed him as well, and I could see him glancing down at the stranger as he organised his papers. Just as he was about to open proceedings, the pinstriped man got smoothly to his feet. He cleared his throat and everybody in the courtroom turned to look at him.

'Anthony Scribner QC, your honour,' he said, 'representing the Ministry of Defence.' He projected an air of stern yet fair authority, and seemed to create the impression that he was the real authority in the courtroom. If the coroner was troubled by this he didn't show it, but I could tell that he was thinking the same thing as I was. Whoever pinstripe was, he was certainly a big gun. So why was the MOD sending a big gun to a routine country inquest? It didn't take long to find out. The coroner cleared his throat gently and everyone turned back to the bench. In a low, modulated voice with a strong country accent, he opened the proceedings, announcing an inquest into 'the death of Robert Anthony Kerr, merchant seaman, of Glasgow in Scotland'.

'Excuse me, your honour . . .' Pinstripe was on his feet again. The coroner looked at him over the top of his glasses. It was a calm, considered look, a look which said that he knew that Scribner would have a very good reason for interrupting his opening remarks, and that he looked forward with great interest to hearing it.

'I apologise for interrupting your honour,' Scribner said, in a tone which suggested only very mild regret.

'Not at all, Mr Scribner,' the coroner said. 'Please proceed.'

'The Ministry of Defence has instructed me to seek an adjournment in this matter.'

'I see, Mr Scribner. And what manner of an adjournment is sought by the Ministry?'

'An indefinite adjournment, your honour.' The coroner removed his glasses and looked at them almost absentmindedly. He turned them over in his hands and put them back on his nose. Somehow the process seemed to ratchet up the tension level in the courtroom until it was at coiled spring level.

'And why does the Ministry consider an indefinite adjournment necessary,' the coroner said, 'considering that the relatives of the deceased have waited over fifty years to learn of his fate, and to have some proper closure?'

'The Ministry has the most compelling of reasons for this request,' Pinstripe said. There was an undertone of impatience in his voice. I thought the impatience was a mistake.

'Are we permitted to know these reasons?' the coroner asked. 'An indefinite adjournment is rather an extreme measure.'

'Regrettably the Ministry is unable to state its reasons for this course of action, although they are of course compelling,' Scribner said, an icy tone entering his voice now.

'Fair enough,' the coroner said, 'but this court has a duty to discharge, both to society and to the deceased, and I do not think that an indefinite postponement answers that responsibility. I will grant a three-month stay.'

'The Ministry of Defence is accustomed to . . .' Scribner said, a definite threat in his tone this time.

'. . . Two months,' the coroner said calmly. Scribner opened his mouth to speak and then shut it again. He rearranged the pens on the desk in front of him. When he spoke again, his voice was urbane, if a snake can be said to be urbane.

'Thank you, your honour,' he said silkily. 'I apologise if any inconvenience has been caused to this court.'

'Not at all,' the coroner said, smiling vaguely, 'not at all.'

'What's happening?' Jimmy whispered, looking bewildered.

'Something quite strange,' I said. 'Something quite strange indeed.'

And the strangeness didn't end there. Jimmy followed me out to the small lobby of the courthouse and went outside for a smoke. As I waited for him the young reporter came out of the courtroom and made a beeline for me.

'Were you the man with Mr Kerr?' she demanded.

'I was sitting beside him. Yes?'

'Where is he?' she said in a slightly accusing manner, as if I was guilty of secreting Jimmy somewhere out of her reach.

'He's having a smoke, as far as I know,' I said.

'Oh,' she said, 'my boss wants me to talk to him, get an interview, ask him about his brother, how he felt.'

'I'm afraid you might in fact be wasting your time, young lady.' The voice interrupting her was dry and precise. I looked around. The lawyer Scribner was standing beside me.

'Why would that be?' I asked, deciding to speak on the girl's behalf.

'Because a D notice has just been issued regarding the proceedings here today.'

'And why would the humble proceedings here today attract the notice of the D notice committee?' I asked.

'Excuse me,' the girl said, 'excuse me!' Her face had reddened and her fists were clenched. 'Don't you two *dare* talk over my head! What is a D notice?'

'A D notice is a cosy little arrangement whereby the press colludes in allowing the government to cover up things that might harm it. It's one of the many ways a government keeps its people in the dark,' I explained, helpfully I thought.

'It is a voluntary mechanism whereby the media assists the government in matters of grave national security. Unfortunately in this case it means that you cannot publish any account of these proceedings, or any statement relating to it,' Scribner said smoothly, with a pleasant if somewhat patronising smile on his face.

'Keeping the poor suckers in the dark,' I added.

'Shut up,' the girl said abruptly. I shut up.

'What is it about this case that is so special?' she said to Scribner. She was fishing in her handbag for a small tape recorder and there were two bright red spots on her cheeks. I knew what she was thinking. She had stumbled on something big, a story that had her passage to Fleet Street written all over it. Scribner smiled. Then he leaned over so that his mouth was close to her ear. He began to whisper. It seemed to go on for ten or twelve seconds and he was still smiling when he had finished, but the girl's face had turned white and she looked close to tears. Scribner turned and walked away.

'Are you all right?' I asked. She turned to me. There was a haggard look on her face. She murmured something faintly and turned and broke into a trot which ended when the door of the ladies crashed shut behind her. I wondered what had led a suave London QC to behave like a Mafia lawyer, and considered following him to see if I could find out a little more. But before I had a chance the door opened and a woman rushed in. She was in her early thirties, dark-haired with expressive hazel eyes and the faintly harassed air of a professional woman with too much on her plate. I envisaged a busy career, balancing children and work, too much to do and too little time. When I glanced down at her hand there was no wedding ring, but I thought I could detect a faint lightening of the skin, which suggested that there had been one there. It's surprising how long it takes for that particular mark to fade.

'Is it over?' she asked breathlessly.

'Hardly started,' I said. 'It's been adjourned.'

'Good,' she said. I raised an eyebrow.

'I didn't mean good like that,' she explained. 'I meant good because I was going to have to ask for an adjournment.'

'Why is that?' She gave me a cool look.

'Have you seen Mr Kerr by any chance?' she asked. I pointed towards the door. Jimmy was coming back in.

'Mr Kerr?' She went over to him. I followed.

'My name is Donna McNeill,' she said. 'I'm a forensic pathologist working at the Royal Hospital. Could I have a word?' She looked questioningly at me as I joined Jimmy.

'It's all right,' Jimmy said, 'he's a friend of mine. What do you want to talk to me about?'

'It's a little complicated,' she said, a slight hesitation in her voice. 'Maybe if we . . .'

'There's a pub around the corner,' I said.

We went outside. It was raining now, and there was a fine spray coming off the tops of the waves. The sea was grey and angry, and even the bravest of day-trippers was inside. I looked across at the promenade, narrowing my eyes against the rain and wind. I could see someone standing in one of the little shelters. I couldn't make out the figure clearly but it looked very much like Scribner, now wearing a raincoat.

'Go on round to the bar,' I said. 'I just want to check something.' Jimmy looked as if he was about to object to being left alone with this unknown woman, but I put my hand in his back and propelled him towards the pub.

'Go on,' I said. 'I'll only be a minute.'

I watched them out of sight, then I started across the street, cursing when a passing car ran through a drain and soaked me to my knees. Crossing the promenade at a diagonal, I made for the pier, creating an angle for myself so that I could see into the shelter. I reached the edge of the harbour. Spray coming over the pier hissed on the water, and the few small boats in the water tossed violently. Panting and soaked through, I found the shelter of the coastguard hut and peered cautiously around the corner. I could see Scribner clearly. He had his back to me and was talking animatedly to someone, but I couldn't see who it was. Water was running down the back of my neck and I started to feel a little foolish. There was probably a good explanation for Scribner's presence at the inquest. I had been out of the intelligence business long enough not to let old paranoias well up in me. I had made up my mind to go back and rejoin Jimmy when Scribner suddenly stepped aside and I saw who was standing behind him. I felt myself freeze to the spot, and the rain running down the back of my neck turned to ice. Moving very carefully, I withdrew my head back to the shelter of the coastguard station and shut my eyes and willed my pulse rate to slow.

For a year or so I had allowed myself the illusion that my past would let me rest. But now I knew that I had been fooling myself. The man talking to Scribner was George Somerville, former head of MRU and once my boss. Somerville liked to cultivate the stereotype English spy look, tweedy and vague. But there was nothing vague about Somerville. The last time I had seen him I had done him some serious damage. For a while after that I waited for him to pursue me, knowing that I wouldn't see the assassin coming. But then I realised that wasn't the way the man worked. He would allow me to live, and would find some way to put me to use, no matter how much he hated me.

I allowed myself one last look around the side of the building. Somerville and Scribner had left the shelter and Somerville was waiting for Scribner to unlock an S Class Mercedes. Hunched against the weather Somerville looked more like the man I knew him to be, a spidery, evil thing.

I waited for them to drive off. On the way back to the pub through the rain I forced myself to think. Again that question: what was Somerville doing here? It was reasonable to assume that an organisation like MRU, with its emphasis on non-attributable covert action, would be deployed somewhere in the Gulf, or more likely against Islamicists in the West. That was where the action was, and where the kudos for a man like Somerville would lie, not in rain-swept little coastal towns. Something was very wrong.

When I got to the Harbour Bar Jimmy looked even more shaken than he had in the inquest. He was drinking a hot whiskey and I ordered one too, ignoring Donna McNeill's prim look. It was early in the day, but I had been soaked and shocked and I reckoned I owed myself a steadier. I sat down at the table. On any other occasion it would have been pleasant to sit in the cosy, wood-panelled bar with wind lashing at the windows, but on this particular day there was too much going on.

'All right, Jimmy, spit it out,' I said. 'What did she say to you?'

Jimmy shot the pathologist a wounded look.

'She wants to take a sample of me.'

'A DNA sample,' she said. 'It doesn't hurt.'

'Why?' I asked. She hesitated.

'When the dog tags were washed up,' she said, 'some . . . remains were washed up as well. Human bones. If we could DNA test Mr Kerr then we could ascertain if some of the bones belonged to his brother.'

'She wants a sample of me,' Jimmy repeated miserably. I sensed that he didn't really understand what she was asking and the implications of it. That he might have something to bury, and a grave to go to.

'Leave it for the minute,' I said. 'I'll talk to him about it.'

'Are you sure?' she said. 'I cleared some time tomorrow morning to do it. Here's the address.' She put a card on the table. She had long, slender hands and surprisingly well-kept nails. Her eyes met mine and I saw green flecks deep in her hazel eyes. She smiled. As she walked towards the door I noticed that she had an elegant walk, when she wasn't rushed. I had the feeling that there was a lot more to Donna McNeill than was immediately apparent.

*

When we got back to the hotel I saw the black Mercedes in the car park. Scribner was obviously staying here, but I doubted if Somerville was. The spymaster had a parsimonious streak. If he was still around, he'd be found in one of the draughty boarding houses along the seafront. Jimmy muttered something about lying down, but I had too many questions swirling around in my head to relax. The *Castledawn* was on the slipway at Kilkeel and wouldn't be ready for another few days, so I had some time on my hands. No harm in digging into the background of things, I thought, no harm at all.

I went up to my room and changed out of the suit I'd worn for the inquest. I knocked on Jimmy's door, but all I could hear was a faint snoring coming from behind it, so I slipped a note under it. As I turned away I almost collided with a figure coming the other way, the small, blonde-headed figure of the reporter who had been at the courthouse. She muttered something in the way of an apology, but went on without stopping. I had caught a glimpse of her face. It was flushed and there was a bright, eager light in her eyes. I almost went after her to demand to know what she was up to. I thought about telling her that she was no Bob Woodward, and that compared to someone like Somerville, Richard Nixon was pure as the driven snow. But I shrugged and let her go. Something about her had rubbed me up the wrong way, and if I was truthful to myself, that something was her eagerness and ambition and her sense of having her whole life spreading out in front of her. Letting her go was just another bad choice in a career that was strewn with bad choices.

THREE

Half an hour later I was on the road in my hired Ford. I stopped in Dundrum for a late lunch. Salt-baked cod washed down with a glass of Entre-Deux-Mers. When I came out the sun was shining and the world seemed a much less gloomy place than it had this morning. It was almost teatime when I arrived in Belfast, and traffic was heavy on the Ormeau Road as I headed down towards the dock. I hadn't phoned the man I was going to meet, but I knew where I could find him.

I had first met Davy McCrink at college in Glasgow. It was the time when student marches and political agitation were at their height and Davy was always at the centre of it. But unlike the rest of us who were barstool anarchists and the like, Davy took it seriously. He took courses in human rights law and corresponded seriously with leading political activists. He travelled to France and to the States and when he had finished college he took off to Latin America, Guatemala in particular, where he worked against the military regime. I lost touch with him then until the mid-1980s. I was at a CND meeting at Greenham Common. I was there essentially as an observer, to look out for known faces, particularly trade unionists who might have connections with the Communist Party. Somerville was looking for smears against the protesters and he made it clear that he didn't care whether they were real or invented.

But I hung back. The Greenham crowd were hardly dangerous revolutionaries, and besides, I sympathised vaguely with their aims. After a few hours watching game housewife types attempting to tear down razor wire with their bare hands, I headed into Greenham proper. I parked the car and was walking towards a small pub when I saw four men get out of another car outside the pub. The men had that air of clever brutality that generally marked Special Branch men on political operations, and as I watched, they began to take baseball bats and staves from the boot of the car, and I thought I saw the dull glint of knuckledusters on big fists.

Agents provocateur, I reckoned. Send them into a pub to start a row then get offside, leaving a gang of angry demonstrators to rampage through the streets. Doubtless some tame media were waiting on a side street to film the mob scenes.

With the kind of curiosity that has almost got me killed on more than one occasion, I followed them in.

They hadn't hung around. Obviously there was some sort of solidarity visit going on and the pub was full of hard-drinking trade unionists. The Branch men just laid into the nearest crowd of drinkers and started to work their way methodically across the room. I saw a blonde-haired girl – a posh politico type – taking the knuckledusters full in the mouth. There was utter confusion at first, men not knowing who was attacking or why. I saw several brawls break out between adjacent groups of drinkers. Through all the confusion I heard a familiar voice. I looked up and saw McCrink's tall, skinny form standing on the bar.

'They're just trying to provoke you,' he was shouting. 'Don't react!'

But it was a bit late for that. It seemed that everyone in the bar was fighting. Worse still, the Branch men had spotted McCrink and were making their way towards him. I backed out of the door and ran around the back. As I suspected, at least some of the bar staff were huddled at the back door. I pushed them aside and darted in, if a man of my build can ever be said to dart. On my way through the kitchen I grabbed a fire extinguisher off the wall. When I got to the bar, two of the Branch men had McCrink on the floor behind the bar and were working him over. The first Branch man got enough dry ice in the face from the extinguisher to give him frostbite. The second got the edge of the heavy casing on the bridge of the nose. I hauled McCrink to his feet. His face was a mask of blood, but his eyes widened in recognition.

'Leave me alone,' he said. 'I was just getting warmed up.'

'I could see that,' I said, half-carrying him through into the kitchen. At the back of the bar I sat him down on a pile of beer crates and cleaned him up a bit. From the street at the front of the pub I could hear glass breaking and angry men's voices. In the distance sirens began to sound. The Branch men had done their work and scenes of mob violence would be appearing on television news bulletins.

I got McCrink out of town, using a warrant card to get past the checkpoints that had sprung up with astonishing spontaneity. It was getting late, but I knew a small Italian restaurant run by a Milanese couple in a nearby village. They were closing when we arrived and they balked a little at McCrink's beaten-up appearance, but I had P-carded them and knew they had been card-carrying Communists in their youth, so I told them McCrink had been involved in a fracas with the fascisti. Within ten minutes we were sitting down to plates of the best saltimbocca alla romana you're likely to get this side of the Trevi Fountain, washed down with good Barbera d'Asti.

College friends can be a disappointment when you meet them out in the real world. It's a matter, I think, of different ambitions, different trajectories. But McCrink had matured into a shrewd political thinker. I knew he had spotted the fake warrant card and had drawn his own conclusions from it. He never mentioned it, neither then nor in all the years since. I think he thought he could win me round with the force of his humanist argument. And in a way, although it took a while, he did.

Over the years I'd met him in Haifa and Beirut and in Guatemala City, and once, memorably, in Sarajevo during the siege. He was equally at home in Harry's Bar in Venice and in Sandinos in Derry. But if you wanted to find McCrink, then the best place was Pat's Bar in the Belfast docks on a weekday evening.

And sure enough, as I ducked into the studied dark from the bright evening sunlight, the first thing I saw was McCrink sitting at the bar. Despite the gloom he was wearing Ray-Bans and he had the customary Golden Virginia roll-up between his lips. There was a copy of Noam Chomsky on the bar in front of him, and a battered pile of papers which looked like a court judgement, and he was studying them both. I walked up behind him.

'I thought all the barstool Guevaras were working for the Human Rights Commission now,' I said. He closed the book and drew on the roll-up.

'Fuck me,' he said, 'you never know what washes up the Lagan on a spring tide. How are you doing?'

I sat down at the bar beside him and ordered a coffee for me and a bottle of Guinness with a Three Castles chaser for him.

'You know the funny thing?' he said. 'There's hardly a bar in the country stocks bottled Guinness any more. It doesn't keep, they say.'

'A modern tragedy,' I said. 'How's things in the customs business?' It had always seemed strange to me that the radical McCrink's day job was as a customs inspector.

'Ah, you know,' he said, 'you open a container at the docks, sometimes you find fridges and TVs, sometimes you find drugs, and sometimes you find twenty half-dead migrants from a village somewhere in China. Keeps you honest, that kind of work.'

'People-smuggling?'

'There's a huge amount of money in it, and a lot of traffic along this coast. Rumour has it that there's some kind of king-pin figure involved. It's hard to know. There's a lot of Albanians active in it, but I reckon there has to be somebody on this side.'

We talked for a while about politics and globalisation, and then, ruefully, about our student days. He asked me about the art dealing which had taken the place of spookery in my life.

'You know,' I said laughing, 'asset-rich, cash-poor.' I had a habit of buying something beautiful and then falling in love with it and finding myself unable to sell it.

In the end he fixed me with a shrewd look, or as much of a shrewd look as I could see through the Ray-Bans.

'Much as I'm enjoying the chat,' he said, 'you're not here to reminisce.'

I told him about Jimmy and the dog tags being washed up. He thought for a moment.

'Where were they washed up?'

'Rathlin,' I said. 'There was a big storm.'

'If I'm right,' he said, 'there was a lot of old munitions washed up at the time, phosphorous bombs and the like.'

'That's right,' I said.

'All that stuff got dumped in the late forties, early fifties,' he said. 'Thousands of tons of munitions dumped in the Beaufort Dyke.'

I nodded. I had often sailed in those waters, and you could smell the foul vapours that rose to the surface for miles.

'Not to mention the radioactive waste that got chucked in on top of it.'

'But you don't know anything about any loss of life?' I said.

'No. It's a long time ago, Jack. I'd say let the man bury his brother and get on with his life.'

'Is that it?' I said. 'No campaign? No public outrage?'

'Ah, Jack,' he said, 'you have to save your energies for the few campaigns that can make a difference.' He took off the Ray-Bans and rubbed his eyes, and I could see tiredness in the lines around them. The kind of fatigue that comes from hard, committed living and seems to go right to the bone. We both fell silent, and I think we could have fallen prey to a kind of glumness that seemed to pervade the bar. Fortunately my mobile went off at that moment – an irritatingly cheerful ring tone which I was unable to change, but which served to lift the gloom all the same.

I went outside to take the call. As soon as I heard the rich, sensual South Armagh tones I had the same feeling of warm honey trickling down my spine as I had the first time I had heard Deirdre Mellows, long ago in the middle of what seemed like a forgotten war. Conversations with Deirdre should have been full of regrets, but she wasn't a woman to indulge herself in recrimination, and I got the feeling that she would take a dim view of my wallowing in the past as well. She'd been working for the UN in New York for several years but, she told me, she had just landed a job in a development agency in London, so was I about, and could I meet up with her? I told her I was in Belfast.

'That's even better,' she said. 'I'm coming home for a visit, so we can meet up. And I've got Kate Elliot with me.'

Kate was an old friend, a mentor of sorts, and she only ventured out of Shetland once or twice a year. But for all that she lived in a windswept croft, she was one of the most sophisticated people I had ever met.

I made an arrangement to meet up in a few days' time and rang off. The conversation had been crisp and pleasant, but the undertones I had been half-hoping for were absent. When I went back into the bar I realised that McCrink had never met Deirdre or Kate, and on an impulse I invited McCrink along. He smiled, looking genuinely pleased. We arranged to meet in the Crown, and by eight o'clock I was on the road back to Newcastle, driving along the coastline with a dark mass of clouds gathering along the horizon. On the way I rang Jimmy and found him in his room. He'd been out for a walk and a meal and had obviously been thinking.

'I'll do it,' he said. 'I'll do her tests.'

'You sure?'

'It'll give me something to bury, son. Even if it's only a bone. I can do that much for him.'

'Fair enough,' I said. 'I'll see you for breakfast at eight.' I hung up. I thought he'd made the right choice. Besides, the prospect of spending some more time with Donna McNeill wasn't entirely unpleasant.

I left the car at the hotel and walked down to the Anchor Bar. A warm fug hit me when the door opened. I went to the bar and ordered a Redbreast. I needed some thinking time. The Redbreast was good and I ordered another. I shouldn't follow this up, I told myself. I should just walk away. The coroner had put up a good fight, but next time they'd be ready for him. The case would be buried and that would be that. There are some forces you just don't take on. But if I *was* going to do something, I thought, what would I do? Start with the ship, I realised. If Robert Kerr had been lost at sea, then he must have been on board a ship. If there was a ship, then perhaps there were old crewmates, records of a sinking. There were good records in the Linenhall Library. There were better ones at Greenwich. I knew a few old seamen along this coast . . . I put it out of my head. I was out of the business now, and that was the way it was going to stay. I finished my third Redbreast. The bar was beginning to empty out. I contemplated another whiskey, then changed my mind. I had an early start in the morning.

As I got to my feet I looked across the bar and caught the eye of the young reporter who had been at the inquest that morning. Her face was pale and pinched. There was an untouched glass sitting in front of her. She lifted her eyes and met mine and almost seemed to flinch. Then I could see determination enter her eyes. She got to her feet and walked towards me, looking nervously around her. When she got to me she grasped my arm so hard it felt like the blood supply had been cut off. I don't think she was aware she had done it.

'I need to talk to you,' she said. 'There isn't anyone . . .' She was breathing hard, still glancing nervously around her.

'Why me?' I said. 'I only came over here to give my neighbour a bit of support. Why would you need to talk to me?'

'You're more than just a neighbour,' she said. 'I don't know how much more, but I know you're more than that.' I looked at her more closely now. She had the air of someone who had acquired far, far too much information in a very short time. She didn't know who to trust, but she had to trust somebody. I stroked my chin. There was a pleading look in her eyes now, and I made her out as a girl who didn't do too much pleading. I made up my mind, thinking, as I usually do at such moments, that feeling sorry for people was exactly the opposite of a good motivational tool when it came to covert action.

'I'm going out,' I said. 'Wait five minutes and then follow me.'

FOUR

Outside, the storm I had seen gathering was beginning to flex its muscles. Litter was blowing wildly down the deserted promenade and I could see the waves starting to build again. The air was full of a fine spray and I could taste salt on my lips. Out of habit I found a doorway and watched the front of the pub for anything unusual or out of place. I couldn't see anything. One car glided past, buffeted by the wind, but otherwise there was nothing. At the end of exactly five minutes the girl came out and stood looking around her anxiously. I crossed the street to her.

'Let's walk,' I said. I turned towards the promenade. She followed. When we got to the promenade she linked my arm. Again I think she wasn't conscious of having done so. I looked down at her. She looked very young, and I had the sense of something precious entrusted to me. I wasn't sure if I liked the feeling.

'What's your name?' I asked.

'Fiona.'

'All right, Fiona,' I said, trying to sound stern, 'what's all this about? And how do you know about me, if you know anything?'

'I broke into his room,' she said simply.

'Whose room?' I said, although I had a funny feeling I knew.

'The barrister,' she said. 'Scribner. My sister is a chambermaid in the hotel. I took her master key.'

'I see,' I said in a gruff, disapproving voice, although I didn't really see at all.

'Could you tell me why you did that?' I went on.

'To find out what was going on, what the cover-up is.'

'Cover-up?'

'Has to be. The D notice and that kind of thing,' she said. I had to suppress the temptation to pat her on the head and send her home. Apart from anything else, her naïvety and earnestness were starting to make my own suspicions seem a little bit juvenile.

'Right, well, let's pass on that for the moment,' I said. 'What do you think you know about me?'

'I heard him talking on the phone.'

'Who?' I said impatiently.

'Scribner, of course.'

'And where were you when this was going on?'

'Hiding. In the bathroom.' She said it casually, but I could see that there was nothing casual about it. I imagined her more scared than she'd ever been in her life, yet caught up in the thrill of the illicit.

'Scribner was talking to somebody about you. He described you and then the other person must have said something, because Scribner got cross and said something about keeping ex-employees on a leash and keeping deadbeat ex-spooks out of his courtrooms.' She said this with the faintest of innocent smiles in my direction. She'd used the phrase 'deadbeat exspook' with a little more relish than I thought appropriate. I was starting to like this girl.

Nevertheless, it was a serious business. Scribner had obviously been talking to Somerville. Which meant that Somerville knew that I was in town and had some connection to the case. Feeling the first drops of rain on my face, I kept on questioning her.

'What did you do then?'

'Waited until Scribner left the room, then had a look in his briefcase,' she said, as if it was the most natural thing in the world to do.

'Did you take anything?' I said sharply. The rain was getting heavier now, great stinging drops that suddenly turned into a downpour. There was a shelter fifty yards ahead of us, but we would be soaked before we got there.

'No,' she said, 'but I think he knows there was somebody in his room. I saw him at reception. He looked pretty cross . . .' The words were tumbling out of her now, and she seemed to be oblivious to the rain.

'. . . but never mind about that, he had these documents in the bag, briefing papers they looked like . . .'

That was as far as she got. As far as she was ever going to get. When people think of a rifle shot they think of a sharp crack. But a modern sniper's rifle can throw a cannon shell over a mile with accuracy, and the sound it makes is more akin to the sound an artillery piece makes. The shooter had obviously waited until the rain was heavy enough to help mask the sound. I was turning towards her as I heard it, and simultaneously a red rose bloomed on the girl's shoulder, a look of terrible wonderment spreading across her face. Without thinking I dived towards her, hitting her hard and carrying her over the low promenade railing. I braced myself, expecting to hit gravel, but instead took a mouthful of seawater. I struggled to get to my feet. The water wasn't deep but the waves were high, and I felt a sucking undertow pull at the gravel under my feet. I staggered under the force of a wave and the girl's weight. As the wave pushed me against the sea wall I realised there was a small alcove in it. I made towards it. As I did so I took Fiona by the right arm. It felt wrong. I looked down and realised, sickeningly, that the girl's arm was only barely attached to her body. She looked at me, her eyes pleading. Her mouth worked but no sound came out. I took her other arm and her body turned in the water so that she was facing out to sea. Half ashamed, half relieved, I started to drag her towards the alcove. I never wanted to see that look in someone's eyes again.

The waves knocked me down several times before I reached the limited shelter of the alcove and wedged the girl into it. The water still swirled up to my waist, but the force of the waves and current was lessened. More to the point, we couldn't be seen from above. I knew I should be thinking of getting Fiona out of there. There was a spit of shingle further down. Providing whoever had shot her wasn't waiting, I should be able to get her there.

'Come on . . .' I said, but the words died in my throat as I looked down at her. There was a dullness in her eyes that I had seen before. And even in the dim light from the pier I could see the dark crimson stain in the water around us. She looked young, even younger than her nineteen years. I touched her face gently and brushed her hair out of her eyes. The faintest of smiles seemed to touch her lips. We were both in the presence of death, a place where a terrible honesty reigned. I could see that she was trying to speak. I put my ear to her lips. I could her breathing, shallow and ragged, but when she spoke her voice was clear.

'Black cat,' she said. 'Black cat.' With her good hand she turned my head to see if I had heard it correctly. She must have seen the puzzlement in my eyes, for her lips formed the words again, and I could see the terrible effort it cost her. I smiled reassurance and put my fingers to her lips. Again she smiled faintly, and turned her head to one side, and like a child falling asleep, she died.

I don't know how long I stood there holding the girl's body. Long enough for the cloud of blood in the water around me to dissipate. Long enough for the cold seawater to numb the lower half of my body. But more than that was the mental numbness of shock. That morning I had expected a relatively straightforward few hours in a provincial courtroom. Now I found myself in a nexus of intrigue and violent death. I looked down at the dead girl's face. I felt a dull anger growing in me. I did nothing to stop it. Anger was good. Anger worked against the torpor induced by trauma. Anger for the young life cut short. Anger in the realisation that the bullet could have been meant for either of us. Anger that my past had once again crept up behind me and placed its cold, bony hand on my shoulder.

I made myself straighten up, loosen my grip on Fiona's body. The tide was full in now and the waves were battering the wall. Great sheets of rain swept across the ocean. I wondered how I was going to get the body to dry land. Then I realised that I couldn't let her be discovered. I had been seen talking to her in the bar. Possibly even seen as I walked along the promenade with her. If she was found dead with a gunshot wound, then I was looking at a tough time, with none of the protection that membership of MRU had afforded me. I knew what I had to do. I bent down and kissed Fiona's cold, dead forehead gently, then I swung her into the tide. The ebb of the tide would carry her out to the edge of the bay, and the great cold current that flowed along that shore would do the rest, carrying her out to sea. As she floated away I knew that I was in debt to her, a debt that would not be repaid until I found out who had shot her and why.

I forced myself out into the waves. There was a big swell coming in now and as I thrust my way through the water I was picked up several times and flung against the wall. It took almost ten minutes and all of my strength to reach the spit of gravel. My ribs felt cracked and I had what felt like a large welt on the side of my head which I didn't remember getting. I found an old bit of timber and propped it against the sea-wall, which gave me a foothold to reach up to the cast-iron railing on the promenade. Almost crying out from the effort, I pulled myself up and rolled through the railing on to the promenade.

Cautiously I raised my head and looked around. There was no one on the promenade, but I could hear laughter and talking as a few stragglers left the Anchor. I looked at my watch. It had been twelve when I'd left the pub. It was just after one now. Just an hour, but it felt like a lifetime. Wearily, I got to my feet and began to half jog, half stumble towards the hotel. Several cars passed, and I shrank into the shadows until they had gone. I probably looked like a drunk staggering home, but there was no point in being conspicuous. I got to the hotel and ducked through the entrance and into the car park. I had left an overnight bag in the car in case I had decided to stay in Belfast. I managed to unlock the car and fall inside. I started the car and turned up the heater. I knew that I needed to get out of the wet clothes, but I didn't have the energy. I stared bleakly through the windscreen at the rain-lashed car park. Fiona had seen puzzlement in my face when she had used the words 'black cat'. But it wasn't puzzlement because I didn't recognise the words. I had recognised the words only too well, and the operation that was associated with them. The problem was that I didn't associate that operation with damp Victorian resorts on the Irish Sea, but with Iraq and the deadly blaze of the desert sun.

FIVE

It was one of my last assignments for MRU, and came in the form of some fraternal assistance for the Americans in the first Gulf War. Right from the start of my career I had had a reputation as someone who could be sent ahead of a military operation in order to make sure that the locals were co-operative. I didn't think there was any great skill in it. Bring an interpreter, don't shout at people and bring cash, or at least the promise of cash in the future. Of course, there was always the chance of getting your throat slit or a Kalashnikov bullet in the ribs, but in general people were friendly and diplomatic, promising all sorts of things, knowing that promises can be cashed in or forgotten, depending on the outcome of the project.

In this case my job was to make contact with a small isolated town about fifty miles behind the front line. The Americans wanted to set up a forward post there, and Somerville had volunteered my services. The Americans wanted to be seen to include MRU, so they went along with it, even giving me fifteen thousand dollars in used hundred-dollar bills to smooth my passage. I was inserted by Lynx, along with Ali the interpreter, and sat at a prearranged spot in the desert in the predawn cool, watching the faint pink glow in the eastern sky grow as the sun came up.

Shortly after dawn the mayor of the town picked us up in his Mercedes. He was a plump man who looked as if he was normally of a cheerful disposition, but this time he was worried. Soldiers were in the town, he said, and senior Ba'ath party members. Something was up, he didn't know what, but he was going to bring us to his tent in the desert rather than to the town. All the while he assured us of his friendship and gratitude. I watched him carefully, trying to interpret his nervousness. In the end I decided he was genuine, and relaxed a little, although the thought of roughing it indefinitely in a tent in the desert heat didn't appeal much.

I needn't have worried. The tent was a magnificent affair lined with traditional carpets. More to the point, it had air conditioning and satellite TV. I gave Mayor Shakil two thousand dollars as a token of my esteem, making sure he saw the Glock tucked in my belt as I did so. In return he was nervous and effusive. I told him there was a lot more where that came from, as long as we were safe. I watched him drive off, his assurances ringing in my ears.

That was it for five days. Mayor Shakil paid several visits to assure me that the townspeople were loyal to the US, but that the troops remained in the town. Ali showed me how to roast lamb in the ashes of the fire and serve it with couscous. Then we would sit out in the evening cool and watch the sunset over the desert, the sky criss-crossed by the contrails of dozens of military aircraft. When it became too cold to sit out we'd watch CNN and try to figure out what was happening in the war, which wasn't easy. Although as the week went on we could hear the distant sound of shelling, and sometimes detect the faint glow of burning buildings over the horizon.

On the morning of the sixth day Shakil arrived once more. He was sombre and serious, and less the parody of the untrustworthy Arab that we had seen before. He told us that the troops had gone, had pulled out suddenly the night before, but that there was something that he wanted us to see. We got into the Mercedes and he drove in silence. We reached the town, which was a surprisingly neat and well-irrigated place with one long main street. I noticed that there was no one on the streets, and that every house had its shutters closed. We passed a small, neat clinic.

'Your two thousand dollars,' Shakil said quietly, 'they will pay for a reconditioned X-ray machine for the clinic.' His English was suddenly flawless.

'Your English is good,' I said.

'Why wouldn't it be good?' he said with a wry glance back at me. 'My brother has an electrical shop in Tottenham Court Road. I worked for him for a few years.'

I looked at Ali. He shrugged. I felt my face turn red, victim of my own preconceptions. He laughed.

'Sometimes it's easier if we just work off the idea we have of each other rather than the reality,' he said. I wondered uncomfortably what stereotype of me Shakil had formed in his mind, and how much of it was true.

We drove for an hour on the other side of town. There was little sign of life save for the odd herd of sheep or goats wandering on the dusty road margins. Here and there we saw freshly burned-out military vehicles. Shakil manoeuvred around these without comment. I could sense the tension growing in him. I began to wish I had some kind of weapon with me. The road climbed a gentle incline for twenty minutes then levelled out. We were on a plateau overlooking the surrounding countryside. Shakil pulled up abruptly and motioned to us to get out. As I stepped out of the car I noticed lorry and jeep tracks on the dust margins at the side of the road. There were discarded cigarette butts and water bottles by the side of the road. When I looked into the scrub at the side of the road I saw a helmet, military camouflage, even a small folding table and chairs. The military had been here, and they had pulled out in a hurry.

'Please,' Shakil said nervously as he motioned to us to follow him. We set off on a small path which wound its way through brush and scrub. It was midday and the sun beat down on us unmercifully. The place where I had lost a finger in the blazing Mexican sun a few years before throbbed with phantom pain as though in sympathy. There was more discarded gear along the track. Water bottles, fatigue caps, even a whole rucksack.

'Not far now,' Shakil muttered. Once more I wished I was armed. Shakil might have been a clever humanitarian, but I also suspected he was capable of playing one side off against the other, and I could have been walking into a trap. As long as it was a trap in the shade away from the blazing sun, I thought sourly, then maybe I would take it.

It took half an hour of exhausting slog before we reached a small ridge. Shakil motioned to us to get down. I did as I was told and crawled on my hands and knees to join Shakil at the top of the ridge.

'Here, look!' he hissed, handing me a small pair of field binoculars. Wiping the sweat from my forehead I put the binoculars to my eyes and focused. The first thing I saw was an aircraft. It was an S3A Viking, usually deployed as a long-range surveillance plane. It was painted a radar-resistant matt black, and there were no markings of any kind on the fuselage. The aircraft had obviously crashed. Two great furrows led across the desert to its resting place. The plane had slid for a long way, but seemed surprisingly intact. It had come to rest with one wing tilted towards the ground and the other elevated. After a moment I realised why this was. There was a large pod-like bomb with fins attached by a pylon under the elevated wing, but the place where another device might have balanced it on the other wing was empty, letting the wing rest on the ground.

There was something very sinister about the jet-black plane with smoked glass windows simply lying in the desert, the ultimate in technology stranded in the most primitive of landscapes. Although in fact I thought there was an inherent cruelty in both.

'Do you see them?' Shakil said urgently. 'Look!' My view of the port wing was partly obscured by a small tree in front of me. I moved to the right and looked again. There was no mistaking what I saw. The corpses of perhaps a dozen soldiers lay underneath the wing or a little way into the desert, lying on their stomachs with their heads pointed away from the plane as though they had been fleeing the plane when they were felled. I could see that the bodies had already begun to bloat in the desert heat.

'What happened . . .' I began.

'The bomb,' Shakil said. 'Look at the bomb.' I focused on the pod under the wing. I saw that one of the mounts holding the pylon was broken, and that the bomb dangled drunkenly from the other. There was a great gouge on the underside of it where it had struck the ground, and from the damaged area a thread of white vapour emerged and hung in the still desert air.

'The soldiers were afraid,' Shakil said. 'Very afraid. They said that when the men approached the plane the nearest ones began to scream and pull at their throats. They fell on the ground and flapped around like fish and then they didn't move any more.'

I looked around nervously. The whole thing had a feel of a black operation about it. I also knew that whoever owned the aircraft would know exactly where it was. The crew had probably been extracted already, and they would be coming back for the rest of their property. If they found us here we would be shot on principle. I told Ali and Shakil what I thought.

'What should we do?' Ali said nervously.

'I think we should leave here very quickly and very quietly, and never mention the fact that we were here to a living soul,' I said.

Both men were very quiet on the way back, and Shakil kept glancing back over his shoulder at me. I realised that he had shown me the aircraft in the hope of extracting more largesse, but now realised that he was in over his head. And people who got in over their head in this part of the world knew what to expect. A bullet in the back of the head and a shallow grave. As we got to the car I caught up with him.

'Don't worry,' I said quietly, 'you'll get your clinic finished.' He gave me a measured look.

'You're certain that the future is yours to give, Mr Valentine?' he said.

*

Back at the camp I raised Somerville on the satellite phone and told him what I had seen.

'Keep it to yourself,' he said. I could hear the excitement, almost greed, in his voice. There was nothing Somerville liked more than finding out other people's secrets.

The Americans arrived in town the next day. First a team of special forces operatives led by a brusque Texan who made it clear that he regarded my presence as superfluous, even when I presented him with Shakil and a group of town elders eager to ingratiate themselves with the liberator. The Texan made it clear that my presence would only be tolerated as long as I stayed out of the way.

That evening I borrowed Shakil's four-wheel-drive and took the road out towards the place where we had seen the plane. I got half a mile. I was grinding my way along a bumpy section of road when I came across a log which had been placed across the road. When I stopped, five or six men wearing ski masks emerged from the scrub at the side of the road. They knew what they were doing and moved fast. Before I had time even to raise my hands I was lying on my face with a Browning pressed to my ear. I kept very still as my hands were tied behind my back with plastic ties. I had seen what the 9mm parabellum shells in the Browning could do to a human skull.

When they had me suitably trussed I was lifted bodily and thrown into the back of the jeep. The vehicle was turned and driven at speed back towards the town. It skidded to a halt outside the town hall and I was thrown out on to the ground. All this time the men had not exchanged a word. It was this sense of deadly intuition of each other's thoughts that special forces always strove for. They achieved it less often than commonly supposed, but when they did there was something terrifying about it. I twisted my head around and squinted up into the sun. The Texan was standing above me looking down. Behind him stood Shakil. Shakil caught my eye and gave an almost imperceptible, apologetic shrug. Of course, I thought. Shakil was going to give the Texan everything he wanted and if that included a nosy covert operative, then so be it.

Worryingly, when I turned my head back to the Texan he had his back to me. As I watched he strode off. Then the jeep drove away as well. Shakil looked at me impassively then turned on his heel.

I lay there until close to midnight. Once the sun had set it began to get cold. My legs and arms were numb and my teeth were chattering when I heard a sound. I looked up. It was Shakil. He didn't say anything, but looked around him nervously. When he was satisfied that there was no one watching he threw a rough blanket over me, then, with another half-shrug, turned and walked off into the darkness.

It was close to midnight when another jeep pulled up alongside me. A hood was forced over my head and I was unceremoniously thrown into the back of the jeep and driven out of town. On the way I wondered just how many people had made this trip and in how many countries, hooded and tied and abducted by night, lying in the stench of their own fear and trying not to think about a shallow grave in a lonely spot. I tried to clench my teeth to keep them from chattering in case my captors would think they were chattering from fear.

We hadn't been driving for long when I heard the noise of helicopter rotors. The sound got louder and louder and I could see bright lights through the fabric of the hood. The jeep came to an abrupt halt and the helicopter noise reached a crescendo then evened out. The craft had landed. Rough hands manhandled me out of the jeep. I was put on my feet, but my legs crumpled under me. I felt the hood being lifted. Around me men were unloading crates from a US Green Giant helicopter, working in silent haste. I turned my attention back to the Texan. He was looking at me as if I was some new species of reptile he had come across in the desert.

'I should get the chopper boys to just throw you out over the Gulf,' he said, 'but I guess you got yourself some kind of fairy godfather, so I got to let you live.' I tried to remember a joke I had heard about Texas being the place where, if you wanted to give the world an enema, you would stick the tube. I decided that now was not the time for levity, so I merely grunted something and tried to get to my feet again. I fell over, almost landing on his tightly laced combat boots. He couldn't resist the opportunity. He drew back one foot and kicked me hard in the ribs. As I blacked out I found myself thinking that maybe there was something in the enema story.

I awoke in a US naval hospital in Saudi Arabia, and was shipped home on an RAF plane next day. Somerville was waiting for me at the airport, eager to get going on the debriefing. He asked me again and again if the plane had any markings and if I was sure that it was a Viking. When he was finished with this he brought another man into the room. A man with heavy glasses over a bland face, wearing a tweed suit. I thought that if you put him in a white coat he would look like one of the cartoon boffins you used to see in children's comics.

In a careful, uninflected monotone he began to ask me about the vapour I had seen escaping, about the shape of the bomb, the fin layout, the dimensions. When he was satisfied with that he moved on to the dead soldiers. What way were they lying? What colour had their skin turned to? How far did I think they had got before the vapour had laid them low? Were their eyes open or closed? There was something obscene about the man's questions, the dreadful lack of emotion. I've always found it hard to look at a dead body. Not from any squeamishness, but from a feeling that I would be violating a fundamental privacy.

That seemed to be the end of it. Until a few months later rumours began to surface about a US black operation in the Gulf that had gone wrong. A plane had been sent in to launch a biological strike on what was thought to be an Iraqi nuclear enrichment plant. The plane had launched one bomb and had then been struck by small-arms fire. It had come down in the desert fifty miles away. The plane had been an unmarked S3A Viking owned by a CIA subsidiary. The unnamed biological agent had been effective for forty-eight hours, and had then lost its lethal function. The mission had been named Black Cat.

SIX

When I woke up just after dawn the following morning it was still raining. I was cramped and sore from sleeping in the back of the car, and the bleakness of my mood matched the bleakness of the day. If I shut my eyes it seemed that I could still hear the sound of the girl's last breath, its tragic sibilance louder than the crash of a thousand waves. And I knew that I wouldn't be able to look myself in the face until I had got to the bottom of her death. I drove to the edge of the town and found a little early-morning truck stop, a mobile grill parked at the side of the road. I got a mug of hot, steaming tea. The woman behind the counter took one look at me and shook her head. She told me to sit in my car with the tea and she'd be over in five minutes. She was there in four with a breakfast which consisted of fried egg, sausage and bacon on a toasted soda, dripping with butter. I looked at it for a long moment. I thought about my arteries and for a few seconds I wrestled with my conscience. Then, as usual whenever I wrestle with my conscience over food, conscience lost and I devoured the lot. It probably shortened my life by about a fortnight, but at least I felt able to meet the day.

I rang the hotel from my mobile, paid the bill by credit card and asked them to send on my hand luggage, then I had them put me through to Jimmy's room. I told him to take a walk to the bus station, where I'd meet him. He grumbled a bit, but I bit my tongue.

I found a public toilet where I washed and shaved then parked beside the old redbrick bus station. I let Jimmy stand around for twenty minutes until I was sure that no one was watching him, then I pulled up alongside him.

I expected him to be grumpy and fractious but he surprised me by being neither.

He got into the car, gave me a long look, then settled back into his seat, facing to the front. We were three or four miles out of the town before he spoke.

'What happened?' he asked. I shook my head. Whatever it was, Jimmy was on the periphery and I wanted to keep him there.

'Bad?' he said. I nodded, without taking my eyes off the road.

'When I was in Kenya,' he said softly, 'you could always tell a man who'd been in bad action when he came back off patrol. It's a look. Like you can see too much of the white of their eye or something. You learn to leave them alone. If they want to talk, you let them. If not . . .' He spread his hands in a resigned gesture which implied that it might not be the ideal thing to be left alone with your pain, but sometimes you didn't have a choice. For that, I stopped at the chuck wagon again and treated him to a breakfast soda, and had another mug of tea for myself. Jimmy insisted on paying. I watched him bantering with the woman behind the counter and realised once again that there was much more to Jimmy than met the eye.

We had reached the outskirts of the city before Jimmy spoke again.

'There's more to this than just my brother, isn't there?' he said.

'There is, Jimmy,' I said. 'Somehow the appearance of those dog tags is tied up with something big. What it is I don't know yet, but I . . . I sort of got dragged into it last night.'

'Whatever it is,' he said, turning to me, 'I want you to know that I'm your man, through thick and thin.' I started to protest but he held up his hand.

'No,' he said, 'I'm serious. I'm at the end of my life, but it feels like I got a message from the past. That there's work for me to do yet before I go. And I was never afraid of work.'

I looked at the old man. He was big-boned still, but his fingers were gnarled with arthritis and his eyes were rheumy, and there was a tiny but perceptible shake in his hands. He seemed to read my mind. He smiled.

'I couldn't wrestle a man,' he said, 'but I could still pull a trigger. I've done it before, y'know. And I will again if needs be. No, Jack, I got the feeling of a call from the past, and I know you got it too.'

And in an odd way I did. From the moment in the croft when Jimmy had been telling me about his brother, I had an eerie feeling that a stern regard from the past had been turned on me, that Robert Kerr had his attention on me, and that I hadn't quite lived up to his exacting standards. We turned into the gateway of Belvoir Park hospital in a thoughtful mood.

Donna McNeill was waiting for us. She was wearing a white coat and gold-rimmed glasses, which suited her. Her manner was brusque and friendly and intimidatingly efficient. In case Jimmy didn't understand, she went through the basics of genetic identification. Jimmy didn't appear to be listening.

'What did you find?' he said abruptly.

'Sorry?' she answered.

'What part did you find?'

'Oh,' she said, 'what body part . . . well, in fact it was a finger bone.'

'I'd like to see it,' he said. She looked at him in surprise, then looked at me. I shrugged.

'Man's entitled to see his brother's finger,' I said, 'if it *is* his brother's finger.' She pursed her lips at the unscientific thrust of my argument, but I could see her turning over the moral weight of it.

'All right,' she said eventually. 'As long as it won't distress you.' Jimmy grinned.

'It won't distress me, doctor,' he said. She went into an annex and returned with a stainless steel tray. On the lid sat an intact finger bone. Jimmy looked at it, then, before she could object, he picked it up.

'That's our fella's finger all right,' he said with an air of satisfaction. 'And I was right about something else too. Look, Jack.'

He held the finger up and I saw that it was crooked with the appearance of beckoning. Don't push it too far, Jimmy, I thought. Your brother isn't really calling us from the past. All the same, I felt a shiver go down my spine. Donna McNeill gave that pursed-lip expression again. She took the bone from him firmly but gently.

'The test will establish that, Mr Kerr,' she said. 'If you wouldn't mind waiting for a moment I'll take a swab.'

When she went out of the room Jimmy leaned over to me and whispered.

'You know how I knew?'

'How?' I replied cautiously, not at all sure if I wanted to hear the answer.

'Our Robert broke his left forefinger at the top knuckle falling off a bogey when he was ten. It was set wrong in the exact shape of that finger there – and it was broke at the top knuckle too!'

Well, I thought to myself, at least events weren't being ordered by some occult force. Then I wondered at the odds against a fifty-year-old finger bone being washed up from the deep, along with dog tags which identified it . . . Fortunately, Donna McNeill bustled back into the room at that moment and I was able to occupy myself with her all too real physical presence. She took a swab from the inside of Jimmy's mouth and put it into a glass vial.

'That can go off to the lab now,' she said, 'but it might be a while before we get results.'

'I know what the results are going to be, doctor,' Jimmy said.

'Would you like a cup of tea after your ordeal, Mr Kerr?' she said, smiling.

'All right, all right,' he growled, 'I made a bit of a fuss. I just don't like being in the doctor's.'

'Funnily enough,' she said, sincerely this time, 'I'm not much of a patient myself.'

'Cup of tea would be good, though,' he said.

'The nurse will show you the canteen,' she said. 'I need a word with Mr Valentine, if that's all right?'

Jimmy went off with a young nurse, muttering a bit. I sat down.

'What do you want to ask me about?' I said. She laughed, half-embarrassed.

'I don't know really . . . it's just that, well, in the courthouse . . . you seemed to be, not quite in charge, but you knew how to handle things . . . There's something funny about this case, isn't there?'

'There is,' I agreed. 'Mind you, it might turn out to be nothing at all. Most of these things do.'

'It's just that . . . well, I spend some time in Rathlin . . .'

'Where the bones were found?'

'Yes, that's right. I have a house up there, overlooking the Sea of Moyle. But the thing is, all the locals say there is something peculiar going on up there.'

'How peculiar?'

'Well, there's never been so much stuff – old munitions – washed up on the beaches. There's a lot of lights out at sea at night. Helicopters, that kind of thing. I don't know why I'm telling you this . . . it's just that that lawyer Scribner gave me the creeps . . .'

'Listen,' I said, 'why don't we take a run up there tomorrow, have a look around?'

I was trying not to sound too eager. She looked into my eyes for what seemed like a long time before she replied, long enough for me to reacquaint myself with those gold flecks in her eyes. There was an honesty in her look, but something troubled as well. There was something more to all of this, I thought. She knew something more than she was telling.

'Yes,' she said, and I felt shaken out of a reverie. 'Yes, that would be a good idea.'

Three hours later I stood on the dockside at Larne watching Jimmy's ferry steam out of the harbour. He stood on deck and waved to me once, then stood watching as the ferry slipped out of sight. I found myself feeling a little melancholy. Ferry ports and airports always did that to me, but there was more to it than that. I realised that Jimmy felt like family now, and that I would miss him. But as I turned away from the dock I pushed those thoughts into a compartment in the back of my mind and turned the key on them, as I had always done. One day that door would burst open and I would have to deal with it, but for now there was work to be done.

Driving back into the city, I rang McCrink at his office and arranged to meet him for lunch. As always, McCrink chose a bar. The Kitchen was one of the oldest in the city, small and atmospheric with a regular crowd, and a place where, as McCrink explained, you got a proper dinner – no fancy herbs or ciabattas or anything like that.

'That's all right,' I said, ordering boiled ribs and cabbage with new potatoes, 'the proper dinner is one of the great civilising influences of the world.' McCrink looked at me suspiciously to see if I was making fun of him, then ordered the same.

'I suppose it's too early to ask if there's any word on Robert Kerr?' I asked as we waited.

'Ordinary Seaman Robert Kerr,' he said. 'Deckhand on the 14,000-ton merchant vessel *Jane Goode*, registered at Newry 1938 and later at Warrenpoint. Employed on Atlantic convoys for several years, damaged by torpedo strike, repaired

Murmansk 1943, and after that plied her trade at various Irish seaports. Attached to naval supply arm Glasgow and Larne until 1951 then . . . nothing.'

'Nothing?'

'Everything's on record until then. I got a bit at the Linenhall Library and I got a contact at Portsmouth to email me the rest. But the record just stops dead.'

'That sounds dodgy.'

'Somebody pulled the relevant file is what it looks like. Happens all the time in the civil service.'

'What's next?'

'Well, all these ships are insured – do you know anybody at Lloyd's List? They keep the best records.'

I thought about it. I didn't know anybody at Lloyd's, but I did know people who could get me any kind of information for a price. It was about time to put in a call.

'The other thing I have is the name of her master.'

'Her master?'

'He seemed to have commanded her all through the war, but the funny thing is that his name isn't on the last manifest. The *Jane Goode* sailed without her captain on her last recorded trip.'

'He's probably dead.'

'Probably. But you have to remember he was appointed in wartime and younger men were given more responsibility in those days. His name's James Baird anyway. I'll try the Seaman's Mission on that one.'

'Thanks.'

'Don't worry about it. I'm doing it in government time anyhow.'

*

After a monumental feed of floury spuds, fresh country butter and ribs we re-emerged on to the street.

'Good pub,' I said.

'I know,' he said. 'It's being demolished in a few months. They're building a shopping centre.' He gave a cynic's laugh and then was gone, striding off through the crowd in his green parka. I shouted after him that we had a dinner date the following night. He acknowledged with a wave of his hand.

Twenty minutes later I was heading into the suburbs on my way back to the *Castledawn*. It took an hour to get to the harbour at Kilkeel. An hour in which to try and find some way of working out exactly what had happened, and why, and then to decide how to move forward. I tried to put the postponed inquest and the nightmare grip of the dying girl together. She had found out something, and someone had thought it worth using a high-powered sniper's rifle in a small seaside town in order to stop her imparting whatever information she had gleaned. And somehow the whole thing was connected to the death of Robert Kerr. But I was tired from the night before, every fibre of my being stretched to the limit and now in rest and repair mode. No time to think or make decisions. I realised I needed a rest in familiar and safe surroundings. Then I had to start hunting. I knew there was information out there. There was always information, unconnected facts perhaps, circulating in the dark. It was a matter of gathering them up and making the connections.

I pulled up at the repair dock and was pleased to see that the *Castledawn* was off the cradle and moored to the quay. The converted trawler was much patched in places, but she had kept her clean, clinker-built lines. Now she had a new navigation system, an engine overhaul and sundry other repairs done, as well as a lick of paint here and there. I could see the boatbuilder, Bill Quinn, leaning on a bollard and looking down on her. Twenty-five years ago every boat in the harbour would have looked like that. Now decommissioning had seen them broken up and burned, to be replaced by new steel-hulled vessels bristling with expensive equipment. I clapped him on the shoulder.

'Thinking about the good old days, Bill?' I said.

'Nothing good about them,' he growled. 'Only thing I can say is that a working boat was a working boat then, not a floating hotel.' I grinned. No matter what Bill might say, I could tell he was admiring the lines of the boat. He had a right to admire it. He had built it.

I looked over at the boat again and frowned. The car on the dock behind the wheelhouse didn't look as if it belonged among the rusted fishing tackle and torn nets. A working dock was no place for such a fine piece of machinery, and a slippery quay was no place for the highly polished brogues of Scribner the lawyer. But there he was, looking down on the *Castledawn* with his face screwed up like, as Bill put it, 'a man with shit on the end of his nose.'

I stepped back out of sight.

'I take it you don't want to see him?' Bill said.

'You'd be right about that,' I said.

'Give me a minute,' Bill said. 'I'll see what he wants.' I watched as Bill crossed the head of the dock. The boatbuilder walked up to Scribner. The lawyer was at least a foot taller than Bill, but as they started to talk, it was the lawyer who backed away until they were out of sight behind the wheel-house. I couldn't see anything for a few minutes, then Bill reappeared, walking briskly away. A clearly furious Scribner emerged then and started to shout after the small man, although I couldn't hear what he was saying. Bill stopped briefly beside a young man who was operating an extremely rusty tracked crane. As Bill walked briskly on, the machine started to grind down the quay, the squeaking and groaning of its rusty tracks setting my teeth on edge. Scribner watched it come as though it was some vehicle come riding out of his worst dream of dereliction and decay, and then realised at the last minute that the machine was headed directly for his gleaming Mercedes. With undignified haste Scribner clambered into the Mercedes and spun it in a wide circle to get away from the inexorable approach of the crane. I wanted to shut my eyes but couldn't, and watched in horrified fascination as the butt end of an old mast scraped a six-foot-long gouge in the side of the car. The car slowed for a moment, then, with a roar that sent it perilously close to fishtailing into the dock, it was gone.

Bill looked relaxed as he rejoined me. He leaned across the bollard and allowed his eye to dwell appreciatively on the lines of the trawler again.

'Don't make me ask, Bill,' I said. 'What was he after?'

'He had a few bits of paper with him.'

'What bits of paper?'

'Well . . .' Bill said slowly, looking impressed despite himself, '. . . let me see. There was the certificate of unseaworthiness, which is a lie because you and me both know how seaworthy she is. And then there was the search warrant. And then of course there was the Admiralty order of forfeiture.'

'What?' I said, incredulous.

'It's all right,' Bill said. 'When he handed them to me I came over all dizzy and dropped them in the tide.'

'Bill,' I said, 'they'll take you into court and skin you.'

'What?' he said, and this time there was a twinkle in his eye, 'an old man like me? Sure, I'm an institution around here. But they're out to get you, son, whatever you done, so my advice would be to steam out of the harbour, set a course up the coast. When you're out of sight, double back and I'll arrange a berth for you at Greencastle. Nobody will find you there.'

I glanced back towards the car.

'Don't worry,' Bill said, 'somebody will drive the car out to Greencastle pier for you.' I looked at him with a question in my eyes.

'Why am I doing it?' he said. 'First of all because I like a man who appreciates a good boat. And secondly . . .' He nodded in the direction that Scribner had taken off in. '. . . I don't like bloody lawyers.'

Twenty minutes later I was swinging round the pierhead in Kilkeel. It felt good to have the deck under my feet and feel the swell lift the boat as she hit open water. There were plenty of people on the pierhead and I made a great show of heading up the coast along the Long Stone shore. When I was out of sight I set a course for open sea, sailed out a couple of miles then doubled back. On my way into the mouth of Carlingford Lough I met the big Ro-Ro ferry on its way in. I stayed on the seaward side of it to hide the boat from the north shore, then rounded her stern and darted into the Greencastle anchorage.

'Carlings fjord' the Vikings had named it, this narrow channel of water between two towering mountain ranges. It was deep in parts and subject to vicious currents, both nautical and political. The Norman castle that dominated the mouth of it wasn't there for nothing. Nor was the navy gunboat patrolling the southern shore. But for all the hardware, modern and historical, Greencastle was a beautiful setting. A row of coastguard cottages overlooked a derelict wooden pier. There was a small beach of gritty sand with quartz glistening in it, and then a deep anchorage, with several fishing boats and pilot boats moored offshore. There wasn't a whole lot of shelter, and you had to watch the currents and a tide that flowed at lethal speed, and a hard salt wind that whipped off the lough. But it was beautiful and isolated and the people weren't given to banter with strangers, and I was as safe there as anywhere. As I eased the *Castledawn* towards the berths a man on the shore got my attention with a piercing whistle and pointed to a berth. When I waved that I understood he turned his back and walked off.

By the time I had finished tying up at the berth I was dead on my feet from fatigue and hunger. I reflected ruefully on the breakfast and lunch and the day's fat intake, and decided to be frugal. But when I looked in the fridge and discovered the piece of fresh-that-day monkfish left there by Bill, I decided that frugality would do for another day. I poured a Redbreast for myself, opened a bottle of Chablis. I made a tinfoil parcel and put the monkfish into it with a glass of the white wine and a pinch of dill. I cut chunky garlic chips from the few potatoes I had left and put them in the oven. Then I poured another

Redbreast and took the phone up to the deck. I made a few calls and left messages, then I pulled the collar of my battered yachtsman's coat around my neck and sipped the whiskey and soaked up the hard, salty green of the sea and the slabs of dark shadow creeping down the steep mountainsides.

After half an hour the food was ready. I put Robert Johnson on the new Bose system that Bill had fitted, poured a glass of the bone-dry wine and thought about nothing else for twenty minutes.

I let the Robert Johnson play itself out, picked up a few books and threw them down again before settling on a Ross McDonald. *Pale Grey For the Shroud*. I'd read it before, but it didn't matter with Ross. I had been reading for twenty minutes before I heard the noise. It's hard to dock a small boat next to a larger one without making some kind of noise. And when you have a boat as long as I've had the *Castledawn*, then intuition as much as experience tells you when the boat has shifted infinitesimally under the weight of someone climbing on board. Within seconds I was in the wheelhouse. I pressed underneath the binnacle. The catch released silently and the Glock dropped into my hand. I reckoned the intruder had come on board the port side so I slipped soundlessly out on to the starboard side of the wheelhouse and circled around, hoping to come up behind him. I ducked under the starboard gantry. When I felt hands on my neck I dimly realised that there had been someone crouched on the gantry. I felt a black wave slip over me.

'Drop the gun, Jack,' someone said, the voice cool and measured with an accent that came from somewhere north of Moscow. I let the Glock dangle and fall, feeling the pressure of thumbs pressed into my carotid arteries diminish.

'Jesus Christ, Sasha,' I said, 'you could have just shouted when you were rowing over.'

The man swung down from the gantry and stood in front of me, a slight creasing around those pale-blue eyes being as near as Sasha Guydarov ever got to a smile.

'It's not often I get a chance to practise on someone as experienced as you, Jack,' he said.

'When I rang you, I had a civil beer in mind,' I said, rubbing my neck. Sasha shook his head in mock reproof.

'Too much beer has made you slow, Jack. And you don't look up.'

I had first met Sasha Guydarov in 1984. I was in the Crown Hotel in Warrenpoint. It was part of that coal strike era. Dock workers were refusing to handle coal imports, so Polish coal was being shipped in with bogus documentation saying it was being delivered to the south of Ireland. Once in the Irish Sea, the ship would make a swift detour into Warrenpoint and illegally offload its cargo. I was there to make sure that no one threw a spanner in the works. One Friday evening I was having a beer in the Crown Hotel and keeping an eye on two young men who were supposed to be dangerous union agitators but who were in fact run-of-the-mill lefty student idealists who skated merrily over the dangerous political undercurrents of the time. As I watched them getting drunk I saw two men sitting quietly together, both with Slavic features.

'Who are they?' I asked the barman.

'Them's the Russians,' he said. 'Been here a few years. They work unloading the boats.'

Later I found out that the older of the two men had connections with the Finnish consulate in the town, which had enabled them to get work permits, but it was the younger man that concerned me. He was obviously being picked on by some of the locals. I heard a few jibes along the lines of 'Russian bastard'. I edged a little closer. The man was pure Slav, with blond hair and slanted, greenish eyes. There was a disturbing air of self-containment about him, which seemed to get the small-town bullies going. For half an hour taunts flew in his direction but he ignored them. Then one of the young men, a fisherman by the look of him, half drunk and spoiling for a fight, put his cigarette out in the Russian's beer. The Russian sighed.

'Now you must buy me another,' he said, without raising his voice or even looking at the young man.

'Fuck you,' the young man said. 'Outside! Now!'

With another sigh the Russian rose from his stool. He walked in front of the young man towards the door. When they got to the door the fisherman shoved the Russian through it. We waited. I saw the older man shake his head.

'What is it?' I asked.

'Very silly boy,' he answered. 'Very silly.'

'Why is that?'

'Sasha is Spetznaz.' I hadn't heard the word for a long time, and I didn't expect to hear the Russian term for special forces in a dock workers' bar in Ireland.

'Where?' I asked.

'Afghanistan,' the Russian said.

'How long have you been here?' I asked. He looked at me. I should have thought that someone coming from the Soviet Union would have antennae for nosy covert operatives.

'I think you have asked enough questions,' he said. 'We have our papers to be here. We want a quiet life.'

I hadn't heard the door of the bar open, but some instinct told me, beyond a shadow of a doubt, that the man called Sasha was standing directly behind me. The older man said something in Russian, and Sasha replied.

'I didn't mean to intrude,' I said. 'It's just my inclination to be nosy.'

'Your inclination, maybe your job too,' Sasha said.

'Maybe,' I said, turning around slowly. Sasha looked relaxed, but you could sense the coiled strength. There was a graze on one of his knuckles, and I knew that once you'd been in a fight, the adrenaline takes a while to dissipate. Unarmed combat had never been my forte, and I had no wish to be thumped silly by an expert.

'I like the quiet life as well,' I said. 'And you're right, by the way. Being nosy is my job, but I'm not nosy about you, so let me buy you a drink.' I saw him relax, or rather I saw him make himself relax, the tension draining out of his eyes.

'Okay,' he said, 'my last drink is a bit spoiled.'

'What about the kid?' I asked.

'Don't worry,' he said. 'Not damaged. Just hit hard so has manners next time.'

I got the drinks in. As I was about to pay, the phone behind the bar rang. The bartender answered it and listened intently, glancing over at us. He put the phone down and came over quickly.

'Listen,' he said urgently, 'that young lad you took outside. His brother's the sergeant in the barracks. He's on his way over, so you better get out of here.'

Sasha headed for the exit but it was too late. The door crashed open and four policemen stormed into the place, followed by the young man who had put his cigarette out in Sasha's drink. The sergeant who led them in was a young man with a Sterling sub-machine-gun in his hand and a hard, dangerous glint in his eye.

'You!' he said to Sasha. 'Up against the wall. And your mate.' To give his words weight he jabbed the barrel of the Sterling into the older man's kidneys, causing him to grunt in pain. I could see the policeman's brother smirking, although it must have been difficult with the swollen lip he had acquired. I had three choices. I could do nothing, which would have been the professional thing to do. I could produce my warrant card, which would mean that my cover would be blown. Or I could get involved. I got involved.

'Leave them alone,' I said, stepping forward. The sergeant gave me an incredulous look.

'They haven't done anything wrong,' I said. 'Your brother was giving them racist abuse. He was lucky to get away with a fat lip.'

I knew before he moved that I was going to be hit. I just didn't think I was going to be hit so fast and so hard. The policeman's fist whipped out and caught me just above the brow. I fell backwards, seeing stars, but managed to straighten myself by holding on to the bar. I saw Sasha step forward, but the other man grabbed him by the arm and spoke urgently into his ear. Perhaps their papers weren't just as good as they had said. He stood back against the wall. I was trying to decide which one of them to hit back when the young brother stepped forward and spat in my face, which decided the issue for me. I hit him harder than Sasha had done, and felt his nose break as my fist connected. Within seconds they were swarming over me. As I fell to the ground I saw the barman usher the two Russians out of the rear door. Sasha looked back and our eyes met for a second. Long enough to let me see that there was now a debt, and he acknowledged it. I stayed on the ground for what seemed like hours, but was probably moments, taking some more damage, although not as much as I feared, for the restricted surroundings of the bar meant that they couldn't get a good swing at me.

After a while I was hauled to my feet and dragged outside to the armoured Land Rover. Presumably to go back to the barracks where they could have a go at me in a more leisurely fashion. But once I was shoved in I reached into my back pocket and stuck a Special Branch warrant card in the sergeant's face. It was a fake, but it was a good fake.

'For Christ's sake,' I exploded, 'I'm one of you. You nearly blew three years of work with those men.' The sergeant looked at me, bewildered. I stormed on, throwing in all the covert terminology that I could think of, talking about agent insertion and network penetration. He looked from the warrant card to me in increasing bewilderment. Eventually he cracked. He ordered two of the policemen to lift me. Then, at his order, they turfed me out of the back doors. He threw the warrant card out after me and the Land Rover took off with a roar. I picked myself up carefully. As I did so, a figure emerged from the shadows. It was Sasha.

'I hang around to see if you are okay,' he said.

'I'm all right, thanks,' I said.

'Why did you do that?'

‘God, I don’t know,’ I said. ‘I don’t like bullies, I suppose.’

‘Thank you. You know, I have papers, but my friend has none. And it is not a good time for him to be sent home. So we are in your debt.’

‘Don’t worry about it.’

As I limped back towards my car I could feel him looking at me, his watchfulness almost palpable. I had a funny feeling that his solicitude was no fleeting thing.

SEVEN

But it hadn't worked like that. Over the years I'd had a few beers with Sasha. We'd gone on a few fishing trips to the west, where he had a delicate and ruthless hand with a fly rod. When we talked it was about art and history, and sometimes about their delicate intersection with politics, but never on a personal level. He never asked me about my work. I had of course checked him out, and the check had revealed a former special forces officer who served with distinction in Afghanistan, nothing more. I knew there were demons there, but I also knew not to tamper with the lid that he kept on those demons. That was our relationship. Until now.

Sasha sat at the table, toying with a bottle of beer. I knew he had something on his mind. I busied myself with the dishes, waiting for him to get to it.

'Dimitri is missing,' he said suddenly, without looking up from the table. Dimitri was the man who had been with him that night in the bar.

'Since when?' I asked.

'Three days,' he said. 'He went out one evening. I think he went to the pub, but he doesn't come back. I ask in pub. No Dimitri.'

'Did you go to the police?' I asked.

'Police don't give damn about migrant workers,' he said shortly.

'What is it?' I said softly.

'I don't know,' he said. 'I got a bad feeling. There are strange things happening at docks. And then your call.'

'Did he ever disappear before?'

'No . . . well, once – a woman, you know. And then sometimes he drinks vodka and does crazy thing. But this is different.'

I sighed. I was tired, but he was asking me for help, and I couldn't refuse.

'Why don't we take a look at his room?' I said. 'There might be a clue.'

On the way to the shore I thought about the way Sasha had automatically assumed that I was the right person to go to with a matter of this kind. Maybe I gave away more of my profession than I thought. It was dark as we rowed to the shore and the wake of the boat glittered with phosphorescence. A cold wind blew down the lough and I pulled my coat around me.

It was ten miles to Warrenpoint. We took Sasha's old Land Cruiser. The vehicle was spotless, but it had two hundred thousand on the clock. Yet when Sasha slipped Jan Garbarek into the stereo and the music washed over us, the old four-wheel-drive felt like a cathedral on wheels.

Sasha and Dimitri shared a house in a cul-de-sac. It was late and there was a car outside every house, so we had to park at the end of the street and walk down. It was a quiet, leafy place. A cat ran across our path as we walked.

'Dimitri likes it here,' Sasha said. 'He likes the quiet.' I wondered if Sasha liked it as much. I've found that sometimes the quiet allows the voices of the past to intrude, voices filled with pain and rebuke. We walked up the path, Sasha fishing for his key. He fitted it into the lock and then he froze, holding up one hand for silence. Looking through the door, which was slightly ajar, I could see a glass door at the back of the house and a light on behind it. Probably the kitchen, I thought. As I watched I saw the shape of a man silhouetted against the light.

'Dimitri?' I asked. Sasha shook his head. He crept forward into the hallway. I followed. I wished I had a gun in my hand. Sasha lifted a heavy torch off the hall stand to use as a weapon. I looked for something, but all I could see was an umbrella. I left it. It's one thing to be in danger and another to look ridiculous at the same time. We almost made it to the kitchen door when it swung open. The man was wearing jeans and a T-shirt, no mask. In his hand he had one of those small, powerful machine pistols. There was a hesitation, but only a faint one before the barrel of the pistol came up and pointed at us. I knew the calculation he was working on. If he fired he would blow the two of us into the street, as well as waken the entire neighbourhood, besides leaving two unexplained corpses in his wake. If he didn't fire we would be able to identify him. I found myself pleading wordlessly with him to make the right decision. Be sensible, a small voice within me urged. He should know, I reasoned to myself, that someone faced with an armed attacker looks at the gun, not at the attacker's face. Evidently he did know this. With a quick, chopping movement of the gun he ordered us on to the floor. We obeyed. Then swiftly he backed out through the kitchen door. Sasha gave him a count of three then leapt to his feet. I was slower.

The back door was open. I followed Sasha out. There was a small backyard then a long alley. The man with the gun and another man were moving down the alley leapfrog style, one covering the other's fallback from a gun-ready crouch, then changing places and repeating the process. The routine was slick and well practised, and we both stood and watched them go. With two professionals in it, the narrow alley was a killing zone and we all knew it. When they were gone I turned to Sasha.

'Let's go see what they were after,' I said.

There were no signs of forced entry on the back door, but I looked at the Yale lock and saw slight, fresh-looking scratches in the metal. The lock had been picked, which suggested not only professionals, but government-trained professionals. There were no signs of the house having been searched until we got to Dimitri's room. The place had been torn apart, floorboards lifted, mattress gutted. A pair of old but good Kef speakers had been disembowelled, and a collection of vinyl records had been strewn on the floor. I picked some of them up and slid them back into their covers. Brian Eno. Kraftwerk. I wouldn't have thought that the carefully ordinary, almost avuncular Dimitri's taste would have run to such spare modern music. Sasha looked around the room and slumped back against the wall.

'Dimitri's dead, Jack, isn't he?' he said. I sat down on the bed. There was something about the pitiless way the room had been taken apart that told both of us that he was in fact dead. I looked at my watch. Was it even twenty-four hours since I had held Fiona in my arms? One of Dimitri's shirts was lying on the floor. Absentmindedly Sasha picked it up and folded it. He wasn't even aware that he was doing it, but there was an intimacy to the gesture that made me look away.

'The first time I met you, I knew you were a watcher,' he said, making it clear that the word 'watcher' was carrying a certain weight. He hesitated for a moment, weighing things in his mind.

'Dimitri was a watcher too,' he said. 'He would report back to the Russian embassy in Dublin. For a few years there was nothing much to report, but recently . . . recently, there has been much activity at the docks. Dimitri used to go out at night, come back tired, with mud on him.'

We sat in the shattered room. I found myself too tired to respond to what Sasha was saying. Abruptly he swung to his feet.

'Come on,' he said. 'I leave you back. Later I look. Maybe I find body. Maybe I find it in water, I think.' Sasha's voice seemed to be coming from a great distance. I followed him obediently out to the Land Cruiser. Before he started it he reached under the dash and brought out a flask.

'Drink some,' he said. The vodka was strong and smoky and caught the back of my throat. He took a drink, then pulled out of the street.

'Did you always know about Dimitri?' I asked.

'Same way I knew always about you,' he said, his lips tightening in what might or might not have been a smile. 'But so what? I am nothing to you spy people, and you are my friends. Or were my friends. My job now is find Dimitri and bury him. But there is another job.'

'Revenge,' I said.

'Yes, revenge,' he said, speaking the word slowly as if he was savouring it. 'That is the word.'

'I have a feeling that our paths are crossing here,' I said.

'I too feel that,' Sasha said. 'So maybe we should help each other.'

'I would like that,' I said, meaning it. Hard, resourceful allies were hard to find when you had stopped working for the government. A few years before, Liam Mellows had always helped me, but Mellows was in New York now.

'Okay,' he said, 'now I tell you what I know.'

Sasha told me that there was something going on in the docks. One of the vast, hangar-like sheds that had been used for storing bales of paper from the paper mill had been taken over. Security was tight. The security men were plainclothes, but as Sasha said, a man walks differently when he carries a weapon, concealed or not. The shed had its own dock and there was activity there most nights, with a rig resupply vessel docking there and cranes working.

'Dimitri was very interested,' Sasha said. 'He go out every night nearly with camera.'

'A camera?' I said. 'Then there will be film. Maybe they were looking for it,' I suggested, taking another pull on the vodka.

'Maybe, but I didn't see film in the house. I think I know where. I'll bring it to you.'

We made an arrangement to meet the day after next. As I rowed back to the *Castledawn* I saw the Land Cruiser's headlights sweep along the shore. I knew that Sasha would be out that night looking for Dimitri. I also had the feeling that he wouldn't find him.

On board, I just managed to get my shoes off before I fell on to the bed and pulled the quilt over me. When I shut my eyes, jumbled images flashed into my mind. The eyes of a dying girl, the barrel of a gun pointed at my head, the haunted look on Sasha's face.

The next morning I woke late, winter sun streaming through the glassed-over hatch above my head. Groaning, I rolled out of the bed and headed for the shower. The old shower banged and creaked and groaned, then produced a torrent of water hot to the point of boiling. I went into the galley and put Doherty's black bacon under the grill, along with a few slices of Clonakilty. I went up on deck and the icy wind blew all vestiges of tiredness away. The sea was deep green with white horses, and I could see the pull of the tidal race against the hull.

When I went down the bacon was almost ready. I slid an egg on to the pan along with a slice of potato bread. There were a few wizened mushrooms left and I fried them with butter and black pepper, reflecting that this was my second fry in as many days. I tried to find a pang of remorse at this, but couldn't. By the time I had finished eating, it was time to leave for my meeting with Donna McNeill. I found myself taking more than usual care with dressing, which prompted a wry grin on the weathered-looking face that stared back at me from the shaving mirror.

It took all of my strength to row my little skiff against the tidal race, and I made a mental note to try and get out when the tide was on the turn. Between rowing and splashing myself with the oars and the wind, I looked a fair bit less dapper by the time I made it to the car.

An hour and a half later I was on the Antrim coast road, heading towards Ballycastle. A few miles outside the town I took a right turn for Shane's Castle and found myself in a cliff-top car park. The only other car there was an old Mercedes, a car just on the edge of what they call vintage, with rich chrome trimmings and seasoned leather seats. Over at the cliff top I saw Donna, leaning over the rail and looking out to sea.

I leaned against the rail beside her.

'Hi,' she said, without looking round. 'I always think what a dreadful place this must have been for the children.'

'Children?'

'The children of Lir. Their stepmother enchanted them and turned them into swans. They had to spend three hundred years in the Sea of Moyle.' She pointed out towards the turbulent water offshore.

'Poor things,' she said.

'Do you have any?' I asked.

'No,' she said, 'it never worked out that way.' Unconsciously she looked down at the place where her wedding ring had been. If I had read her right, then Donna McNeill had a certain old-fashioned streak to her. That ring was meant to be for ever.

'I'm sorry to hear that,' I said. She looked away for a moment. When she turned back to me, her voice was brisk.

'I want to show you something. A place, in fact. Let's go.' I followed her down the steep path that led to the ruins of what was known as Shane's Castle. We went down past it, down to the very edge of the water, where there was a little landing stage. She stood by the edge of the water and looked down, as if meditating.

'Donna,' I said gently, 'you were going to tell me something?'

'Sorry,' she said, 'I was dreaming. This is where they brought him ashore.'

'Who?' I said.

'The man,' she said.

'What man?'

'The man they found in the bay – the pilot,' she said.

'Hold on a second,' I said, drawing her back from the water's edge. 'Start from the beginning.'

She told me that she had received a call one night at her cottage, which was nearby. It was from one of the local fishermen. They knew she was a doctor and they had been unable to find the local GP. She had asked them what was wrong, and they told her to come quickly. One of the fishermen met her in the car park. It seemed they had been returning from fishing and they had heard a sound in the water. When they shone a light they found it was a man. He was floating in a lifejacket and seemed barely conscious. They hauled him aboard. When they did so they realised that he had trouble breathing and that an overpoweringly sweet acetone smell emanated from him. Every so often he would go into spasm. They had brought him to the little pier and called an ambulance, but it would be half an hour before the ambulance was there, and it seemed to them that he was almost beyond help, and that time was of the essence.

Donna had knelt beside him, but there was little she could do. His breathing was shallow and he was panting. His face felt feverish, and the spasms were coming closer together now, great shuddering events that arched his back so that only his head and heels were touching the ground. He murmured something, and she pressed her ear close to his lips to hear.

And as she did so she realised that his breathing had stopped.

The men stood around him, the scene lit by a torch, as they waited for the ambulance to arrive. They had seen lights at the top of the cliffs, but it wasn't the ambulance. They saw more lights coming rapidly down the path, then suddenly they were surrounded by men, hard-faced men with civilian clothes, some of them carrying guns. The fishermen and Donna were unceremoniously pushed back against the wall. Donna demanded to know what was going on, but was told brusquely to shut up. Within minutes they had the body strapped to a stretcher and were gone, without a backwards glance, leaving Donna and the fishermen standing, awkward and a little frightened, on the pier.

'There was nothing in the papers about it or anything,' she said.

'How did you know he was a pilot?'

'He was wearing one of those jump suit things. And he had goggles round his neck.'

'Any badges or anything on the jump suit?'

'Nothing that I could see.' It had all the hallmarks of a black operation, I thought. The fact that the man wasn't wearing any identifying marks, which would have been normal for a military or civilian pilot. The swiftness of the response from the hard-faced men with guns. The news blackout.

'What did he say?' I asked. Donna was staring out to sea again.

'Sorry? I was thinking about the swan children again.'

'What did he say just before he died? The thing that only you heard.'

She frowned.

'It was a funny thing to say. I'm not even sure if I heard it right.'

'What did he say, Donna?'

'He said two words: black dog.'

Black cat, black dog. I turned the words over and over in my head as I climbed the cliff path. Four words from the mouths of the dying. What did they mean? A gust of wind blew a few drops of cold rain in from the sea. I shivered and turned up my collar. When we were almost at the top Donna slipped. Reaching out to stop her slide, she grabbed at the cliff face, but the stone she had gone for came away in her hand. I reached out to stop her, catching her around the waist and losing my own footing at the same time, so that I came down hard on my knee.

'I'm sorry,' she gasped.

'It's all right,' I said, feeling a stabbing pain from my knee. 'Are you hurt?'

'No,' she said, 'I'm okay, but you've hurt your knee.' Both of us suddenly became aware that I still had my arms around her waist. She flushed slightly, but she held my gaze with a steady look of her own. I took my arms away and stood up. The knee was sore, but I could walk on it. She crouched down to look at it, deftly rolling up my trouser leg.

'You have a bad gash there,' she said. 'You'll have to come back to the house and get something on it.'

When we got to the car park the wind had risen and the rain was driving in hard from the sea. I followed Donna's Mercedes up the coast road for a few miles then we turned left on to a narrow lane. Hawthorn and elder brushed the side of the car as we drove up a hill, then down into a dip. The house was a stone-built cottage set in a hollow. There was a small orchard beside the house and a well-dug vegetable plot. An iron gate opened into what looked like a kitchen garden.

I parked behind the Mercedes and waited as Donna unlocked the door. The interior of the house was comfortable and well used. One set of shelves held books. There was a fine Delargy over the fireplace and other, smaller works by local artists.

'Would you like coffee?' she said. 'O God, I forgot your knee.'

'Don't worry about the knee for the time being,' I said. 'I'd murder a coffee.'

She went into the kitchen. I examined her books. She had a good collection of contemporary fiction mixed in with scientific books. There was a fair bit of true crime stuff as well, not the rubbish, but the well-researched serious authors like Gita Sereny and Gordon Burn. They might have belonged to a husband or friend, but somehow I didn't think so. She came to the kitchen door.

'Come in and we'll have a look at that leg,' she said, then giggled in a girlish way that I liked. 'That sounded a bit country GP, didn't it?'

'Very reassuring, Dr Finlay,' I said. I went into the kitchen. There was an old pine table and an Aga and all the things you would expect in a country kitchen. She had a first aid kit open on the table. I rolled up the trouser leg again and leaned back against the sink. The cut was deep but hadn't bled much. She started to clean it with warm water. I was looking down at the nape of her neck. Her hair was up, but a few strands had escaped and fell across her neck. I had to resist the temptation to brush them out of the way. She dried the knee, then frowning with concentration, she put a dressing on it. She stood up from where she had been crouched. I suddenly realised how close she was standing to me. In the corner the bubbling coffee maker suddenly seemed very loud. Outside it seemed that more rain had swept in, as drops struck the windowpane behind me and the room suddenly darkened. She was looking directly into my eyes now, and I thought that if I moved a muscle or even breathed, the spell would be broken. Then she closed her eyes and lifted her face to be kissed.

She led me, not to her bed, but to the big sofa in front of the fire. There was uncertainty there, the sensation of being touched by other than familiar hands, but there was a fierce hunger as well and in the end the hunger and need transcended everything. Her body was toned and supple and her touch was sure. At the end her eyes opened as though in wonder and then we held each other and were lost to the world.

We lay listening to the rain drumming on the roof as the afternoon wore on and the dark began to close in, telling each other our stories, both surprised at the ease with which we talked. I didn't tell her much of the detail of my former job, but she seemed to know I was holding back and was content for the moment with what I told her. Her life was one of grammar-school girl going to college, acquiring the job and the husband. Obsessed with her job and inattentive to the husband, who meets another woman. 'Not younger,' she said, with a rueful laugh. 'She's a year older than me.' As she talked about it, I liked the way she refused to assign blame.

'I'm supposed to hate him, and officially I do, but, you know, we were together a long time, and only soulmates can last that long. And soulmates don't come along that often, do they?' I looked into her eyes and thought silently that I could indeed be your soulmate, Donna McNeill, and I kissed her again, and she kissed back and together we slipped out of the world again. And when we came back we held each other. I heard her breathe and knew she was sleeping and then, it seemed, I slept too.

When I awoke she wasn't there, and I heard her in the kitchen. I looked at my watch. Five o'clock. I felt lazy and rested for the first time since I had arrived in the country. I looked up from my watch to see Donna standing in the kitchen door, stark naked, a cup of coffee in each hand.

I put a match to the fire in the grate, which had already been set. She sat down opposite me and pulled the drape of the sofa around her shoulders.

'This afternoon,' she said, seriously, 'when I said "black dog", you looked funny, like it was something you had heard before.'

'In a way it is,' I said, 'but I can't really explain at the minute.' She looked into the fire. There was a troubled look on her face.

'There's something about all this that you're not telling me,' I said. There was a long silence and then she began to speak.

'You're right, there is something that I didn't tell you. When I was called out that night I grabbed a bag of medical kit. I don't really have stuff you'd use in an emergency, but at least there were dressings and things that might have been useful.' She paused. The fire crackled and hissed as raindrops came down the chimney.

'Anyway,' she went on, 'when I saw the man I knew there was nothing that could be done outside a hospital. I felt a bit useless, to be honest, so . . . so I took a blood sample.'

'A blood sample?'

'To save time,' she said defensively. 'I had a feeling we were dealing with something unusual. I could have taken it over to the lab and analysed it for them. Then those bloody men arrived and took him away.'

'So where is the blood sample now?'

'In the lab.'

'Are you going to analyse it?'

'I already have, Jack.' Her voice was serious and I could see fear in her eyes. 'I wish I hadn't, but I did.'

'What was in it?' I asked.

'The man died from exposure to a combination of three compounds. Sarin, cyclo-sarin and tabun.' Her voice was shaking slightly.

'Sarin and cylo-sarin are nerve agents.'

'Used in the Tokyo subway attacks,' I said. She nodded.

'Tabun is a slightly less powerful agent, although just as lethal. I'm scared, Jack'.

I found myself wishing that I could reassure her, but I knew that I couldn't.

'Can these things be made outside a lab?'

'No, Jack. Somebody with the right equipment could make sarin all right, but this is a sophisticated cocktail. It's my guess it is designed to have a life span.'

'In other words, it would lose its effect after a certain length of time?'

'Yes. Forty-eight hours or so is the norm. You need to do a lot of work in a good laboratory to manufacture these awful things.'

In other words, the nerve agents had to have been made by somebody who had access to sophisticated facilities, which made it unlikely that a subversive group was involved. The only other people who had access to this kind of thing were government agencies. A mental picture of my former boss, Somerville, came unbidden into my head. Whatever was going on, it had his fingerprints on it. I looked at Donna and realised suddenly how scared she was. I reached out and drew her to me.

'What do I do?' she said.

'First thing, don't tell anyone about this. They have no way of knowing that you have it.'

'They might,' she said. 'The fishermen saw me take the sample.'

'That's true. Is there any of it left?'

'Yes. In a fridge, a secure fridge, in the lab.'

'We have to get it out of there. As soon as possible.'

'I can't do it now. I have to do a lecture at the university.'

'And I've got something to go to . . . We'll have to do it later tonight.'

Somehow the darkening of the evening air that had seemed so romantic now became sombre. Donna slipped off to the bedroom to get dressed and I got myself ready to go. For some reason, when Donna came out we spoke to each other in low voices, almost in whispers. We arranged to meet later that night outside the lab. Looking at Donna I knew that she had the hard metallic taste of fear in her mouth. As I walked out towards my car I took her hand. She held on tightly.

'I don't know how I got into this,' she said, almost to herself. 'A week ago the world seemed a simple enough place.'

'We'll get to the bottom of it,' I said, thinking as I said it that we had to get to the bottom of it or she would never be safe again.

When I reached the car she kissed me lightly on the lips and turned away. There was none of the earlier passion, but as I drove away I saw her standing in the doorway of the cottage, arms folded, watching me.

EIGHT

On the way to the city I rang McCrink. We were due to meet with Deirdre and Kate at half eight. I asked McCrink to meet me at the Crown an hour earlier. I parked the car in a multi-storey and walked down Victoria Street. It was wet and rainy and the warm, gaslit fug of the Crown seemed almost infinitely appealing when I pushed through the ornate stained-glass doors. The old pub had been built by the Italian craftsmen who had been brought over to build the cathedral, and it showed in the elaborate plasterwork and ornately carved timber. The old gas jets had been retained to add to the atmosphere, which was somewhere between a cathedral and Dickensian London. McCrink's angular face hunched over a pint of Guinness seemed to fit perfectly. I bought a coffee and waved him into one of the large snugs that lined the rear wall. Once the door was closed it seemed a perfect place for tales of intrigue.

McCrink's face grew serious as I related what had happened to Donna. His pint sat untouched at his elbow. When I told him about the compounds that had been found in the pilot's blood, he sat back in the seat and closed his eyes. I waited.

'Do you remember when we were at college?' he said. 'We

were convinced that Armageddon was just around the corner. Nuclear weapons, chemical weapons. We were convinced that the world was on the brink. Then the Cold War ends and most people just forget about it. But all that stuff is still out there. They're still making it.'

'We don't know what is going on yet.'

'Well, obviously, whatever it is something has gone wrong. Either there has been an attack or an accident. Whichever it is, there's nothing in the papers.'

'We can't go public,' I said urgently.

'No,' he said. 'For a start they would probably suppress it. Secondly, it might land your doctor friend in a lot of trouble with very unpleasant people. Particularly if she still has some of that blood. We have to think about this, Jack. We have to think hard.'

I looked at my watch. It was time to meet Deirdre and Kate.

'Let's not take too long thinking,' I said as we got up to go.

Outside, the evening traffic had died down. A cold wind blew down the avenues between the buildings, but it had stopped raining. We walked along, both sunk in our own thoughts, then I heard someone calling. Deirdre and Kate were standing on the corner of Royal Avenue. They walked quickly towards us, Kate laughing at something Deirdre had said. I put an arm around both of them and hugged them both, but it was Deirdre's eyes I ended up looking into. There was warmth there, and something else – melancholia, regret, I couldn't tell. I had a lot of history with Deirdre Mellows and with her brother Liam, who was now in New York. But my work had got in the way, to the extent of almost getting her killed. Any chance we had together was gone, I knew, but you can't stop yourself looking at somebody and wondering.

I complimented them both on how well they were looking. Deirdre was wearing a tailored black suit with severe lines that set off the fineness of her features. Kate was as usual wearing an unusually cut black skirt, vintage shoes and a hat resembling a velvet fedora. Deirdre said she was the best-dressed woman she had ever met, and wondered how she did it from a croft in the Shetlands.

'An introduction would be nice,' Deirdre said.

'Sorry,' I said. 'This is Davy McCrink.' They shook hands. Davy looked a little ill at ease, so I walked ahead with Kate and left him to walk with Deirdre. I knew that he was better on a one-to-one basis and that he had a sly sense of humour, which Deirdre liked. Kate told me she had built an office on to her croft and had built up a business trading vintage clothing on the internet. She asked me about my art dealing, and I recommended a few painters to her. Then she looked at me with a sly smile.

'Who is she, Jack?'

'Is it that obvious?'

'To me it is. Written all over you.' I glanced back at Deirdre and McCrink. They were chatting animatedly together. I told Kate about Donna, then quickly sketched the situation she'd found herself in.

'Jesus, Jack,' she said, 'you have a knack of bringing trouble in your wake.'

'She was already in trouble when I arrived,' I said, more sharply than I had intended.

'I'm sorry, Jack,' she said, touching my arm. 'I didn't mean it like that. I just worry. For both of you.'

The meal at Rankins went past in a blur. I was driving so I couldn't drink, but I took a paternal interest in ordering wine for the others. Deirdre was by turns entertaining and fiery about her work at the UN and the fiasco that was Iraq. This was of course music to McCrink's ears, and she was able to bring an insider's knowledge to his broad political perspectives. Kate watched them, half-amused. Rankins managed to rustle up a decent macrobiotic meal for her, while I indulged in crubeens with sausage and a mustard crust. It was warm and companionable, and I settled into a long conversation with Kate on the value of baroque art. When coffee arrived I looked at my watch and realised I needed to leave soon to meet Donna. I ordered the bill. Kate yawned.

'I think I'll walk back up the road with you.'

'What about you two?' I said. Deirdre looked at McCrink.

'I think we might sit on for a while, have another drink,' she said. We split the bill and I got Kate's coat. When I got to the door I turned. Deirdre and McCrink had their heads together, talking animatedly. I knew I had no right to the feeling that flared up inside me, no right at all, but that didn't stop it. I turned away to see Kate watching me. There was nothing but sympathy in her eyes. We didn't talk much on the way back to her hotel, but when we reached it she kissed me on the cheek and laid her head on my shoulder for a minute, too wise to say anything.

Donna's lab was in the northern suburbs, where the city started to give way to big houses with long, leafy drives. The laboratory itself was a 1970s concrete and glass structure, showing its age. There was no security guard, but there was a code to open the gates, which Donna had given me. Once you got through the gates there was a long drive before you reached the building. The whole place was surrounded by fir trees, probably to shield the eyes of the privileged locals from the dated architecture. Donna's car was in the car park and one light burned in the building, otherwise there was no sign of life. I got out of my car. The cold wind moaned in the trees. I shivered and pulled my jacket around me. I used to be able to see the romance in being alone in isolated places. But now, on nights like this, give me crowds of people and well-lighted streets.

The door was open. The building was cold and had that smell of stale chemicals that all such institutions possess. I walked down a long corridor until I saw a light under a door. I pushed it open. I could see Donna at the far end of the lab, her head bent over a book. The dim lighting reflected from laboratory glassware and various kinds of expensive-looking equipment.

'Donna,' I called out to her. She looked up, startled.

'Sorry,' she said. 'I was lost to the world.' She came over to me and put her arms around me. It felt good, and the small cold dagger I had felt in my ribs when I saw McCrink and Deirdre melted a little.

'I think it would be a good idea to get hold of this blood and get out of here,' I said. There was something about the stark shadows of the laboratory that made me feel uneasy.

'Come on,' she said, detaching herself. She lifted a small cool-box with a handle from the workbench and led the way to a large gunmetal-coloured fridge. It looked like a normal fridge except that it had a dial on it. She bent in front of it and entered the code.

'I feel like a safe-cracker,' she said in a whisper. The door opened. I saw serried rows of phials filled with blood or with clear liquid.

'None of it is all that dangerous,' she said, 'apart from our own of course.' She reached into a separate compartment at the back and removed a phial of blood. It seemed an impossibly dark, rich colour, almost medieval, and for some reason I found myself thinking not of ultra-modern chemical compounds, but of the subtle poisoners of the Middle Ages. It struck me that Donna handled the deadly thing with excessive casualness, and I breathed a sigh of relief when she placed it in the foam-lined interior of the cool-box and closed the lid. Like most people, it's the things that I don't understand that frighten me most. She shut the fridge and spun the dial.

If we had left then, we might have made it out safely. Then again, it was more likely we would have been caught in the open. As it was, she brushed against me as she stood up, and next thing our lips met. I don't know how much time passed, then she pulled away from me. She rubbed her chin thoughtfully.

'You need a shave, mister,' she said. 'My chin hasn't felt like this since I was seventeen. Mind you, there's lots of parts of me feel like they were seventeen again. Including my libido if today is anything to go by.' She laughed, and it seemed a light-hearted sound in that forbidding laboratory. Then I heard the car engines. I hushed Donna and pushed her into a crouching position. Keeping low I looked out towards the car park. Two cars were pulling to a halt in the middle of it. They could have been innocent, but several things told me that they weren't. Innocent visitors would have pulled into parking spots instead of stopping in the middle of the car park. Innocent visitors would have had their headlights switched on. And innocent visitors wouldn't be carrying guns when they got out of the car.

'What is it?' Donna said. Her voice was level but I could see the whites of her eyes in the darkness.

'Is there another way out of here?'

'Out the back,' she said. 'The fire door.'

'Come on,' I said. I wasn't moving fast enough or reacting quick enough, and I knew it. I hadn't expected this, and my gun was in the car. We made it into the corridor just as I heard the front door open. They knew we were here, but they were still moving cautiously. Or at least they knew Donna was here. Her car was outside. I thought it unlikely that they would pay any attention to my anonymous Ford.

'Run!' I whispered. We were both wearing light shoes and our feet made no noise. There was a turn in the corridor and we needed to make it. We did, but only just. There was no shout of warning as I saw bullets lift plaster dust off the wall in front of me. And no muzzle report either. They were professionals using silenced automatics.

As Donna rounded the corner she slipped and fell to the ground. I lifted her and urged her on. I needed time to evaluate the situation, examine the options. Even a few minutes would have done, but I didn't have a few minutes. I could see the fire door in front of us. It had a panel of reinforced glass in it, and in that panel I saw the shape of a man's head in silhouette. They had covered the rear entrance as well. As any good pro would, I thought. Without thinking, I yanked Donna into the nearest room and closed the door.

'What is it?' she whispered. Her breathing was fast and shallow.

'They must have got to the fishermen,' I said. 'They're looking for the blood.' And looking for you too, I thought. I looked around us quickly. We were in a storeroom full of janitor's materials. Not much scope for weaponry in the collection of brooms and paint cans and mops. It was only a matter of time before they started trying door handles. There was an industrial vacuum cleaner near to the door. With all my strength I yanked the flex out of the back of it until I had a length of the wire. Fumbling at it I stripped out the positive and negative wires. I wrapped them quickly around the metal door handle and motioned Donna back. I put the plug into the wall and crouched by the switch. I watched the handle. The seconds seemed to stretch out into minutes. Then I saw the handle start to move, infinitesimally, as though somebody had rested their hand on it preparatory to kicking the door in. I hesitated a microsecond, then, just as the door started to fly open, I flicked the switch. There was a flash of blue and a fizzing sound and I saw the figure who had been coming through the door flung upwards and backwards. I rolled through the door, knowing there would be two of them. The first man was slumped against the back wall. The other, who was standing to one side of the open door, reacted quickly, but he hadn't expected me to come through at floor level. I kicked his legs out from under him, but he squeezed off a shot as he went down, sending splinters shooting up from the floor.

I tried for his gun hand but he wrapped his legs around me to stop me getting at it and tried to take aim. Every time he seemed to have me in his sights I managed to throw him off, but I knew I wasn't going anywhere. He got off another shot and I heard the bullet sing past my ear and crack into the door post. Suddenly I heard him scream. He writhed and I kicked free. He was clutching at his face and moaning now. I looked up. Donna was standing over him with an open can of drain cleaner, which she had just tipped into his face. She was staring at him with horrified fascination. I looked around. The other man was moving slightly, but there were burn marks on his fingers. I grabbed his Beretta sub-machine-gun from the floor. It was hot to the touch from the jolt of electricity. I went to the corner in time to see two of the others emerging from the lab. I squeezed off a burst at them and they ducked back. When I turned back to Donna she was still in the same position, still staring.

I pushed her hard in the back, forcing her towards the door. The wiring I'd wrapped around the door handle was still there, but now the wood around the lock was starting to smoulder. As I watched a flame flickered along it.

I shoved Donna through the open fire door and forced her to run. We found ourselves on a path running round the building, a path overgrown with neglected shrubs. We pushed through them, then I forced my racing brain to think. I grabbed Donna and made her stand still, just off the path. She obeyed like a child. Sure enough I heard someone else coming the other way, pushing the dripping branches aside. I saw the figure and then I saw the gun. I fired three shots. The figure dropped. I grabbed Donna by the hand and pulled her after me. I'm not sure if she registered that the operative I had just shot was a woman. I didn't regret her death any more or any less than anyone else I had shot. Less, perhaps, because she would have killed me without flinching, and celebrated it with drinks that night in a special forces drinking den at an army base prior to being airlifted out. There would have been no inquest.

Suddenly and unexpectedly we burst from the shrubbery into the car park. The whole thing had the look of a special forces operation that had gone wrong. The man who had been left to cover the car park and our cars had gone to the doorway of the lab and was peering in. To the rear of the building smoke and flames were beginning to shoot into the night air. The man looking into the lab should have kept to his brief, which would have been to stop us escaping. I dropped to one knee and fired a burst at him, hitting him somewhere in the lower body. He grunted and fell, the weapon in his hand clattering to the ground.

When we got to the cars I realised that he had done part of his job properly. One of their cars was blocking both of our cars. As I hesitated a burst of gunfire sent sparks flying from the chain-link fence beside me. I looked back and saw a man silhouetted against the flames that were starting to shoot from the rear door of the building.

'Come on,' Donna said, surprising me. We dived into her car. She stuck the heavy Mercedes into reverse and backed into the attacker's car. Metal ground against metal as the big car pushed the other car aside. Another burst of gunfire starred the windscreen of my Opel. Donna gunned the Merc across the car park, hitting the kerbs hard, but she kept going.

I leaned out of the window and sprayed bullets in the general direction of the building, hoping to keep heads down rather than hit anything. Then we were on the drive and the trees closed around us, hiding us from the pursuit. I turned to tell Donna to keep her shoe to the board, but realised I didn't have to say a word. Her driving was fast and controlled, and she took the final corner of the drive in a long four-wheel drift. We hit the road hard and Donna opposite-locked the big car, swinging it perfectly into line and gunning the engine.

'Hey, hey, slow down,' I said. 'They're not going to follow and I don't want the traffic branch on our tail.'

It took a visible effort for her to slow down and unclench her hands from the wheel.

'Where did you learn that?' I asked.

'Driving?' she said. 'I had four car-mad brothers. We used to do a bit of rallying, stock car racing, that kind of thing.' She turned her face to me. 'I don't want you to say anything for five minutes, okay? I just need to drive and to think.' I held up my hands to show assent.

We drove on in silence. After the allotted five minutes she pulled into a lay-by and turned off the engine.

'Look,' she said, 'I've known you for two days. In that time I've been pulled into . . . into . . . I don't know, some kind of web of conspiracy. I've been shot at, been in car chases . . . I don't want this to go any further, Jack. I want my life back right now.'

'Just wait a minute,' I said, aware that my voice sounded harsh in the confines of the car. 'Your problem started the minute you were called out to that dead pilot. That's what happened, not me arriving on the scene. It's true, there would have been one major difference if I hadn't been here.'

'What's that?' she said, her voice defiant.

'If I hadn't been here, you would be dead by now.'

'I wouldn't be . . . anything like that . . . I would have gone to the authorities . . .' There was uncertainty in her voice now.

'For God's sake, Donna,' I said, 'these people *are* the authorities.' I had seen the expression on someone's face many times, an ordinary person trying to adjust their perception of the world, suddenly seeing it as a much more complex and dangerous place than they had always assumed, realising that the safety nets we take for granted are no such thing.

'The contract with the state,' I said.

'What?' she said, looking bewildered.

'The notion that if we fulfil our obligations towards the state, then it will fulfil its obligations towards us. Most people believe that without really thinking about it. But it's not true.'

'But surely those people aren't the . . . the state . . . the government . . .?'

'The state has a lot of faces and a lot of ways of expressing itself, and I'd bet my life that we've just seen one of them.'

'Listen,' she said, 'I'll drop you where you're going, and then I'm going home.'

'You don't get it, Donna. You can't go home now.'

'I can and I will,' she said, but there was no conviction in her tone.

'You have to come with me.'

'I'm afraid,' she said. Her tone was suddenly desolate. I put my arm around her shoulders.

'Once these things start you have to follow them through to the end,' I said. 'But there always *is* an end, Donna.'

She didn't look at me. She turned the key in the ignition and the engine started.

'What direction do we go in?' she said in a hollow voice.

She said nothing when we met a fire engine speeding the other way, its siren going. Nor did she speak when I directed her to the quayside at Greencastle, then helped her into the little dinghy. It was only when we got inside the main cabin of the *Castledawn* that her strange reserve broke. She looked around her quizzically, then looked at me.

'You live on a *boat?*' she said. She started to giggle. I watched as she collapsed helplessly on to the banquette, gasping for air. I poured two Redbreasts and handed one to her.

'I'm sorry,' she said, 'I'm not laughing at you.'

'You are, you know,' I said, 'but I don't mind.' She looked down at her clothes. Her trousers were torn and there was a burn mark on her jacket. She got up quickly and went to the mirror. There was a smear of soot on her face and her hair had fallen from its tight bun. I thought it looked attractive.

'A sweet disorder in the dress,' I said.

'Sweet disorder my eye,' she grimaced. 'I look a sight . . . There's an overnight bag in the back of my car.'

'I'll get it for you in the morning. I don't think I'm fit enough to row back over there again.'

She gave me a dubious look, but stopped short of demanding that I jump into the skiff forthwith.

'There's a shower in there,' I said, nodding towards the stateroom, 'and there's a bathrobe on the back of the door.' She took a long drink of the whiskey. For the first time I noticed the dark rings under her eyes.

'I want you to sit down with me and explain everything that happened tonight,' she said. 'I want to know why you acted the way you did and how you live with it. Secondly, I want to know how I get out of it. And lastly, put that phial of blood into the fridge if it's so precious.'

She didn't exactly slam the door of the stateroom behind her, but you knew that slamming was on her mind. I put the blood in the fridge as I was told, then set about a quick bow-to-stern check of the *Castledawn*, looking for obvious signs of an intruder. I couldn't find anything. I secured and locked anything that could be locked, checked the lines and went below. I poured myself another Redbreast. After a while I realised there was no sound from the stateroom. I knocked gently on the door. When there was no answer I eased the door open. Donna was fast asleep on the bed. She was wearing the bathrobe and her hair was still wet. She looked like a teenager dreaming teenage dreams, and I left her to them, drawing the cover up over her gently and kissing her forehead. I took sheets and a quilt from the old steamer chest and closed the door gently behind me.

NINE

I woke early the next morning with a crick in my neck and an aching back. I'd turned the old bunks into an office and the banquette wasn't meant for sleeping on. Grumbling to myself I went into the galley and put on a pot of Colombian. While that was brewing I sluiced myself down in the decktop head. It was a fresh morning with a brisk north-easterly blowing up the lough. I heard the compressor start up for hot water below, which gave me about twenty minutes before Donna appeared. I threw on a jumper and swiped her car keys from the banquette. By the time she had appeared, her overnight bag was sitting on floor outside her door.

'Thanks,' she said, a little stiffly, and disappeared back into the stateroom. I took some frozen English muffins from the freezer, and started into a hollandaise. Five minutes later I was putting eggs Benedict on the table. Donna came out again, wearing a black cashmere ensemble that looked elegant enough for a good film première, and understated enough not to look ridiculous at breakfast time on a converted trawler. I moved over to let her sit down. As she passed behind me she bent down and planted a chaste kiss on the top of my head. At least the thaw has started, I thought.

When we had finished eating we brought coffee up to the wheelhouse. It was cold and I turned on the heaters. The cold always made the finger I had lost in Mexico ache. Losing that finger wasn't an episode I liked to think of all that much, and I jammed the hand firmly in my pocket, using the other to log on to my email on the new iMac I had just installed in the wheelhouse, and of which I was inordinately proud. While I waited for the wheelhouse to warm up I told Donna about Sasha and Dimitri and the activity at Warrenpoint.

'I'm convinced that all these things are connected,' I said. 'We just don't have enough information. I'm hoping that I can get some answers now.'

A few years ago, when I needed fast, discreet and, it has to be said, expensive intelligence I would put in a call to Paolo Casagrande in Torino. Then Paolo had lost his daughter to a big-time drug dealer, and we had gone after the dealer. We'd got Alva back, but I'm not sure if she would ever be described as wholly intact after that. Paolo had lost his legs in an under-car bomb, and since then he had dedicated himself almost wholly to his love of fine art. Alva had taken over the intelligence side of things. She was young and beautiful and subtle in a dangerous, unknowable way, and each time I was in contact with her I had to remember the friendly little girl I'd seen every summer in Fiesole. I'd sent an email off to her containing a series of questions, but now her reply consisted of two words: Call me.

I picked up the phone.

Alva answered almost instantly. Her voice was low and modulated, her English almost accentless.

'Jack, *caro*, how are you?'

'Not too bad, Alva. In trouble as usual.' Her laugh was soft and musical and almost entirely without humour.

'Yes, I did wonder about your questions.' Here the tone became businesslike. 'And I thought I should talk to you directly.'

'Why is that?' Something about the way this was going worried me.

'Let me answer your questions and then I will tell you. Firstly, there is a great deal of electronic traffic associated with the area of sea known as the North Channel. Much of that traffic is coded, which would suggest that someone has something to hide, no? Second, the compounds you mention, crypto-sarin et cetera, are of course key chemical weapons compounds. Third, Major Somerville has not been seen since September of this year, which is unusual.'

'So why did you want to talk to me directly about this, Alva?' I said. She laughed, a cool, amused little laugh. Characteristic, but worrying. When other people got scared, Alva just seemed to get a little more arch, a little more ironic. I often wanted to ask her if that was really her personality, or if the couple of grams of good Burmese heroin she took every day had anything to do with it.

'The rumour is that some action of a very serious kind was planned for Iraq, or rather the political circumstances surrounding Iraq.' I listened intently. To anyone in the trade, the word 'action' had a technical meaning, referring as it did to a covert action. 'It seems that this action has been undertaken. The consequences have not yet come to pass, but no doubt they will.'

'So?'

'So, Jack *caro*, this information comes to me. Next thing you come to me asking about chemical weaponry, which is one of the great themes of the Iraq war. So I put the two together.' She hadn't actually asked a question, but the words hung in the air as if she had.

'I don't know,' I said. 'I don't know what is going on, Alva.'

'Then be careful,' she said, and this time there was no irony in her voice. 'There are big interests involved here, the biggest. Don't get in their way.' I was already in the way, but I didn't say that.

'Let me know if you find out anything else,' I said.

'Sure,' she said.

'Payment in the usual way?' I said.

'No, Jack, actually it is my father's birthday in four weeks.'

'How is he?'

'Good. Lost in his art and his garden and talks about many things as though they were far in the past.'

'Give him my best.'

'I will. But for payment I want you to find a good work by a young artist for his birthday. That will cover my fee.'

'It'll be a pleasure. I'd rather give an artwork than pay money.'

'Normally I take the money. For you I make an exception.' I laughed. Maybe, buried deep, there was still something of the Fiesole girl.

'*Ciao*, Alva.'

'You are forgetting your last question, Jack.'

'God, of course, the ship.'

'I checked with Lloyd's. No ship of that name could have been in that place at that time.'

'My source is good.'

'Maybe not good enough. The *Jane Goode* was lost with all hands in a storm off Cyprus in 1950 according to Lloyd's List. The ship did not exist at that time, Jack.'

I hung up feeling more confused than ever. I told Donna everything that Alva had told me.

'This gets worse,' she said. 'An international incident.' I hushed her. The local radio was on quietly in the corner and it was coming up to news time. We listened. There was no mention of gunfire or arson at the laboratory.

'I can't believe it,' Donna said. 'That should have been the headline! They can't just make things not happen!'

'They can.'

'What about my job?'

'Forget about it for the time being,' I said. 'They've probably cordoned off the building anyway.'

'How long is this going to go on?' she asked, miserably.

'Until I find out what is happening,' I said. I looked across at the shore and saw a car pulling up at the quayside. The occupants got out. It was Deirdre and Kate. I felt my heart sink. Even at this distance Deirdre looked radiant, or at least I imagined she looked radiant. They waved across the water.

Five minutes later I was sculling across the water to them, thinking that it was about time to hitch my old Seagull outboard motor to the skiff.

'Davy told us where you were,' Deirdre said. 'He's coming down later. We're staying at the house in Edentubber.' I was sure I didn't change the expression on my face when Deirdre talked about McCrink, but Kate gave me a wry look which told me that I had. Nor did I like the reference to the house in Edentubber. It was Deirdre's old family home and it was where we had spent most of our best times.

'Are you coming across?' I said, trying not to sound abrupt. Kate slid easily into the bow of the skiff and held it while Deirdre climbed aboard. On the way across I gave them a quick sketch of what had happened, including the events of the previous night. Deirdre shook her head slowly.

'Jesus, Jack, not now, not again.'

'I'm sorry, Deirdre,' I said, and I meant it. Deirdre had been drawn into my operations before, had almost been killed in fact, and would carry the physical reality of that for the rest of her life. Kate watched us sympathetically. I wanted to say that I hadn't asked for this. That a promise to an old man and a debt to a dying girl had put me here. But I knew that wasn't the whole truth. Some part of me attracted this kind of chaos like a magnet, and some part of me embraced it. Deirdre let her fingers dangle in the water, then looked up at me with a sudden sly smile.

'Ah well, since Liam isn't here to look after you, I suppose I'll have to. Besides, I don't like people dumping their chemicals in the sea.' I felt my heart leap. After all these years, she still had the capacity to surprise me.

Donna was standing on the deck as I pulled alongside. The wind was blowing her hair back and moulding the cashmere dress to her body and I could see Deirdre looking at her with an appraising eye. I made fast and we climbed on board. Without waiting for an introduction Deirdre took Donna's hand.

'Deirdre Mellows,' she said.

'Donna McNeill,' Donna replied. 'Sorry I'm a bit on the glam side – this outfit is all I had.'

'Tell me about it,' Deirdre said, with a glance at me. 'Life with Jack Valentine is full of surprises. We can go shopping later, if you like, and get you some stuff.'

Chatting away as if they'd known each other all their lives, the two women went below. I gave Kate a bemused look. She just shook her head and laughed, then followed the other two. I gave up, grabbed my mobile and rang Sasha. The news wasn't good. There was still no sign of Dimitri.

'Some people see him,' Sasha said, 'walking to docks. He had bag with him. That is all. I need to get into restricted area.'

'So do I, Sasha,' I said. 'So do I.'

'Will you help?' he said.

'I'll see you this evening at eight,' I said. 'I think we could take a look at what they're hiding.'

I hung up and opened the spring-loaded panel under the wheel. I took out the spare Glock pistol I kept there and checked it. I hadn't used it for a while, but it had been cleaned and oiled and was ready for action. I put it back. I wouldn't need it until later. What I did need was a car. The car I had left at the lab had been hired using a fake driving licence. It would keep the police off my track, but it would certainly send out a signal to anybody with an interest in the covert. I regretted not having torched it. It might take a while but eventually someone would track my prints. But that was a problem for the future.

The mobile went again. It was McCrink.

'I'm coming down on the one o'clock train,' he said. 'Any chance you'd pick me up?' I agreed, reminding myself that I'd known the man for twenty years, and feeling a little ashamed of my jealousy.

When I went down to the galley I heard talk and laughter, which stopped the minute I went in.

'We're taking Donna shopping,' Deirdre said. I looked from face to face. I did wonder if there was something contrived about the apparent friendship between Deirdre and Donna, but it didn't seem so.

'Then I'm going to stay with them,' Donna said. She looked me straight in the eye, but reddened a little, high on her cheeks, and the room went quiet, everybody aware of what was hanging in the air between us.

'That's good,' I said, trying to sound brisk. 'That's the right thing to do.' And in many ways it was. Deirdre and Kate were smart and streetwise. Donna would be safe with them and it would free me up.

Kate, who was the strongest rower, took me across. Donna kissed me with surprising warmth before I left, then hugged me and turned away. Kate said nothing on the way over, maintaining an enigmatic, almost Zen silence. As I watched her row back, I decided that I needed male company.

Donna had agreed to lend me her Mercedes. As I got into it I looked with envy at the car Deirdre was driving. She had always liked fast cars, but this time she had excelled herself, with a two-year-old Alfa Romeo GTA. I had thought about asking her for it, but a steely look came into her eye when I broached the subject of cars and I thought better of it. She had seen what had happened to cars that I had brought on operations. I coaxed the Merc into life and cruised the twenty miles to the railway station in retro Teutonic luxury. McCrink was waiting when I got there, an ancient rucksack slung over his shoulder. He slung the rucksack into the boot and jumped into the front seat, commenting that I had at last developed good taste in cars.

We cleared the traffic and got on to the dual carriageway leading towards Warrenpoint, making small talk as we did so, but I knew he had something on his mind.

'Listen,' he said at last, 'I know that you and Deirdre used to . . .'

'Listen,' I interrupted. 'Before you say anything else, it's fine. That was a long time ago. I think she's a great woman and a good friend and I'm glad to see her happy. You too, for that matter. All right?'

'All right,' he said. He fished the pack of Drum from his top pocket and rolled a cigarette. He drew on it with an air of contentment.

'She is a great woman, isn't she?' he said, with a grin.

'The best,' I said, meaning it. I let him have his cigarette and whatever fond memories floated through his mind as he lay back in the Merc's leather seats with his eyes half-closed and a smile on his face, then I got down to business. I told him everything that had happened since I had last seen him. The laboratory, the information I had got from Alva, the presence of chemical weapons. By the time I had finished he was sitting bolt upright.

'I have to ask you one thing before we go on,' he said. I nodded.

'I've never asked you what you did before and I'm not going to start now, but I need to know if you are working for any government agency.' I shook my head.

'Not any more,' I said.

'Then what is your interest in all of this?'

'It's personal,' I said. I thought about the girl Fiona. But as I did so Somerville's face came to mind. McCrink examined me thoughtfully.

'All right,' he said eventually. 'And I need to tell you my own motivation. It's simple, Jack. I've always hated these people and what they've done to the world for the worst of motives. And this might, just might, be a chance to expose them. Also, you know what kind of work I've done on the environment. The thought of those people pouring this stuff into the sea. More than that, it's the fucking arrogance of them.'

'This could get very hairy,' I said.

'It's all right, Jack. I'm ready for some direct action.'

I parked the Merc in the square in Warrenpoint and we walked across to the Crown. It was a dark, moonless night with drizzle drifting in sheets up the lough. Ideal for our purposes, I thought, but I found myself wishing I'd brought some proper wet gear. Sasha was waiting in the bar. He looked up suspiciously as I entered with McCrink.

'He's an old friend,' I said. 'A very old friend.' Sasha didn't look convinced. We sat down. I ordered a Guinness for McCrink and a Redbreast for me. It was too early to go snooping around the docks, and a bit of internal warmth wasn't going to do us any harm. I was worried about the way that Sasha was eyeing McCrink, but I didn't have to. By the time I had waited the compulsory six minutes for the Guinness to settle, and arrived back at the table, they were engaged in a passionate discussion about the future of ethnic Russians in the new Latvia. I sat back and left them to it, the Glock shoved into my waistband reminding me of the night's work ahead.

We allowed ourselves two drinks. By that time the big Ro-Ro ferry would have turned around and steamed out of the harbour, and the docks would have quietened down for the night. The rain had intensified by the time we got out into the square. I pointed the Merc towards Narrow Water. We passed the docks on the left, the acres of containers lit by towering arc lights. For some reason I thought of the lights of a prison camp and I shivered.

I pulled on to the first lay-by of the dual carriageway. It was a popular spot for courting couples and another car parked there wouldn't arouse any suspicion. Sasha unslung his bag and produced two military-style ponchos and a pair of Maglites.

'I only plan for two,' he said, apologetically.

'I got one in my bag,' McCrink said, going to the boot. When he was out of the car, Sasha slipped a slim Russian-made K6 pistol into his pocket. I didn't comment, although I wondered what he needed it for around the docks. McCrink came back.

'Right,' I said, 'let's get going.'

Waiting until the road was clear, we slipped over the fence and down to the water's edge, in the shadow of the old watch-tower that had stood guard over this narrow inlet for centuries. As we passed under it I remembered the legend of the prince who had put his daughter's lover to death by drowning him, and how she had flung herself in despair from the top of the tower into a pair of ghostly drowned arms that rose from the dark waters to embrace her. I fixed my eyes on the arc lights half a mile in front of us. It was the wrong time to start telling myself ghost stories.

The shore of the lough at that point was sheeted in mud and covered in flotsam and jetsam from the docks. Within minutes we were all mud to the waist. We pushed on, not daring to use the Maglites. The other side of the shore, less than a hundred yards away, was heavily wooded, old-growth pines and oaks reaching right down to the water's edge, and Sasha kept glancing over there, as though something was watching us from the ancient shadow of the trees. We rounded a small point and suddenly the lights were directly ahead of us. It made the going easier but we were also more visible. We went along the back of a group of scattered warehouse units until we could see the back of the container yard. We were close enough to see the mesh fence with razor wire enclosing the yard.

'We must go around shore to get to big shed,' Sasha whispered. I could see a small security hut near the entrance of the container yard, but there didn't seem to be anything else and we skirted it, running as fast and low as the mud underfoot would permit. I could feel my heart hammering in my chest. I knew that the docks proper were around the next point. Sasha got there first. I joined him, peering cautiously around the corner, almost recoiling at the sudden scene of light and activity that confronted us. The shed we wanted to look at was a massive building, almost the size of an aircraft hangar. It stood right on the dockside and opened on to it. Moored alongside was a rig supply vessel, a 120-foot steel-hulled ship. There were objects on the deck of the ship covered in tarpaulin and its crane stood ready, although I couldn't work out whether the material under the tarpaulin was coming from the warehouse or going into it. There was plenty of activity on the deck of the ship and on the quayside, men moving about in a purposeful way, some of them with guns slung over their shoulders. Whatever was going on, this was no rig supply operation.

I nudged Sasha and was about to speak when, to my horror, I saw, from just around the corner, a cigarette butt arch out on to the water and extinguish itself. I felt Sasha tense beside me. We waited for several seconds, not daring to move. Then I heard the familiar metallic rattle of a gun barrel striking a solid surface, then one voice saying something and another replying with a laugh. There were guards here and we had almost walked right into their arms.

I put my finger to my lips to tell McCrink not to make any noise, but his attention seemed to have been caught by something in the mud. I lay down on my stomach in the ooze and carefully stuck my head around the corner. People's attention will be caught by an object at eye level, but not as easily by an object at ground level, but it didn't stop a shiver of disgust as the evil-smelling mire oozed into my clothes. Looking up into the night sky I saw two men. They were both wearing bulletproof vests over civilian clothes. They had night-vision goggles around their necks and they carried sub-machine-guns low on their hips, in the casual manner of men accustomed to using them. I turned to Sasha. There was a question in his eyes. I shook my head. The only way to get past the two men was to kill them, and I wasn't about to take two lives just to get a look at what they were guarding. I slid back around the corner and motioned to Sasha and McCrink to go back. If we were to get into that part of the docks, we would have to find another method.

As Sasha turned he saw what McCrink had been poking at in the mud. He motioned to him to show it to him. McCrink held it up. It was a camera. Sasha wiped some of the mud off. I knew by his expression that this was the camera his friend had owned. Sasha put it in his pocket.

It seemed much longer on the way back, our feet continually slipping in the mud and on the seaweed-covered rocks. I was starting to pick up bruises, and my left leg was numb from the knee down where I'd fallen over a discarded fish-box, but if it hadn't been for the treacherous mud, Sasha would have shared whatever fate had befallen his friend. For just as we were in sight of the castle Sasha slipped, and simultaneously something gouged a foot-long strip of concrete out of the sea wall above his head. As I hit the deck I caught a dull metallic glint in the trees across the water. Sasha was on his belly in the mud as well, but McCrink hadn't moved. It was his first time under fire, I realised, and he was doing what most people did. Absorbing the information. Trying to process the fact of someone trying to kill you. Finding the situation strange, almost preposterous. Two things happened then. Sasha hit McCrink around the waist and brought him down, and another silenced rifle shot lifted more concrete from the wall behind us. I squeezed off a couple of shots at the place where I had seen the gleam of metal, although I didn't have much confidence that I might hit anyone.

We lay in the mud then, breathing hard. I was working through the options, and I knew that Sasha was too, but I could see the numbness in McCrink's face. He kept turning to look at the marks the bullets had left on the wall behind us. I was sure that they were caused by heavy shells from the same gun that had opened fire on me in Newcastle. Experience told me that the sniper would be gone by now. That was the historical modus operandi of the sniper. Fire one or two shots and get out before your position is identified. However, a certain caution that came with age prevented me from poking my head above the large slimy rock where I had positioned myself to test the sniper's knowledge of his own role.

'What do we do?' McCrink said, trying to keep the fear out of his voice.

'Nothing,' I said. 'He's probably gone, but we lie low for a while. Just in case he's still out there.'

'I think we do not have that choice,' Sasha said, inclining his head laconically in the direction we had just come. At least two shapes were making their way across the rocks, low and fast. I moved to get a better view and must have exposed myself momentarily, for another shot from the sniper's rifle added to the already considerable damage to the sea wall. Obviously the man behind the rifle was trying to keep us pinned down until the other two got to us.

'There is that,' Sasha said, indicating a large metal disc on the wall, a glorified lid in fact, concealing an outlet of some sort, a stream or a factory waste disposal pipe. I could see the problem immediately. There was no way of knowing where the pipe ended up, and if all three of us climbed into it, it would be a simple matter to stick the barrel of a sub-machine-gun into the end of the pipe and empty a few magazines into it.

'One of us must go,' Sasha said urgently. 'One man who can get firing point, attack these men. You go. I stay with McCrink.'

I opened my mouth to object but Sasha spoke first. 'You go. I train for this many years. I know to fight like this.'

'Okay,' I said. Fire zones weren't a place to sit around arguing. Not if you wanted to stay alive. McCrink looked between the two of us. He seemed bewildered. We both knew he was safer where he was. I couldn't afford a passenger.

'The clock is ticking, Jack,' Sasha said urgently. I nodded and counted it in.

'One, two, three!' On three I flung myself towards the outlet. Sasha got to his feet and fired two aimed bursts, one across the river and one towards the approaching men. As I reached the outlet, return fire stitched holes across the wall above my head and my nostrils filled with acrid cement dust. I grabbed the edge of the heavy metal lid and it creaked slowly open, its massive hinges creaking in protest. I felt rather than heard the impact of another bullet from the sniper's rifle against the wall. Ignoring the foul-smelling water cascading down my front, I rolled in and let the lid slam shut behind me. None too soon, as the dark tunnel filled with the sound of bullets ricocheting off the metal. It was then I realised that I had ignored one vital element. There was no light in the tunnel, and I found myself plunged into darkness, a darkness so intense that it seemed light must never have penetrated this terrible place. I groped for the Maglite, but when my fingers found it I felt the sharp edges of shattered glass. I twisted it to turn it on, but it was well and truly broken.

For what seemed like an eternity I slogged forward on my hands and knees, sinking into sludge time and again, disorientated to the point where I found myself crawling up the sides of the pipe. Each time I put my hand down I flinched at the thought of what it might encounter, and once, evoking a jolt of primal fear, I did indeed put my hand on something furry and alive, which squirmed out from under my hand with a shrill squeaking that was magnified by the pipe walls into a terrible and seemingly endless squeal.

As I went upwards, the pipe seemed to get narrower and the surface rougher under my hands. I realised that the pipe had changed into a square stone conduit. Every few metres I stopped and felt either side of me and above my head, but even so I nearly missed it, my fingers just catching the edges of what seemed to be a stone slab. I heaved against it but I could not move it. Again and again I tried, feeling now as if the tunnel walls were closing in on me. In the end in desperation I lay on my back in the stinking mud and put my feet against the slab. I felt it move. Inch by agonising inch I edged it to one side, and at last felt a draught of damp night air on my face. I heaved once more, then turned around and felt my way to the space I had opened. There was just room to squeeze through. I pulled my aching body up, using the walls of the conduit for leverage, and fell on to my face, feeling damp grass against my cheek and smelling the good earth once more. I rolled over on to my side and realised I had emerged only fifty yards away, in the grassy inner courtyard of the castle.

My body crying out for a rest, I stumbled to my feet. There seemed to be renovation work going on, and part of the side wall of the castle had been removed. I ran for the gap, fetching the Glock out of my waistband. Inside the castle a narrow stone staircase wound upwards and I ran up it as fast as I could, my lungs crying out for oxygen. And as I did so I passed each ancient room of the small castle, and seemed to sense the unquiet souls of those violent men who had built castles to quell the wild natives.

Half-dead with fatigue, I burst out on to the castle roof. I staggered as much as ran to the parapet. I found myself looking down the lough towards the docks. In the shadow of the castle, fifty yards away, Sasha and McCrink were crouched behind a rock. Only ten yards away two men had taken cover behind a line of rocks. I noted that one of them was lying with his back to the action, his right leg stretched out in front of him. At least Sasha had hit one of them, I thought grimly. But they were still too far away for accurate shooting. I looked across the lough. The sniper was still there. Confidence or arrogance had made him ignore normal sniping procedure. He was kneeling with his back to me. The rifle rested on a fallen tree trunk. The castle jutted out into the lough a little, but it was still a difficult shot. Firing downwards is always difficult to judge and the Glock was intended to be a close-quarter weapon. I steadied the gun on the parapet and fired a short burst. I didn't hit the man, but one of the bullets clipped the complex-looking telescopic sight on top of the rifle. Almost instantly the man rolled sideways and out of sight. I turned my attention to the other two, firing short bursts in what can only be described as their general direction, since it would have been a miracle to hit them at that range. Sasha looked up and waved in my direction, then squeezed off three single shots at the men. I looked across the river again. I saw the flash of brake lights in the trees and then saw headlights bumping through the forest, heading towards the narrow main road. The other two men were in retreat as well, one being half-carried by the other as he kept his injured leg off the ground. I stood on the parapet and waved to Sasha. He understood and I saw him clamber wearily to his feet.

With a respectful nod to the memory of the ghostly princess, I left the roof. It would have been a difficult climb to get out of the keep if the workmen hadn't left a ladder against the wall, and even with that, I had trouble. Sasha and McCrink were sitting beside the car when I arrived.

'Everybody all right?' I asked. They nodded. Without making it obvious, I scanned McCrink for signs of shock. He seemed okay, but dog-tired. I fished for my flask of Redbreast and we all took a long draught.

'Bit of a waste,' I said. 'We didn't get anywhere – and now they know we're out here.'

'Not complete waste,' Sasha said. 'We got camera.'

'At least we know he was here, I suppose,' I said.

'Maybe more,' Sasha said. 'Maybe he drop it on way out, not on way in.'

'And maybe the film is ruined,' I said. 'But let's develop it.'

We got into the car and swung around into the northbound carriageway. No one spoke.

'Are you sure you're okay?' I asked McCrink.

'First time anybody ever shot at me,' he said, with a kind of wonder in his voice. He fished his mobile out of his pocket and turned it on. Almost immediately it rang.

'I'm all right' was the first thing he said. 'Slow down, I'm all right.' I knew, with a pang, that it was Deirdre. And when we got to Sasha's house and McCrink told us he was taking a taxi to Deirdre's cottage, I knew why. Coming close to death had that effect on many men, causing an electric, life-affirming priapism. I tried to shut the thought out of my head. I had no rights over either of them, and particularly not over Deirdre.

I was dog-tired and covered from head to foot in evil-smelling mud. Sasha lent me some clothes and I showered. When we were both cleaned up we had a shot of vodka each at the kitchen table. Sasha produced the camera. We cleaned it up as best we could, then we opened the back and took out the film. There was some moisture in the film compartment, but we decided it was worth giving the film to a friend of Sasha's to see what could be saved. Sasha was pale and troubled, and looked as if he hadn't slept since Dimitri had disappeared. I made him go to bed.

'Let's see what happens when we get the film back,' I said. 'After that, I have an idea.'

Sasha had left a sleeping bag on the sofa and I clambered in. It was after three but I still couldn't sleep, and lay awake listening to the occasional hiss of a car passing, and the waves grinding the shingle on the shore. Black dog. Where had I heard the phrase before? Then it occurred to me. Black dog was the name that the writer Samuel Johnson had given to the terrible black depressions that afflicted him from time to time. And then Winston Churchill had adopted the phrase to describe his own depression. But there was a piece of this puzzle that I hadn't got. There was no point in the exercise unless the truth was hidden somewhere, no matter how oblique the reference was. I fell into a troubled sleep, haunted by images of falling princesses and pipe-smoking covert operatives.

TEN

When I woke the next morning Sasha had gone but there was fresh coffee in the kitchen. I washed and dressed, drank the coffee and was on the road for nine. As I drove towards Greencastle I realised that I had forgotten about one chess piece in the game. I pulled in and hauled out my mobile. I dialled Alva's number in Turin. As always, she answered almost immediately. I wondered if she sat beside the phone, immaculately groomed and composed, for twenty-four hours a day.

'Alva,' I said, 'can you get me anything on Anthony Scribner QC?'

'I'll be back to you later this morning,' Alva said and hung up. I had parked at Killowen, looking down over the lough. It was a fine morning and I could clearly see the big ferry steaming up the lough with the little pilot boat from Greencastle sailing alongside her. There were several yachts out on the water as well, and far in the distance, the grey hull of the naval vessel which patrolled these waters.

The skiff was neatly tied up at the pier and I rowed across to the *Castledawn* quickly. I heaved the old Seagull outboard out of its deck locker and fastened it to the stern of the skiff.

If I was going to be living here, I needed to get in and out from the boat a little more quickly. When I'd done that I went down to the fridge and fetched the phial of blood. I took five or six frozen sea trout out of the freezer and secured the phial in the middle of them with a bungee cord.

The place had been left neat, but somehow the absence of the three women hung in the air and depressed me. I put the phial and the fish into a cold bag and went back on deck. After three or four pulls the Seagull sputtered into life and I headed for the shore. Once there, I drove back into Kilkeel, passing the remnants of the old wartime air base as I did so. All that remained of the tens of thousands of airmen who had passed through were a few windswept sheds, walls made from dug-up concrete and empty, flat expanses where runways had once extended in every direction.

Bill Quinn was supervising a winch overhaul on a new trawler when I got there. I explained to him that my freezer had packed in and I needed a place to store some fish before they defrosted. If there is one place in the world where there is no shortage of cold storage, it is a harbour. Within ten minutes the deadly phial was safely secured in the corner of a vast chill room. I thanked Bill. He waved me away, but not without a shrewd glance. Considering my former vocation, a disconcerting number of people seemed to be able to discern when I wasn't telling the whole truth.

The next step was a twenty-five-mile drive to a bleak border police station, still surrounded with blast walls and anti-rocket steel netting hanging from rusty stanchions. It seemed a poor place for a policeman of the calibre of Wesley Whitcroft to end his career, but there was a dour, unconventional streak in the man that probably didn't sit too well with his superiors. I waited to be buzzed in by the battered station intercom, but to my surprise the steel door creaked open and Whitcroft himself stepped out. A little more grizzled than the last time I had seen him, even more suspicion of the world and its motives evident in his impenetrable brown eyes, but for all that he moved with the puggish vigour of a man twenty years younger.

He didn't put out his hand or acknowledge me with anything more than a nod, but I didn't expect anything else. We had been through enough together to make us blood brothers, but that wasn't the way Whitcroft played it. For all his cynicism he could see a harsh but just morality at play in the world, and I knew he disapproved of the morally elastic universe that I inhabited.

'Let's walk,' he said. We walked down the deserted main street of the village to the old stone bridge where a footpath led along the side of the river. Whitcroft didn't speak until we were out of sight among the hanging alder and willow branches.

'Talk,' he said, 'but don't tell me anything that I don't need to hear.'

'I just want to ask a few questions,' I said. He sighed.

'I suppose I'm better off not knowing what you're up to,' he said.

'I'm looking for information about any unusual activity along the coast, specifically around Warrenpoint docks.' He was quiet for a few moments.

'There's an ongoing operation around Warrenpoint.'

'What is it?' I said, trying to keep the eagerness out of my voice.

'People smuggling,' he said. 'Eastern Europeans mostly. We've been after them for ages, but we can't seem to break into the ring.' I frowned. Whatever was going on with the rig supply vessel, it wasn't people smuggling.

'You know,' he said, 'I always hated crime. Really hated it. But some actual criminals, you could quite like.' I said nothing. There was one man, a criminal who had become a friend, who had died fighting alongside us, and I knew that, no matter how much Whitcroft disapproved of me, that memory was a bond.

'But I can't feel for these people,' he said. 'I despise everything about them. They trade on people's desperation. They put men, women and children in mortal danger. They ship country girls to brothels and laugh while they're doing it.'

It was the biggest speech I'd ever heard Whitcroft make. And when I looked at him I could see how worked up he was, his jaw clenched, his hands balled into fists.

'I tell you what, Valentine,' he said, 'I don't know what you're up to and I don't want to know, but if you can find out anything about these people, I'll give you all the help I can, within reason.'

It was a big commitment and I thanked him for it. He shrugged my thanks away.

'According to my information, you're out on your own now, Valentine. There is no protection. So if I find out that you're up to any cowboy stuff, you'll find yourself going away for a long time. That's a promise.'

He turned and walked away, suddenly looking older, his

shoulders hunched, burdened, I suppose, with the desire to see justice done that he had carried about with him for decades. When you got to his age you realised that, to paraphrase Oscar Wilde, justice, like truth, is rarely pure and never simple. And then you had the people like me who wanted to stand next to him in the hope that some of his hard-earned integrity would rub off on them.

I went back to the car. There was a text on the mobile from Donna. It read: 'Can I have my car back please?' I decided to call on Sam McKeown on the way back to see if I could pick up a car of some description. As I was getting ready to pull out the mobile went again. It was Alva.

'Anthony Gerard Scribner,' she said without preamble. 'Born Hertfordshire, 1950. Eton and Oxford. Entered prestige London chambers 1980 and has been there ever since. Has specialised in cases involving SIS, MI5 and other covert agencies. Has defended the Home Office in several high-profile cases involving whistleblowers . . .'

'What happened to the missing years?' I interrupted. 'He would have left Oxford in perhaps 1972, and he didn't join his legal chambers until 1980.'

'I thought you might spot that,' she said, sounding faintly amused. 'And the answer is interesting. He was in the Coldstream Guards. A family thing apparently. But not only that, he was also Det.' Det referred to being detached from your regiment and seconded to a specialised unit.

'Detached?' I said.

'Indeed. To the SAS. His father was close to David Stirling.' Stirling was the founder of the SAS and had been involved in a string of right-wing conspiracies in the 1970s. Somerville had been floating around the same strange organisations at the time. At the very least it suggested that the QC wasn't averse to a little parapolitical action when the circumstances called for it.

'Thanks, Alva,' I said. 'That's helpful.'

'My pleasure,' she said and hung up.

I drove east then turned south towards Sam McKeown's. Outside Newry I ducked down a side road and wound my way down to McKeown's. Sam was working on a car inside his shed, his pipe clenched between his teeth. He climbed out of the pit, cleaning his hands with a rag and casting an approving glance over the Merc.

'It's not mine, Sam,' I said, 'but I do need a car.'

'Never thought it was yours,' he said. 'Too much class.' Sam wasn't a man inclined to mince his words. But he knew his job and he knew his cars and he was discreet to a fault. His membership of an increasing band of close friends who thought I needed taking down a peg or two was a cross that I was just going to have to bear.

'Right,' Sam said, 'you need something fast, not too flashy . . .' He cast a withering glance over the ill-fitting clothes I had borrowed from Sasha. '. . . and cheap.'

'Something like that,' I agreed, with bad grace.

'Give me twenty minutes,' he said. I slumped against the Merc and prepared to wait, but Sam took the pipe out of his mouth and pointed towards the bungalow where the McKeown family had been raised. I slouched towards the back door, which was opened by Mrs McKeown before I got there. In five minutes' time I was working my way through fresh pork ribs, home-grown cabbage just brought to the boil and taken off the heat, and local Kerr's pinks, bursting from their skins, the whole thing lathered with guilty pats of fresh butter. A huge mug of tea and apple tart with cream finished the whole thing off. A cardiologist might not have agreed with it, I thought happily, but it didn't seem to be doing the McKeown family a whole lot of harm.

As I was trying to turn down a third slice of apple tart I heard an engine outside. It had a throaty, boy-racer kind of sound, but when the driver blipped the throttle I heard the vicious, highly-tuned whine that you get in a rally car. I was almost afraid to go to the door and look. When I did, I saw a Subaru Impreza with full body kit sitting there, a young man of about twenty behind the wheel. The car was polished to a fault, but I could see signs of hard driving, dents in the alloys, gouges in the skirting. I didn't blame him. If I was twenty I would want to drive a fast car hard as well. But I wasn't twenty, and I could tell by the grin on Sam's face that he was, as usual, having a little fun at my expense. These cars weren't made for middle-aged men.

However, my embarrassment faded when I took the car on a test drive. I insisted on Sam coming too. No matter how hard I pushed, the car was impeccably behaved, the acceleration blistering. I took it right to the edge. Not because I wanted to impress anybody, but simply to see if I could wipe the smile off Sam's face. I didn't succeed, although I fancied that the grin became a little more fixed as I gunned the car through a downhill series of sharp bends, slamming it from one opposite lock to another. When we coasted back into the yard I told him I was happy. We agreed a price with the young man and I wrote him a cheque.

I asked Sam to drive the Merc up to Edentubber for me, while I followed in the Subaru. When we got there, Deirdre's car was gone. As I pulled up by the orchard wall, I saw Donna. She had been kneeling by the flowerbed with a trowel in her hand, and as she looked up, brushing a lock of hair out of her eyes, I realised that I had forgotten how beautiful she was. Sam had cattle to look at in a field near by, so I promised him a lift back in an hour and went into the house with Donna.

'Deirdre and Kate dropped McCrink back to the train,' she said. 'They're not back yet.'

It had been a few years since I had been in the house, but it still retained its atmosphere of refuge. There was a slightly musty smell in the air, as if no one had been here for a long time, but the windows had been opened and fresh flowers placed on windowsills. Donna put on the kettle and I fetched cups from the dresser. But we didn't make it as far as tea. Donna looked at me, and there was something different in her eyes, a kind of respect, for want of a better word, which hadn't been there before.

'Kate told me a lot about you,' she said. 'An awful lot.' She walked over to me and laced her arms around my neck. But this time when she looked into my eyes her look was direct and brazen. She locked her lips to mine and pushed me back against the dresser. I reacted in kind, pulling at the buttons on her blouse, so that they spilled on to the floor. The violence in her lovemaking was a kind of retribution for the way I had torn her life apart, the way that death had intruded on her in a visceral way. She pushed me on to the floor and knelt on top of me and in the end she emitted a long animal moan, rising to a keening sound, ending abruptly as she knelt above me, her head thrown back, taut as a bowstring, and then, as she took her release, she sank slowly into my arms.

I held her like that for a long time. When she lifted her eyes to mine, they were wet.

'I never . . . it's a long time since . . . I don't know . . . I let go like that.' I tried to sit up, but a muscle in my back which hadn't been used for a long time told me to stay where I was for a moment.

'Worn out?' I shook my head.

'Surrender?' she said, smiling this time.

'Never,' I said. 'The Valentines never surrender. It's a family motto. *Valentine non surrendare*.'

'Is that a fact?'

'From medieval times. The Valentine family goes back a long way, you know.'

'I knew you were aristocratic from the moment I met you. I'm going to be looking for a ransom for you, high-born stranger.'

'Better do it soon then.'

'Why?'

'Deirdre's car just pulled up outside.' She jumped to her feet and looked down at the ruined blouse.

'I only bought it yesterday,' she said. 'God, I'd better run.' She darted into one of the bedrooms and I tried to straighten myself up, as the door opened and Deirdre and Kate bustled in carrying bags of shopping.

'Like the car, Jack,' Deirdre said. I glared at her suspiciously, looking for a tone of mockery. They dumped their bags on the table. As they did so I surreptitiously swept a couple of buttons from Donna's blouse under the dresser with my foot. When Donna reappeared five minutes later, she had changed and showered, although there was a colour high up in her cheeks that couldn't be attributed to make-up. She gave me an old-fashioned disapproving look. I glanced in the mirror and realised I was a bit dishevelled-looking.

I sat them down at the table and told them about what had happened the previous night. It seemed important to include them. I told Donna what I had done with the contaminated blood. If anything happened to me she might be able to use it as a bargaining counter. Then Sam knocked on the door and I wasn't able to tell them any more. As I left with Sam Donna followed me out.

'Are you doing anything tonight?' I asked.

'REM in the King's Hall,' she said. 'We're staying the night.' Then, seeing the look on my face, 'Please, please don't ask who REM are.' I grinned. My musical memory was a junk-yard of Dylan and Ewan McColl and Sandy Denny with the odd rock icon thrown in.

'Give my best to McCrink,' I said. 'I'm going to see if I can get hold of Sasha and get a look at these photographs, if they came out.'

Traffic was heavy and it was just before four when I got to the docks. Sasha would knock off at four, so I waited near the gate. Men appeared, walking in groups or driving towards the exit. I saw Sasha in the distance, talking earnestly to a couple of other men with an eastern European look, one of them a strikingly good-looking man in his early thirties. Sasha saw me at the gate and shook hands with them. He smiled fleetingly when he got to me, but he was preoccupied and looked blankly at me when I asked about the photographs, before understanding dawned on him. He motioned me into the First and Last bar. We took a seat in the corner and ordered a drink. He took an envelope from his pocket.

'I got some photos – not good, though,' he said.

I looked at the photographs. Somehow his friend had managed to develop them, but they were hopeless, the original film having been attacked by damp. All you could see were vague shapes in black and white, with what looked like all sorts of stains spread over them. Sasha still looked edgy.

'Are you all right?' I asked.

'I get call from Dimitri's brother today. I have to tell lie that he is ill. What about blood?' he said, changing the subject abruptly.' Did you hide blood?'

I told him what I had done with it. He nodded in approval.

'I have to go,' he said abruptly. He reached for the photographs and scooped them up before I had a chance to say anything. I watched him leave, his shoulders hunched in his thin jacket. I looked down at the table. The negatives were still there. I thought about running after him with them. Then I thought about Paolo, Alva's father. He had retired from the intelligence game, but he was an authority in the restoration of old photographs and manuscripts, and I knew that he was still incapable of turning down a challenge. If the photographs could be enhanced . . .

I went to an internet café down the street. Using the disk I emailed the photographs to Turin. There, my old friend, I thought. There's something to take you out of the garden for a while. I finished the last of my drink. It had been a long day.

Time for a shower and something good to eat, I thought. With that in mind I turned the Impreza towards Kilkeel harbour, thinking I'd pick up a bit of monkfish off one of the boats, or at least a half-kilo of prawns.

It had just turned dark when I got to the harbour. The sky had cleared and the wind had turned to the north-west. It was suddenly bitterly cold and you could smell the Arctic on that wind. But there was something I liked about the harbour this time of the evening, the small offshore boats coming in under lights so that you could look out to sea and see a fan of green and red running lights coming in from the darkness, converging on the harbour. A chip van parked on the quayside had attracted a queue of fishermen and warm scents rose from it, so that I half-considered abandoning my original plan for a warm, soggy bag of chips and a bunburger smothered in ketchup. Instead I bought a cup of tea from the van and sat on a bollard watching the boats coming in. Fishing was a hard life and many of the boats were now crewed by immigrants rather than local people, but you knew by the way the men stood with exaggerated casualness on deck as the boats swept past the end of the pier, that there was still a glamour associated with facing the sea that the landlubbers on shore would never feel.

My moment of romance faded quickly. As I looked up towards where the main road bifurcated to make two roads that ran either side of the main inner basin, I saw something that shouldn't have been there. More than one thing, in fact. Three four-wheel-drives, travelling in formation and swinging round the other side of the basin with military precision, keeping perfect distance from each other. Please don't stop outside the cold store, I said, please don't stop there. But of course they did. Car doors opened and men began to spill out, five to each vehicle. None was carrying a weapon openly, but you didn't doubt the existence of concealed weapons, with custom stocks for concealment perhaps, or cut-down barrels.

Using a pair of bolt cutters they had the store open in seconds. It wasn't hard. The quality of the lock took account of the fact that no one was particularly interested in stealing fish. They filed into the building purposefully, in teams. Two of them took up positions at the door. There would be no way in or out. I didn't start to think about how they knew about the blood. For all I knew it was a tail, or the Merc had in fact been jarked – the covert term for secret bugging – with a high-frequency bug on board. For all I knew, everywhere I had visited in the past twenty-four hours had teams of men descending on it – hard-eyed, ruthless men. There was only one thing I could do. If they wanted the blood that badly, then I had better try to make sure they didn't get it. I looked down at the dark, oily water. In between two steel-hulled trawlers I saw a paint-streaked raft, no more than a few planks strapped on top of oil barrels for the purpose of painting boat hulls.

I clambered down the steel ladder bolted to the harbour wall. It was a different world down there, the oily water full of debris, the hulls of the boats shifting and groaning as they rose and fell. It was dark as well, the hulls blocking the light. If I kept to the shadow, no one would know I was there. I jumped on to the raft, which swayed alarmingly as I landed on it. I cast off and took hold of the primitive sweep oar at the stern. For a minute or two it seemed as if the raft was barely moving, then it seemed to pick up a bit of momentum. I squeezed between the trawlers and the harbour wall, picking up fragments of conversation and snatches of music from the quayside above.

It took ten minutes to get from one side of the harbour to the other, as I tried to make the raft go in the direction I wanted it to go. Once or twice I crashed against the harbour wall, wincing at the dull metallic boom from the oil drums that made up the base of the raft. But finally I was under the loading dock of the cold store. I grabbed one of the steel ladders that scaled the harbour wall and swung myself up from the deck of the raft. I climbed the ladder as swiftly as I could and peered cautiously over the edge of the dock. There was no reason for them to post a guard out here, went their deadly logic, so there was no point in wasting a man. The dock was empty. However, I was faced with four large aluminium sliding doors, closed down to the ground and locked with padlocks. There was no way I could break the lock without making enough noise to waken the dead. Fortunately I didn't have to. When I examined the nearest lock I saw that it was broken and useless, and had only been made to look as if it was secure. Obviously they thought it was even less likely that someone would try to steal fish from the harbour side of the cold store.

As carefully as I could, I raised the door just enough to let me slip inside. I found myself in a kind of cold lock between the doors and the store itself, heavy strips of plastic hanging from the ceiling to stop the cold escaping when the doors were opened. I carefully moved one of the flaps aside and peered in. It was like a scene from some kind of cold hell. The outside doors had been left open, causing great clouds of condensation to wreath the vast spaces of the store, through which men with guns appeared and disappeared. The noise of the massive freezer units dominated everything, but through their backdrop I could hear curt barked orders. I moved cautiously down a row of pallets stacked to the ceiling. The phial of blood in its cold-box was diagonally opposite me now on the other side of the store. It was colder than I remembered in the store, and I could feel it in my bones already. I wondered if they knew exactly what they were looking for. Perhaps I had been seen carrying the cold-box into the store. In which case, it might take a while, but they would find it eventually.

It was almost impossible to see through the wreathing condensation. As cautiously as I could, I rounded the corner of the pallets and almost walked straight into the back of one of the men. Quickly I darted back – and then almost ran into one of them coming the other way. I ducked into a gap between two towers of pallets and held my breath. A trickle of sweat ran down my back and turned uncomfortably cold as it did so. This was no good, I thought. There was no way I could negotiate the entire store and hope not to run into one of the men. I looked upwards. I was in a kind of canyon between a dizzy pile of pallets containing, according to the labelling, blast-frozen prawns. It was then it occurred to me. I couldn't get across the floor, but there was another way.

Five minutes later I was halfway up the pile of pallets, wondering if I'd done the right thing. The climbing itself was relatively easy, but the slats of the pallets were ice-covered and treacherous, and once, when I grasped a pallet too firmly, the whole tower swayed menacingly. It wasn't the fate I envisaged for myself – to be buried underneath tons of prawns. I held my breath until the swaying stopped, then climbed diagonally on to the next tower, which seemed more stable. By the time I reached the top, my fingers were frozen and useless and my feet felt like two clubs. As fast as I could, I climbed over the top of the frozen fish in the pallets, slipping and slithering and trying not to look down into the deep canyons between the towers. I don't know how long I spent up there. It felt like hours, pinned down by the merciless beam of the big halogen lamps a yard over my head, and by the huge ducts out of which poured frozen air.

At last I reached the far side. I lay on my stomach and looked cautiously over the side. As I did so I saw that the front doors had been closed. I closed my eyes and listened. There was no sound except for the freezer units. I realised that I hadn't heard the men for a while. I groaned. It seemed that I could simply have waited and walked across the floor. I wondered if they had been disturbed. Then my frozen brain came awake. There could only have been one reason why they had stopped their search. They had found the thing they were looking for. I crept to the edge again and looked down. The little corner where I had left the cold-box was empty. The blood was gone.

It was a long, laborious climb down. I forced the outside doors open by the simple expedient of leaning against them, then spent the next twenty minutes hopping up and down and blowing on my hands, trying to bring some life back into them, before I could start the long walk back to the car. I was troubled by the disappearance of the blood. It had been the proof that there was something seriously amiss. It had represented some security for Donna, and now she was the only evidence for the finding of the pilot and for the way he had died. It meant that she was now in serious danger. It now became imperative that we get a closer look at what was going on in the docks.

This time I succumbed to the lure of the chip van and sat in the car eating fresh haddock and chips, soaked in malt vinegar. When I'd finished I drove slowly out to Greencastle. The newly-engined skiff had me on board the *Castledawn* in a few minutes. I changed out of Sasha's clothes, by now fairly battered and smelling of fish, had a shower and poured myself a stiff Redbreast. I turned on the Imac then and checked my email. There was one from Turin, not from Alva this time, but from Paolo, telling me to phone him when I got in. I dialled the number. As it rang I realised that there were attachments to the document.

'Jack, *caro*.' Paolo answered the phone, his tone as warm and civilised as ever. When I had first met Paolo he was the epitome of the handsome Italian, with flashing brown eyes that women, it seemed, could not resist. His first great love, Alva's mother, had been killed and I think he had never replaced her. Now he was a legless cripple in a wheelchair and had withdrawn to his art dealing and his garden, but the bomb that had removed his legs had not dented the essential quality of the man.

We talked about art for a while. Paolo had developed an interest in Japanese art and had built a Zen garden at his otherwise baroque villa in Fiesole. He talked about it with passion and I wished I was there – not in the Zen part, but on the old terrace looking out over Florence. Finally I nudged him round to the photographs. Paolo chuckled.

'You know I am retired, Jack. You also know that I could not resist the temptation to look at your photographs. I was able to enhance them. Did you open my attachments?'

I clicked on the first attachment. It was still fairly murky, but I could make out a geometric shape. He told me to open the second one. It was sharper and was clearly the tail fin of an aircraft.

'The danger with enhancement is that you work towards what you think you see, but in this case, Jack, I am fairly sure. It is the tail fin of a Tupolev 30.'

A Tupolev 30. The mammoth jet was the workhorse of the old Soviet fleet. The design was pretty old now, but there were still plenty of them in service. The next attachment was a close-up of the tail fin that seemed to show nothing.

'No markings, as far as I can see,' Paolo said. The whole thing had become even more intriguing. A Tupolev 30 on a black operation? Meaning that whatever it had been carrying was substantial. The Tupolev had a payload of 33,000 pounds.

'I could only clarify two more images,' Paolo went on. The next attachment showed a fuzzy rendition of a five-pointed star in close-up. There was something familiar about it, but I couldn't place it. The final image was of what appeared to be a standing man with some bulky object about four feet tall beside him.

'I will leave you in peace now, Jack,' Paolo said, and there was the hint of a smile in his voice. 'You have a big puzzle, no?'

Paolo was wrong. I had about ten big puzzles. My head reeled as I tried to take it in. Where did Dimitri take the photographs? If he did take them in the port, then what was a Tupolev doing there? Crashed, I thought, it had to be crashed, and they were taking the wreckage ashore. It had to be, but why? What was on board that would justify a massive covert operation by such an efficient, obviously governmental, agency? I poured another Redbreast and logged off. I felt a serious need to see a friendly face, and in the absence of that, to hear a friendly voice. I checked the clock. It was half-eleven, which meant that I might catch Liam Mellows at home in New York. I tried the number. He picked up almost instantly. His voice was warm, relaxed. He was probably with his feet up with a beer after work, watching baseball. Liam had a bloody past, and we had fought a few campaigns together, but he had left that behind him and was now running a building firm in New York. He was loyal and intuitive, ruthless when he had to be, charming when he wanted to be. There was no better man to turn to when you were floundering in the dark.

'Jesus, Jack,' he said, 'I hear you're campaigning again. You like trouble, that's your problem.'

'Used to like it yourself, Liam.'

'Used to, Jack. You mind what I told you last time we talked?' He'd quoted a veteran Republican who had fought for thirty years. He had said that you carry your own dead easily – your comrades who had died – but that once the war was over, the other dead rose up in front of you. Men you'd killed or seen die.

'I know what you mean, Liam.'

'Ah, you don't really, Jack. It's not until you stop and start a normal life that it happens to you. Maybe that's why you can't stop, Jack.'

'You think I'm afraid of that?'

'Who knows, Jack? We're getting old. We're all afraid.' Then he laughed, not sounding afraid at all.

'I hear our Deirdre's pleased with herself.' He knew all about my history with Deirdre and had been careful not to interfere, although in the end, I knew, family was all where Liam came from.

'If she's happy, that's all I care about,' I said, and meant it.

'I know that, Jack,' Liam said. 'I know that. So tell me, what has you ringing me at this time of the night?'

I filled him in on everything that had happened to date. He gave a low whistle.

'Jesus, Jack, you can pick them, can't you?'

'What would you do?'

'I tell you what I would do, Jack. I would pick up a phone and ring Somerville. Tell him you have the blood, and do a deal to get this girl Donna and yourself off the hook.'

'That's the bit I didn't tell you, Liam. I don't have the blood any more. They got it earlier this evening.' There was a long silence before he spoke again.

'Then you don't have anything, Jack, do you?'

'To tell you the truth, a deal was never on my mind – for my own sake anyway.'

'Why is that?'

In my mind's eye I could see Fiona's face, the life fading from it. I wondered if I would ever stop seeing it.

'The dead rise up in front of you, Liam,' I said. 'The dead rise up in front of you.'

'Is that the way of it?' he said. 'You always had that streak in you.'

'Did I?'

'You did. Now,' he went on briskly, 'what you have to do is follow things through, find out what is in that shed and what it is doing there, and see what leverage you can acquire. And, along the way, maybe you'll find your sniper.'

'That's what I had in mind.'

'There's another thing, Jack – either you've been having some very bad luck or information is leaking somewhere.'

It was a possibility that should have occurred to me. I watched for tails, of course, and every so often practised anti-surveillance measures, but what if they were following Sasha, or McCrink?

'That's not what I'm thinking, Jack,' Liam said gently. I think I knew what he was getting at from the start. I just didn't want to think it. An informer in the camp. My heart resisted the idea, but my head told me that it had to be a possibility. That they always seemed to be one step ahead of us. Suddenly I felt very tired. I rubbed my eyes and sat back. But the evening hadn't finished with me yet. As I went to put the Imac to sleep I noticed that there was an unread email in Outlook Express. The email was from Whitcroft. It was brusque and to the point, telling me to inform him if I saw either of the two men whose jpegs were attached. I opened the attachments. The photographs were mugshots, taken against a grimy wall in poor lighting. The two men looked hard and sullen, and one of them had bruises on his face, as if from a recent beating. But there was no mistaking them. They were the two men I had seen Sasha talking to earlier that day.

ELEVEN

The next morning I got up early and took a long walk along the beach, passing the vast caravan park at Cranfield, deserted now in midweek, sand blowing through it in the cold north-westerly airstream. I rounded the next point and walked the small sandy inlets. Out at sea big freighters moved along the horizon like cardboard cut-outs. In the covert business one of the first things you must think about is the lack of loyalty. You have to watch for the men and women to whom betrayal is a business. But I realised that I'd probably spent too much time in the company of Liam and Deirdre and absorbed their iron rule of loyalty to their friends and family. And once you started to feel that loyalty yourself, then you started to expect it from others. A dangerous expectation.

There were two incidents where I had been compromised. The first was when we tried to enter the docks. The sniper had known that we were going to be trying to enter the docks that way and had time to get himself into position in the trees at the far side. The second was my placing of the phial of blood in the cold store. And Sasha was the only person who knew about both. It wasn't conclusive evidence, but he had been troubled the day before, and somehow he was connected with the two men Whitcroft was seeking.

When I got back to the *Castledawn* I rang Whitcroft.

'Tell me who I'm looking at here,' I said.

'Roman Kovitch, ex-member of Arkan's mob in Bosnia, and Georgi Stanovitch, a Romanian native – he's the good-looking one. Both seriously involved in people trafficking and prostitution. Charge about four grand a skull to get people over here. Then there are the girls. Promise them a job abroad, confiscate their passports, rape them, brutalise them, then set them to work as prostitutes. To be honest, I thought it was a yarn till I went over to Rotterdam and heard some of the girls speak for themselves.'

'So listen to me, Valentine,' he went on. 'I don't give a damn what you're up to. I'm near enough retirement and all that political shit doesn't mean anything to me, but if you got anything on these boys, you'd better tell.'

'I'm not sure if I've got anything,' I said, 'but if and when I do, it's yours. Are these two political?'

'Depends on whether you think people trafficking is politics or not. But no, not in the sense you mean.'

When I got off the phone to Whitcroft I printed the two photographs off and drove to Warrenpoint. It was coming up to lunchtime and I knew that Sasha normally ate in Bennetts. When I went in he was sitting on his own at the bar. I pulled up a stool beside him and ordered a coffee.

'Any word of Dimitri?' I asked. He shook his head silently. I took the printed photographs out of their envelope and slid them across the bar to him.

'Seen either of these characters before?' I had to give him his due. His eyes slid across them with not the slightest hint of recognition, and he shook his head.

'Never saw them before.' I put the photographs away. For the first time I noticed the vodka glass at his elbow. He beckoned to the barman, who brought him a double. He raised the glass to his lips, glancing at me as he did so. There was a thin smile on his lips, but the look was entirely without humour.

'Tell me this, Jack,' he said, 'what gives you the right to be judge? What gives you the right to go out at night like a thief with gun in your hand? Are you the sheriff?'

I'd put the same question to myself many times and hadn't come up with a satisfactory answer. I slipped off the barstool.

'See you later, Sasha,' I said. He gave a harsh laugh in reply.

I sat down on a bench facing the sea and tried to think of the things I would need for what I had planned for that night. I went to an outdoors shop and bought a wet suit, goggles and a waterproof torch. There were several missed calls on my mobile, but I ignored them. Once I'd bought what I needed I had the afternoon to kill. I thought I'd try to follow up the Kerr story. Jimmy had told me that his brother had lived in Larne for a while. Maybe there was something like a seamen's mission, or even a bar where seamen drank, where I might glean some information. Maybe there had even been a woman.

It took an hour and a half to drive to Larne. I went down to the ferry port and asked one of the men at the gates if there was a seamen's mission or something of the sort. There wasn't, but they pointed me towards the British Legion. The Legion was in an old prefabricated building on a side street. It looked dilapidated on the outside, but it was surprisingly cosy on the inside, with carpet and worn leather banquettes. There were horse brasses over the bar, and regimental insignia and photographs covered one wall. I noted that there were a lot of naval pennants, and that many of the photographs had been taken on the decks of naval vessels.

There were a few men sitting at the banquettes, most of them with that ex-serviceman way of holding themselves. I went up to the bar. The barman was a small, red-faced man in a white coat. I told him I was researching an historical project on local seamen and I was interested in finding the crew of the *Jane Goode*. The man looked at me and grinned.

'You come to the right place in a sort of a way,' he said. 'I don't know of no crewmen, but there's a photograph of her on the wall there.'

I went over to look. He was right. There she was, an anonymous freighter, battered and salt-stained, tied up at a dockside.

'Where was this taken?' I asked.

'Here,' the barman said. 'You can see the harbourmaster's office in the background.'

I saw that someone had inked in the date on the bottom right of the photograph. It said 1953. That was a year after she was supposed to have sunk in the Mediterranean. I peered more closely at the photograph. There was nothing unusual about the ship, except for the fact that part of her foredeck railing had been removed, but that might have been for repair.

'The man that took that photo still lives around here,' the barman said. 'Davy Wilson.'

*

Wilson lived in one of the bleak tower blocks that dominate the town. I took the foul-smelling lift to the eleventh floor and got off on to a surprisingly clean and well-kept corridor. I found Wilson's door and knocked. It took a long time for him to answer and when he did I realised why. He was a frail, elderly man who walked using a Zimmer frame, but the eyes in the shrunken face were shrewd and alert. I introduced myself as a naval historian.

The living room was full of seagoing memorabilia, and as neat as a new pin, the way I suppose you would expect an old sailor to keep his quarters. He motioned to me to sit down and sat himself down opposite me.

'The *Jane Goode*?' he said. 'I've been waiting for the day when somebody would come round asking questions about her.'

'Why do you say that?'

'Because she sailed out of here one day and never came back. I was working in the docks at the time and we were told to hold a berth for her, that she would be back in three days. But she never came back.'

'When was this?'

'The end of 1953.'

'Did you know that she was listed as sunk with all hands in the Med in 1952?'

'Somebody made a mistake, mister, for she was here in '53.'

'Do you know what she was carrying?'

'She went out of here empty, but I do know she was bound for Holy Loch in Scotland. The naval base.'

'Anything else you can tell me about her?'

'There was one funny thing. She had all single men on board. They made sure of it. In them times there wasn't much spare manpower, so you didn't go turning down men that was married, but the *Jane Goode* did.'

'What do you think she was up to?'

'Don't know. It was different in them days. You did what you were told and you didn't ask questions. You saw something strange, you just looked the other way. But I tell you something. There were thirty-five men on that vessel. I suppose their families would all be dead by now, and that's all the more reason why somebody should try to find out what happened to them. Now, mister, since I know you're not a naval historian, maybe you'd tell me what you are doing here?'

The last line was delivered with a pointed finger and a rising quaver in his voice. He was a brave man, I thought. He knew he was helpless if things turned ugly, but he was still prepared to challenge me. I told him the truth, how Jimmy had asked me to find out about his brother. He nodded slowly.

'I tell you what,' he said. 'I'll try to find out what I can here. By the look of her she could have been dumping munitions.'

'There was a lot dumped in the North Channel.'

'Tens of thousands of tons. Maybe something went wrong.'

'I don't want to trouble you,' I said.

'It's no trouble,' he said. 'It gives me something to do with my days, and being an ex-serviceman opens doors for me that wouldn't open for you, if you know what I mean. And I know the archives inside out. If there's anything there, I'll find it for you.'

As I crossed the car park at the base of the flats I looked up and imagined I saw Davy Wilson watching me, then turning those bright, inquisitive eyes to gaze across the sea. I pulled out of Larne and hit rush hour traffic immediately, which meant it was almost seven before I got back to the *Castledawn*. There were calls on my mobile from Donna, and from McCrink, but I ignored them. Tonight I was going to operate on my own. I threw together a quick bruschetta and salad and wolfed it down as I checked my gear. Then I put on the wet suit and attached the waterproof torch to the belt, along with a large diving knife I had bought some years previously. The knife was too big and made me feel vaguely ridiculous, but it was better than nothing. Finally I wrapped my little box of lock-picking tools carefully in several plastic bags, then tied the whole thing to my belt.

I went up on deck. The night was perfect for my purposes. It had been clear, but a bank of drizzle had pushed up from the open sea and visibility was down to about twenty metres. Being careful to keep to the seaward side of the *Castledawn* so that I couldn't be seen from the shore, I climbed over the trawler's rail and slipped into the water. Even with the wet suit on, the water was freezing. I held on to the side of the *Castledawn* for a moment to let my body acclimatise itself, then I let go.

I had worked it out carefully, but even so, the strength of the current took me by surprise. I had intended to float gently down towards the pilot boat that was moored about a hundred yards away, but now I realised that it mightn't be quite that easy. As I left the lee of the *Castledawn*, an eddy in the current seemed to catch hold of me and spin me around several times, so that it took a moment to reorientate myself. I was slightly inshore of the pilot boat and bearing down on her fast. I knew that if I missed there was a very wide, dark expanse of water beyond, and that the current could carry me miles out to sea. There was nothing for it except to swim, which I did, propelling myself closer and closer to the sturdy pilot boat. As she loomed above me I made a grab for the cable that held her to her buoy. I missed. I grabbed for the hull, but it was smooth and there was nothing for my cold, numb fingers to get a purchase on. In fact, by trying to grab I was pushing myself back out into the current. I looked up and saw an inflatable fender hanging over my head. With one desperate lunge I launched myself from the water and caught hold of it. Then, using what remained of my strength, I hauled myself arm over arm over the rail and collapsed, exhausted, on the deck.

I lay there for a few minutes, trying to get my breath back, my stomach heaving with a sick rush of fear. That was supposed to be the easy bit of the night's work, I thought ruefully to myself as I levered myself into a sitting position, then blew on my hands to get some life back into them. I took out the lock-picking tools and started on the solid brass Yale lock of the wheelhouse door. It took me half an hour, and made me wish I'd paid more attention to the instructor at the intelligence centre in Kent all those years ago, as he tried to impart his lock-picking skills to me.

Once I was in the wheelhouse it was a relatively simple job to rip out the ignition and leave it ready to start the engine. I didn't spark it up yet, though. The sound of the heavy diesel had a way of travelling across water, even through the mist and rain, and I was pretty sure the pilot, who lived on the shore, would recognise the engine note of his own boat. I went on deck and cast off, allowing the boat to drift a quarter of a mile along the shore before I dared start her up. Once the engine was going I steered a course for the centre of the lough, keeping an eye out for the freighters and ferries which plied their trade there.

When I judged that I was sufficiently out of earshot, I steered back towards the northern side of the channel and cranked the engines up full. Unlike the *Castledawn* the engines were new and full of torque, and the pilot boat soon had foam piled up at her bow as we sped towards Warrenpoint. After twenty minutes I spotted the big ferry as she lost way in order to dock at Warrenpoint. I slowed a little. I wanted to arrive just after she docked – the dockside would be busy with trucks and freight being unloaded, and with luck I could slip in without exciting much comment.

I slowed to walking pace as the ferry backed into position. I watched her doors being lowered and suddenly the quayside was alive with activity, lorries grinding off the boat, cranes lifting containers from her deck. I opened the throttle a little and sailed quietly under the bow of the ferry. I doubt if anyone even saw me round the corner. The next dock was deathly quiet compared with the one I had just left. There were piles of fresh timber and huge rolls of paper stacked high here. I couldn't see anyone, but I made a great show of motoring up the dock and mooring the pilot boat at the small jetty, checking the cables thoroughly so that a watcher would think I was tying up for the night. Wearing the skipper's yellow oilskins I sauntered across the dock in the direction of the gate. When I reckoned I was out of sight I ducked into a doorway and removed the oilskins. Using one of the piles of timber for cover I moved to the edge of the dock and climbed down the darkest section of ladder I could find.

The water smelled acrid and I had to push aside debris as I moved along the water's edge, using the pilings to push myself along. It took fifteen minutes to reach the corner. Cautiously I peered around. There was no sign of the rig supply ship, and the doors of the vast shed were closed, but the frontage on to the water was brightly lit, and I could see two figures standing by a four-wheel-drive in front of the shed. Keeping low to the water and trying not to leave a wake, I swam across so that I was directly under the men. There was a dog-leg in the dock which meant that one side of the shed was also on the water. That was where I wanted to be. From a distance this part of the shed seemed to be disused and was certainly darker than the front of the building. The problem was that it was by a long thin channel with a narrow entrance, and the water in it was filthy. There were oil drums and paint tins and rotting fruit and vegetables probably discarded from one of the freighters. As I swam through it the wing of a dead gull brushed my face and I recoiled from the touch.

There was a ladder here as well, but this one had obviously had an encounter with a large ship. It was twisted out of shape and some of its rungs were missing, so that it was all I could do to get to the top of the dock. I emerged into the kind of area that every industrial building has – the place where they keep the rubbish, the discarded equipment and the redundant stock. I was happy to see the tangle of broken machinery and pallets and general junk. It meant for a start that it wasn't guarded. The professionals that I had seen when we had approached the other night would have cleared this area for visibility and field of fire if they thought it was vulnerable. The second thing was that the rubbish was piled against the wall of the shed, so I might be able to get up to roof level. It's a truism of burglary that the higher you go, the less security you encounter.

I thought my best bet was an old crane which had been parked up against the side of the building. I waited for ten minutes to see if there was any sign of guards, but it seemed clear. Keeping low I ran across to the crane. It had shed one of its tracks and the jib was tilted drunkenly over the lower part of the roof. I scaled the jib quickly, easily finding hand and footholds in the crane structure. When I got to the top I realised that the roof was further below me than I thought. A cold wind whipped off the lough, chilling my face and hands. There was a length of cable dangling from the jib. I pulled it towards me and examined it. The hemp was almost gone and the steel core of the rope was visible, with sharp strands poking through, but I didn't have much option. I had to reduce the twenty-foot drop to the roof below. As I lowered myself on to the rope I felt one of the sharp strands spear into the fabric of the wet suit, tearing it and digging into the flesh beneath. I could feel blood trickling down my leg. I lowered myself gingerly down the cable until I could go no further and then I jumped. I hit the roof hard. It was a long, gently sloping area of asbestos sheeting, about half the size of a football field, and I bounced and slid twenty feet before I managed to stop myself. I could see the ventilator structure on the ridge of the roof and assumed it would be easy enough to climb up the gentle slope. But I hadn't reckoned on the age of the sheeting, or the fact that it was coated in an evil green slime, so that every time I attempted to get to my feet, I came crashing down on to my face.

In the end I had to crawl it. At least the ventilator looked like it would provide the access I was looking for. I giddily started to work out a fifty-fifty ratio for things going right as opposed to things going wrong, then decided to quit the exercise on the basis that standing on a windy rooftop, about to descend into the bowels of a deadly covert operation, was probably the wrong place to start tempting fate.

The slats of the ventilator were corroded by the salt air, and broke like twigs when I started to tear them off, being careful not to let them fall on the inside. When I had a sufficiently big hole I peered in. I was right at the top of the building, among the webbing of ducts and electrical assemblies and piping. Through all of it, I could see lights from the floor far below, but there was just too much in the way to get a clear view. I half climbed through the vent and looked for something I could stand on. There was a maintenance gangway just below the ventilator and I lowered myself on to it. It felt warm and quiet compared to the freezing rooftop. It would have been tempting to sit down for a few minutes, but I didn't want to lose my adrenaline charge. I moved further along the gangway. I could get tantalising glimpses of the floor, but couldn't get a full picture. As far as I could see, there seemed to be wreckage on the floor. I had to get closer.

A steel ladder led vertically down to the gangway on the next level. It was risky. I would be in full view from the floor while I was on it, but if I didn't try it, the whole expedition would be a waste. I swung out on to the ladder as quickly and smoothly as possible, making sure the gear at my waist didn't bang against anything. I was sure I had made it, as I launched myself into the lower gangway, when all of a sudden something seemed to go off in my face, something bursting upwards, blinding me and sending me staggering backwards. I stifled a cry and instinctively hit the deck. And then I realised what it was. When I was young I had gone on a major expedition to London with my father. There is a photograph of it. I'm standing in Trafalgar Square holding a container of birdseed out, and dozens of pigeons are swirling around it. I seem to be smiling, but I know that in fact my smile hides a grimace of fear, for I was terrified out of my young mind by those pigeons. And as I lay on that gangway, the same primitive fear came rushing back as the pigeons I had disturbed fluttered around my head as they tried to escape from the enclosed space.

Everybody has their phobias, and pigeons were mine. I lay still as that seven-year-old schoolboy for what seemed like an eternity, until they had all slipped into the space below me and disappeared into another roost. My heart was pounding and the palms of my hands were wet. As I cautiously looked around, I reflected that I would rather be shot at. Looking nervously around for more pigeons, I inched to the edge of the gangway.

I had seen the way air accident investigators reconstruct an aircraft after an accident, laying it out on a hangar floor in the exact dimensions of the original plane. It looks like some misshapen parody of the original sleek aircraft, the chunks of metal twisted and torn, the engines mangled, the wings shattered into fragments. That was what I saw here. The crushed fuselage of the plane was in five or six pieces, each with great holes torn in them. One wing was almost intact, the other was almost entirely absent. As in many crashes, the tailpiece and the cockpit seemed to be almost intact. It was the tailpiece that identified it as a Tupolev 30, presumably the same one I had seen in Dimitri's photograph. I had seen them in Africa and in the Balkans – anywhere the Russians went, their workhorse had gone as well. She was obsolete now, but there were a few hundred battered examples out there still. But this one would fly no more.

I scanned the tailpiece and what was left of the fuselage for identifying insignia, but I could see nothing. I sat back against the gantry. There was something almost surreal about the scale of the operation, in what was essentially a small provincial port. It pointed to astonishing arrogance on the part of the operatives behind it, or to the fact that this was something of huge significance, attracting serious high-level support. I shut my eyes and formed a picture of the aircraft in my mind. There did not seem to be any serious fire or missile damage that I could see – not that this meant anything, considering how much of the plane was missing. I leaned out for another look, this time around the periphery. Somehow first time round I had missed the guards, but this time I counted five in my line of vision. Guarding a heap of inanimate metal would normally be considered a dull job, and you would expect a bit of banter between the guards to relieve the tedium. But there was no banter here. Each man was alert, his eyes flickering about the place, hands on triggers.

I was about to pull my head back in when my eye was caught by something which did not seem to belong. It was a four-wheel-drive that was obviously part of the cargo, as it had been heavily damaged. On one door panel I saw a partly obliterated insignia, the first I had seen. The same five-pointed star that had been in Dimitri's photograph. Obviously he had thought it significant as well. Then I realised there were more objects sitting around the plane. Crushed machinery with a scientific look. A massive centrifuge, I thought, the remains of something which looked suspiciously like an isolation tank. And any amount of smashed, waterlogged computers, filing cabinets, lab benches – all the equipment needs of a medium sized laboratory. I began to wonder whether the plane or its cargo was the most important thing now.

Then a whirring noise transmitted itself up through the rafters. As I watched, an electric wheelchair moved smoothly into view. The occupant was facing away from me so I couldn't see his face, but I didn't need to. I had been there the day he had been put in that wheelchair for ever. Liam Mellows had blown out his knees when most of us there would have simply shot him in the head and be done with. But Liam had a highly developed sense of retribution, and he intended that the man in the wheelchair should remember Liam Mellows every day for the rest of his life. Harry Curley was Somerville's right-hand man and a stone killer in his own right. He was also a technical genius, adept at killing people in all sorts of cost-effective ways. There was an old joke about the Americans and the Russians and the effect of gravity on writing instruments. The Americans spent a million dollars on inventing a pen where the ink would flow without being influenced by zero gravity. The Russians used a pencil. Curley was a man who improvised parsimonious death for scores, perhaps hundreds of people, a man who never, ever went over budget. He had always reminded me of the type of gamekeeper who killed eagles and stoats, and hung their bodies without discrimination on home-made gibbets to discourage other vermin. I felt a shiver run up my spine when I saw him. For my money, Liam had made the wrong decision.

As I watched, two other figures stepped into view. At first their faces weren't visible, but then one of them stepped back into the light and I recognised him from Whitcroft's photograph. I felt a chill run down my spine. Not because of the way the light caught the man's face and gave it a sinister aspect, but because I had seen him with Sasha, and here was a line which led all the way from Sasha to whatever had been going on in the shed. The night we went out we were never intended to get near the shed. Sasha had led us straight into the sniper's sights. I wasn't meant to be here. I was meant to be dead. Curley seemed to say something, and the older of the two men laughed, a harsh laugh that echoed in the roof space around me. Time to get out of here, I thought. Liam Mellows and Deirdre had always talked about evil as an almost tangible thing, and for a moment it seemed that this huge shed was filled with a dark substance, heavy and clinging. It seemed that I fled before it, for I had no great memory of finding my way on to the roof.

The cold night air seemed to clear my head, and I needed a clear head to get down the slippery roof. I slid and slithered down it, trying desperately to keep my balance. When I got to the bottom, mainly by virtue of being unable to maintain my grip, I realised that I would never be able to reach the crane jib again. I think I had always known this, but had studiously avoided thinking about the alternative. Now I had to face it. The water in the harbour below looked cold and oily, but it looked more inviting than the ten feet of debris-strewn dockside that I would have to clear in order to get to the water. I dithered on the edge until a small ironic voice in my head told me that I wasn't going to get any more athletic just by standing there. Using as much of a run-up as I could get, I launched myself off the roof.

As it happened, I had no trouble clearing the dock, but almost struck the opposite wall. I hit the surface just in time, and felt the filthy water close over me. I sank and seemed to be down there for a long time. I felt the piling wall of the dock beside me and used it to propel myself upwards. I didn't realise that I was coming up under one of the ladders. With an impact that sent a wave of nausea through me, my head struck the bottom rung. Dizzy and sick, I floated up behind the ladder so that I was squeezed between the bottom rung and the wall. When my sight cleared, I froze. A man stood on the opposite dock, peering into the darkness. He must have heard the splash as I hit the water, I thought. If he saw me I was a sitting duck, pinned between the ladder and the wall, but perversely, this was the thing that saved me. I was in the dark fold of the steel piling, and I knew to turn my face away from him, so that the black helmet of the wet suit blended in with the dark surface of the piling. I knew that nothing stands out more against a dark background than a white face, but I could feel a prickling sensation between my shoulder blades and it took all of my mental strength to keep my back to him.

I stayed like that for what seemed like hours, without moving, for movement also attracts attention, while the cold crept up my legs. I judged that I had stayed still long enough, then forced myself to do another fifteen minutes. If the man on the opposite dock was a professional, he would be mirroring my thought processes. I never got the opportunity to find out. He was gone when I turned around.

The cold made the journey back to the pilot boat hard and long. I skirted the guards on the dock easily, but it took a long, long time to cross the inner dock and I barely made it over the low gunwale of the pilot boat. Other men my age had given up fieldwork long ago. Deirdre would have asked me what I was trying to prove. She would have said there was a juvenile, competitive part of me which would not allow me to give it up and grow old gracefully. She would have said that this was half my problem, and the reason why I left mayhem in my wake. Had she been there, she would have told me all this, and I wouldn't have been able to give her a satisfactory answer.

I got to my feet and made my way wearily to the wheelhouse. As I did so, I cast off. I fired up the engines as the slight current turned the bow towards the entrance of the basin. But before I could do anything I heard a thump on the deck. I spun around. One of the two men I had seen with Curley, and with Sasha, was standing in the stern. He had a pistol in his hand. I couldn't make out what it was, but it looked like one of those expensive machine pistols that are all the rage in the drug business. He grinned in an unpleasant way.

'This ship never tie up here. Never,' he said.

I learned two things from what he had said. Firstly, that he had a strong east European accent. Secondly, that he was no seaman, because anyone used to the sea could not possibly refer to the sturdy pilot boat as a ship. On an impulse, and because I still had my hand on the throttle, I jammed the lever forward. There was a brief hesitation and then the screw started to turn. The boat put her bow in the air and leapt forward. If I hadn't been so tired, and if there hadn't been so much at stake, I would have laughed. The man, off balance, took two steps backwards, which was one step too many. The backs of his knees caught the low gunwale, he swung his arms wildly to try to maintain his balance and then he was gone.

I could see him floundering in the water behind me as I joined the channel. I wondered if he could swim. I decided I didn't really care. If what Whitcroft said was true, he deserved everything he got. However, something told me he would be all right. You don't get rid of men like him as easily as that.

A sudden wave of exhaustion and depression swept over me. I had to talk to Whitcroft and I had to talk to him about Sasha. I didn't feel much like standing in judgement on the Latvian. People's lives took unexpected turns, they got lazy or tired or greedy, and they found themselves in places they had never intended to be, with no way out. If there were moral absolutes out there, I had yet to come across them. But Sasha was involved with these people. He was a danger to the wretched asylum seekers and he was a danger to me and those close to me, Donna in particular. Still, I didn't feel good about it. Sasha had told me how he had been brought up, his parents lost in a sea of alcohol. Running wild, then being given a choice of joining the army or going to gaol. How the army had given him back his self-respect. How Afghanistan had taken it away again.

He hadn't told me much about that war at the start, but he made it clear that it had been hard and brutal. One night he did open up to me. As a special forces soldier he was reasonably well equipped, but the same couldn't be said for the average soldier. He had been serving in the southern provinces. It was mid-summer and very hot. He had been sent with a colleague to make contact with one of the warlords in the high passes, who was considered an ally as long as his opium trade was not interfered with. They had been inserted by helicopter, but still had to walk for two days. For that two days they walked through poppy fields, the smell of the flowers heavy and drowsy in the air, so that the whole trip began to take on a hallucinatory quality. They rendezvoused with the warlord's men at a lake high in the mountains and they were taken in a gleaming four-wheel-drive to the man's summer lodging, where he fled from the heat of the plain below. They handed over their delivery to him: an envelope full of bearer bonds drawn on a Zürich bank. In return, they were well looked after with food and drink, and women too if they wanted them, but they were also closely watched and were not allowed to stray from the compound. The warlord, who was plump and laughed a lot, made it clear that he was waiting for something, a special treat of sorts for them.

On the third day he called them out to the small plateau in front of his mud-built residence. A container truck had just arrived. The warlord motioned Sasha over to the container. The first thing he noticed was the vile smell emanating from the container, so strong that he had to cover his mouth and his nose. Then there were the flies, great buzzing clouds of blowflies.

The warlord gave an order and two armed men ran to the back of the truck, and threw open the doors. It was like a scene from a Bruegel painting, as Sasha described it. The container was full of men, some dead, others dying. They had obviously been in the container in the searing heat for several days. The doors and sides of the container were streaked with blood and filth.

'Taliban!' the warlord said with an expansive grin. As he spoke, one of the men in the truck stirred, then another and another. They stretched out their hands beseechingly and a thin wailing began to rise from the truck. One man stretched out a trembling hand and grasped the edge of the container floor as though to pull himself out of it, but one of the guards smashed the butt of his rifle down on it, then the doors were slammed shut again.

On their way back Sasha and his friend did not go through the poppy fields. Instead they climbed upwards until they were in a position high above the road which led away from the warlord's house. There they waited. It did not take long. At dawn they heard engines in the distance. Far up the valley they could see the lorry with the container still attached coming down the mountain. There was an escort of four-wheel-drives and a Land Cruiser with the warlord himself in the passenger seat. Sasha watched the procession for a minute or two, then quietly unpacked the radio and called in an air strike from Kandahar. It took the Mig-19s just over ten minutes to arrive, by which time the convoy was below Sasha's position. The aircraft came up the valley fast and low, four of them, firing rockets in salvos of two. The lead jeep disintegrated. The warlord's Land Cruiser veered into the side of the road and men jumped from it, but it was too late. Two rockets struck the rock face just above them, obliterating the jeep and men. Two other jeeps exploded. Only the lorry, abandoned by its driver, escaped. It sat, momentarily unscathed, in the middle of the road. Then the last Mig screamed down the valley. Sasha could see the pilot's helmet. He imagined him fixing the target, thumbing the missile release. Then the projectiles streaked out from under the plane's wings and the container lorry exploded in a fireball, delivering its wretched cargo from their living hell.

It was a strange time after that, he said. They were sent out in four-man teams, travelling cross-country and living off the land, picking out targets and either taking them out themselves or calling in air strikes. It was a barbaric period. There was hand-to-hand fighting. There were attacks on camps full of sleeping men. All belief and morality drained from him until the only imperative was to kill. And then even the lust to kill was gone, and you killed from habit.

Winter came and the four men fought on. A silence seemed to have fallen between them, and they communicated in staccato military phrases or hand signals. Then the end came. They had called in an air strike on a convoy going through a high mountain pass. They were observing from a snowy bluff above the pass. Perhaps it was a mistake, although Sasha thought there was a peculiar glint in the radio operator's eye when he had radioed in the co-ordinates. For the co-ordinates given were not those of the convoy far below, but of the bluff on which they lay. They heard the scream of the Migs coming in hard and fast. Sasha looked up and, through the cold, misty air, saw points of light burning under the jet's wings as the rocket motors ignited. Then he remembered no more.

When he woke he was lying in a snowdrift beside a strip of burned ground. One of his boots had been blown off, and he could not move his left arm. Of his three companions there was no sign. The air strike had blasted them into oblivion, a suicide of sorts. He searched around for equipment. He could find no rations, but he did find a ripped and bloodstained battledress, which he tore into strips and wrapped around his foot. He still had his service knife and some matches. As he shuffled away, it began to snow.

He wandered in the snow for most of that day. As dusk began to fall he knew he would not survive the night. It was then that he found the cave. It was a hole in the rock face about eight feet high and fifty deep, and in the back of it he found several crates of tinned food, rice and millet. He thought that it must have been a shelter for the people who herded animals on the high mountain during the summer.

He spent that winter alone with the mountain. At night it was bitterly cold and you could hear wolves howling, and if you ventured outside you thought you were among the stars, so bright and clear were they. His arm got better, and he became hardened to the cold. But more than that he emptied his mind of all that had gone before, of all the death and butchery, and found a still place where he could go. That was how a Russian patrol found him the following spring. A bearded, wild-haired man sitting on his own in front of a cave, who did not acknowledge or even glance at them when they approached, but seemed to be roaming in some far distant place.

He kept that space fixed in his mind, he had told me, and he would retreat to it on the nights when he would awake sweating, with screams ringing in his ears and the smell of burning flesh in his nostrils.

Perhaps the coldness of the mountain had spread to his heart. Perhaps the lure of the people smugglers' money had proved too much. I knew that I would have to ring Whitcroft in the morning.

I stopped alongside the *Castledawn* and untied the skiff. Then I re-moored the pilot boat and fixed the ignition casing back as best I could. I rowed quickly back to the *Castledawn*, too exhausted to care whether I was seen or not. I stripped off the torn wet suit and showered. Then I poured a Redbreast and put Jimmy Rodgers on the CD player. My phone beeped with a text. I tried to ignore it, but in the end I glanced at it. It was from Deirdre. It said simply: 'Ring me'. With a sigh I turned Jimmy Rodgers down and dialled her number. When she answered the phone she sounded furious.

'Jesus, Valentine, you're some piece of work.'

'What did I do?' I protested.

'Apart from what you've always done, you mean? You've dragged this poor woman into your scheming, then you leave her sitting on her own, worrying herself into a nervous breakdown without even a call from you.'

'Firstly,' I protested, 'I didn't drag her into anything. She got into it herself. Secondly, I was off trying to sort things out.' In the sort of place where a mobile going off at the wrong time could get you shot, I thought, but didn't say.

'Just because you can't content yourself with the ordinary things in life doesn't mean that other people don't want to.'

This was from a woman who had once driven an armoured car through the wall of an aid warehouse because the food wasn't getting to the starving quickly enough, but I knew where she was coming from.

'If I don't find out what they're up to, then none of us is safe, you included,' I said.

'I suppose you're right, Jack,' she said softly. 'Just when I had a chance of a bit of happiness, I suppose you had to pop up with your spooks and spies.'

'Can Donna come down here tomorrow?'

'I'll ask her to ring you.'

'I'm sorry,' I said. 'I really am.'

'You always are,' she said sadly. 'You always are.' She hung up. I looked stupidly at the phone in my hands for a few minutes and then put it down. I drank my Redbreast, looked at the level of the bottle, then decided on another one. What were the words she had used? A chance of a bit of happiness, that was it. She must mean McCrink. If she wanted him, then she should have him, I thought, and impressed by the grandeur and generosity of my own sentiment, I finished the bottle of Redbreast and stumbled off to bed.

TWELVE

I was awoken the next morning by the chirping of the mobile. My body was aching and my head felt as if it had been sandbagged. I looked at the number on the mobile and didn't recognise it, so curiosity got the better of me.

'Morning, Mr Valentine,' a frail voice said. 'It's Davy Wilson here, from Larne.'

'Morning, Davy,' I croaked.

'I haven't got anything on the ship yet,' Wilson said. So why the hell are you ringing me at this hour, I thought savagely.

'But there is something you might be interested in,' he said.

'What?' I said ungraciously, hoping I hadn't lumbered myself with a pest.

'Well, I was talking to the boys down at the Legion last night, and it seems there's a small rig out there, near the North Channel.' I sat up at this.

'Go ahead, Davy,' I said.

'They say it's doing seabed tests for the interconnector, the new gas pipeline they're building. That could have been the thing that disturbed the poor man's final resting place.'

'Makes sense, I suppose,' I said.

'Aye,' he said, sounding puzzled, 'the only thing is this – the rig is about fifteen miles south of where the connector is supposed to be going. And they got this kind of exclusion zone around it. You're not allowed within ten miles of it. Supposed to be a safety thing.'

'And is it?'

'Safety? If you can't see a bloody oil rig and crash into it, you shouldn't be at sea in the first place,' he snorted. 'Anyhow, I'll keep digging into it.'

I thanked him and hung up. I had a shower, then turned the water to cold to try and wake myself up. There were bruises all over my body and a gash on my leg where the wire core of the crane cable had come through. When I'd finished I defrosted some McNamee's brown bread from the freezer, and ate it with scrambled eggs laced with smoked salmon. I felt as if I owed myself a luxury. All the time I was cooking the phone sat at my right hand, and I kept throwing glances at it as if it would be able to tell me the right thing to do. By the time I'd finished eating I knew that I had to ring Whitcroft. He answered on the first ring.

'Remember those two photographs you sent to me?' He grunted assent.

'Well, I've seen both men in Warrenpoint.'

'When?'

'Yesterday . . .' I said.

'There's a hesitation in your voice, Valentine. What is it?'

'They're knocking around with a friend of mine.'

'Why does that not surprise me?' Whitcroft said.

'Knock off the weary, cynical cop routine, Whitcroft,' I said. I wasn't in the mood for it.

'Did you find out where these two jokers were staying?'

'No, but Sasha is dealing with them. If you follow him, you might find them.'

'Pull him in?'

'Yes,' I said. I needed Sasha to be neutralised.

'I appreciate you doing this,' Whitcroft said, with unaccustomed grace.

'It's leaving a bad taste in my mouth,' I said.

'Too much of this fucking business does.'

'Just do me a favour and handle it yourself. Don't send any amateurs in, either. The man's a pro.'

I gave him Sasha's address and other details, and put down the phone feeling depressed. I should have been angry at Sasha's betrayal, but I wasn't. And the professional part of me knew that he had to be got out of harm's way before he got me killed. At least this way he was staring at a jail sentence rather than a bullet. So why, I asked myself, did I not feel better about it? I was about to feel worse.

The phone rang again. Deirdre's number came up. I ignored it for a while. I wasn't in the mood for another lecture, but it rang again and then again, and a funny feeling started to steal over me. I lifted the phone. I think I knew what she was going to say before I heard her voice.

'They've got her,' Deirdre said, pain in her voice. 'They've got Donna.'

I used everything the Impreza had on the coast road before I hit traffic in Rostrevor. It was slow going through Warrenpoint as well. There were police cars at the dock gates, and people were slowing to have a look at whatever miscreants might be having their collars felt. As I passed, I saw

Whitcroft's men leading Sasha out. He was limping and his face was covered in blood, but he had a half-smile on his face. I thought about the place he said he went in the high mountains, that place in his head.

It took another half an hour to get to Edentubber. My heart sank as I pushed through the front door, which sagged from its hinges, the lock expertly sledged off. Apart from that, there was little sign of violence at the front of the house. Deirdre and Kate were waiting for me. Deirdre was pale. Kate said nothing.

'What happened?' I asked.

'We went out for an hour,' Deirdre said. 'The bastards must have been watching the place. Donna stayed behind. She wanted to do some baking.'

'She must have been in the kitchen,' Kate said. We went on to the kitchen. There was flour on the worktop, dough rising in a bowl. I saw that the kitchen door had also been sledged. She must have had time to lock it. I saw Kate go down on one knee. She was looking at a pool of blood on the floor. I told myself that it didn't mean anything, that a small cut will produce a large amount of blood. I didn't feel very reassured.

'Anybody see anything?' I asked.

'We tried all the neighbours,' Deirdre said. 'Nothing.'

I started looking around for clues, knowing my chances of finding anything were slim. I checked the lane outside for tyre marks, or anything that might have been dropped. I examined the marks on the shattered doors. I found some more drops of blood, but nothing useful. I went back into the kitchen, angry at myself for neglecting Donna's safety, at the same time telling myself that anger was no good, that if I was to help her

I had to stay cold and sharp. But I knew the men I was dealing with, and knew that the stakes were high. Donna could already be dead. I could tell by Kate and Deirdre's faces that they were thinking the same thing. I leaned back against the sink, trying to put my thoughts in order.

'She must have seen them coming and locked the kitchen door to give herself time,' I said.

'There was a black Pajero at the bottom of the lane earlier,' Deirdre said.

'It's still not much,' I said. 'There must be thousands of black Pajeros on the road.'

'I know,' she said. 'Where would we start?'

'I have an idea,' I said, 'a very good idea.' I scrolled through the numbers on my phone until I found Whitcroft.

Ten minutes later I was on the road, heading towards Newry. In twenty minutes' time I was walking through the foyer of the Canal Court Hotel. Whitcroft was waiting for me.

'They gave me a room upstairs,' he said. We went up the stairs, Whitcroft carrying the VHS tapes I had asked him for.

'I'll leave you to it,' he said. 'Leave the tapes with the desk.'

'What about Sasha?' I said, the words out of my mouth before I realised I'd spoken them. Whitcroft smiled tightly and shook his head. I wasn't getting any more information on Sasha. I knew what he was doing, and he was right not to implicate me any further, but it still rankled.

The tapes were the security videos from the dock entrance. As it happened, they had been picked up by Whitcroft's men every day in order to watch for the two people smugglers. Like most security footage, it was of poor quality, but I was still able, after a few hours, to pick out a black Pajero coming and going perhaps three or four times a day. The quality of the images was too bad to make out the driver or the registration. One of the better shots came on the final video, and I played and replayed it, straining my eyes to make out the shadowy faces in the front seat. In the middle of this Deirdre rang. She was in the foyer with Kate. I told them to come up. They sat in silence as I rewound and stopped the video. In the end I sat back and rubbed my eyes. Deirdre moved towards the television and pointed at something on the windscreen.

'What is that?' she asked, pointing to a smudge on the bottom right-hand corner of the screen.

'I don't know,' I said. 'Tax disc?'

'No,' she said, frowning, 'it's the wrong shape. The mark below it is the tax disc.'

'I know what it is,' Kate said quietly. 'It's a disabled sticker.' And as she said this the face in the driving seat seemed to take shape. It was Harry Curley, Somerville's wheelchair-bound lieutenant. It would please Somerville to save a few pounds on parking charges by using a disabled sticker. It had to be Curley. My mobile bleeped. I took it out and saw a text from Alva, saying: 'Call me'. Which meant don't call me on your not very secure mobile. I went downstairs and found a payphone. I started to feed my credit card into it, then changed my mind. Maybe I was being paranoid, but why let them know that I had made a particular call at a particular time? I went to the bar and got a pile of change and fed it into the phone instead. Alva answered on the first ring.

'Hi, Alva,' I said.

'Jack, *caro*,' she said. I might have been mistaken, but I

thought I detected a tense note in Alva's normally imperturbable voice.

'What is it, Alva?' I asked.

'Jack,' she said, and I had the impression that she was picking her words carefully, 'things are very tense at the moment. There is much talk about a big operation that has gone badly wrong. There is talk about a plane crashing in the north Irish Sea. Everybody is trying to get a look, but the cloud cover is low and satellites cannot get an image. Jack, please stay away from this. I cannot help you any more.' There was a click and a buzz. Alva was gone. I turned around. Kate was leaning against a pillar behind me.

'Come on,' she said, 'let's get a coffee.'

'I've got things to do.'

'You might be better sitting still and thinking a little, rather than rushing off in every direction.'

She was right, of course. We went into the bar and ordered coffees. We sat down at the window. I started to talk about Donna, but Kate held up her hand.

'Talk about something unrelated for a while. Let your mind absorb the information it has got. Tell me about your art dealing.'

I had to fight to do it, but I trusted Kate's intuition. I told her about the young artists I had been buying up, lending the paintings to friends to hang on their walls since I had no room for them myself.

'What about your Venetian lady?' she asked. The Venetian lady was a portrait, oil on board, by an unknown hand. The woman was a seventeenth-century courier, a beautiful woman who looked out of the portrait with a corrupt, amoral stare.

The painting and its fusion of beauty and evil had always fascinated me.

'In a bank vault,' I said. 'It's too valuable to leave at home.' Kate smiled at me. I think she realised what I was thinking – that having the Venetian lady's stare follow me around the room reminded me uncomfortably of my own compromises.

'I thought of something,' she said suddenly. 'It might mean something and it might not.' I nodded for her to go on.

'The reason I ended up living in Shetland is part of . . . part of a search, I suppose, that started when I was young. I suffer from what they call clinical depression, always have done.'

I could see the pain in her eyes at the mention of it. Deirdre had hinted at something in Kate's life, but this was the first time I had heard what it was.

'In a way, it destroyed part of my life,' she said. 'I'm ill – lost is a better word – for months at a time. I was . . .' She hesitated. '. . . either irresponsible or cowardly. Satch was, I thought, the only man who could have lived with me and I never looked for another.' Satch, her husband and my friend, had been killed in a quayside accident.

'And I was afraid to have children, in case I couldn't care for them. Anyway,' she said, going on briskly, 'the reason I'm telling you this is that I heard you use the phrase "black dog" and I know it is the phrase that Samuel Johnson used to describe his own depression.'

'Churchill,' I said.

'What?'

'Winston Churchill. He suffered from depression as well. He used the phrase "black dog" to describe it.'

'Churchill would have read Johnson.'

'Of course. Hang on a second.' I shut my eyes. There were links here if I could see them. An image of the five-pointed star I had seen on the military vehicles in the dock, beside the wreckage of the plane, came unbidden into my head. I realised what it was. It was the insignia used by the Iraqi army.

'Iraq,' I murmured. 'Iraq and Churchill.' Kate watched me. 'Churchill administered the League of Nations mandate for Iraq way back in the twenties,' I said slowly. 'And the way he did it was by using aerial bombardment of towns and villages to keep a lid on it.'

'Go on,' she said.

'And he advocated using chemical weapons on the same villages as being more cost-effective,' I said. 'It has to be Somerville behind all this. He is a Churchill buff. He would know all this. And it's exactly the kind of trail that he likes to lay down. He just can't resist leaving a complicated clue behind. Feeds the ego, I think. Look how clever I am.'

'It's all a bit far-fetched, Jack,' Kate said, looking doubtful.

'Not if you know Somerville,' I said.

'Still,' she said.

'I tell you what,' I said. 'I'm going to make a phone call. If I'm not talking to Somerville within five minutes, I'll admit that you're right.' She shrugged. I picked up the mobile and rang the SIS switchboard. My former employee had no formal identity and thus no office or phone, but I knew that I could use the MI6 switchboard.

'This is Jack Valentine,' I said. 'I'd like to speak to George Somerville.'

'I'm sorry, sir,' the girl said, 'there is no George Somerville listed in this building.'

'Jack Valentine for George Somerville,' I said. 'Tell him I'm on the mobile – he should be able to find the number.' I hung up. We waited. It was almost four minutes before the call came, and I heard Somerville's voice for the first time in several years.

'Good afternoon, Jack,' he said. 'I have to admit I was a little surprised to hear from you.' If he felt any rancour over our last meeting he wasn't showing it. The voice was as level as ever, rational, civilised, with a slight West Country burr. The kind of voice you might hear at a cricket match on a village green. The kind of voice that more than one man had heard in a windowless interrogation room in one of the many dark, conflicted places where Somerville had operated.

'Cut out the surprised bit, Somerville,' I said. 'Did you and Curley take the girl?' He chuckled. It wasn't a comforting sound.

'You know I never confirm, never deny, Jack.'

'I suppose there is no point in asking what you're up to?'

'No point at all, Jack. Let me put it this way: I have something you want.'

'Donna.'

'I have something you want,' he continued patiently, 'and you have something I want. So perhaps we can deal.'

'What do I have that you want?' I said, genuinely perplexed.

'Come, come, Jack,' he said. 'A little glass jar with something red in it?'

The phial of blood, I thought. But Somerville's men had taken it from the cold store in the harbour. He already had it in his possession, or so I had thought. The phial was the cold, hard evidence that something was amiss. Without it no one would believe Donna's story. But if Somerville hadn't taken it, who had? One of his own men involved in an elaborate double-cross? I doubted it. Anyone who worked for Somerville knew he was devious beyond measure, and vengeful in the same way. I decided to play it as if I had the blood.

'We need to talk face to face,' I said.

'I don't quite see the necessity of that,' he said, in a chiding tone.

'I do,' I said. If it were anyone else I would have asked if Donna was still alive, but from dealing with Somerville I knew that he wouldn't kill her. People like Somerville didn't burn an asset unless they had a good reason for doing so. Donna was alive. The downside was that Somerville would be absolutely indifferent as to her condition.

'Where do you want to meet?' Somerville said, sounding languid, even a little bored. I thought hard. If I had Liam Mellows with me, or even Sasha, I thought bitterly, there were a hundred places I could have chosen with back-up and a good field of fire. McCrink was a thinker, a man of action to some degree, but he didn't have the hard-won field experience of the other two men. I realised I had hesitated too long. Somerville laughed again, a low, soft laugh full of malice.

'You don't have back-up, Jack, so let's not think about all this gladiatorial business. Let's have a good walk on the beach where that fascinating trawler of yours is anchored. You see, Jack, if I had wanted to deal with you I would have done so already.'

I stifled the impulse to swear at him. Better pretend that I wasn't trying to hide the *Castledawn* from the world.

'I'll see you there in an hour,' I said, trying to wrench what little advantage I could from the conversation.

'Fair enough,' Somerville said. He had the air of a man who was being magnanimous in victory. I hung up, but it seemed like juvenile rudeness rather than the act of a man fully in control of the situation. I looked up and saw Deirdre come in with McCrink. McCrink was white-faced and intense.

'I have some more information,' he burst out. 'Important stuff, Jack.' Inwardly I half-groaned. It seemed that I already had more information than I could deal with. It must have showed in my expression, because I could see an injured look on McCrink's face.

'Sorry,' I said. 'It's Donna being lifted . . . I didn't mean . . .' McCrink immediately put a hand on my shoulder.

'Fuck . . . sorry, Jack . . . I should have . . .'

'No,' I said, 'but everything helps. What did you find out?'

'Jesus,' he said, 'it sounded important when I found out . . .' Suddenly there was a tone of doubt in his voice.

'Come on,' I said, 'spit it out. Everything helps.'

'Right,' he said, turning serious. 'There is a small oil rig moored near the North Channel. They're taking stuff up by crane from the seabed. Fishermen have seen it. Also there is an area around the rig that is dead sea – birds, fish, fauna, you name it, they're all dead. Anybody who goes within ten miles now gets an army boat on them within minutes and some very rough boys warning them off.'

'Good work,' I said. 'Anything more?'

'Well, yes,' he said. 'I tried a few newspaper editors, boys sympathetic to environmental stuff. All dead enthusiastic, then next thing you know, they don't answer the phone. I tried to post it on the web – you know, there are a few sites like cryptome that don't take any shite off anybody. Next thing you know, the servers have pulled the plug on them.'

I gave a low whistle. It took a fair bit to bring down that kind of site, as far as I knew. I began to think about Alva's nervousness. I began to wonder if we were in too deep ever to see daylight again. The room seemed to grow dark and silent for a moment. When I looked up again, Deirdre and McCrink were talking urgently. But Kate was looking at me with a steady, troubled gaze. She came over to sit beside me.

'I want to come with you,' she said.

'No,' I said, 'I can't put another person in harm's way.'

'That decision was taken a long time ago,' she said. 'Let me put it another way: I'm coming with you.'

Many years ago, after I had watched Kate's husband die in that stupid dockside accident, I had stayed with her and watched her deal with pain that, as a young man, I couldn't really understand, rawness piled upon rawness. One night, when it seemed she had found some equanimity, she had reached for me and taken me to her bed. I was young and callow, a mixture between two things – a shallow primness and a rage I didn't know I had – with a desire to dominate and, if I was truthful, to hurt. She let me dominate and let me hurt, and then in the early hours of the morning, with the early northern dawn streaming through the windows of the croft, she conquered me with gentleness and wisdom, and a wantonness that took my breath away. And then, later that morning, as I slept the sleep of the young, she packed my bags, and when I woke, told me that she had booked a ticket for me on the afternoon ferry. I remember standing there, fresh from the shower, wearing only a towel, with tears in my eyes as I pleaded with her. She did not give in, but she let me take her one more time and this time it was sweet and simple and equable. Kate didn't owe me anything.

It took twenty-five minutes to get back to Greencastle. We drove in silence for a while. I had to stop myself thinking about Donna as if she was already dead.

'What did Donna talk about when you were staying at Edentubber?'

'I suppose she talked about herself,' Kate said. 'She was going through . . . what way do I put this? You know, some women take a sabbatical when they're Donna's age, go off and think about themselves. Donna met you instead.'

'Some sabbatical,' I said.

'Indeed,' Kate said. 'But the effect was something similar. You challenge everything you've done, everything you are.'

'Sounds a bit self-indulgent,' I said.

'Maybe, but at least it's normally a gentle process. I wonder what sort of woman Donna McNeill will be at the end of this.'

I found myself hoping that, if there was a Donna McNeill at the end of this, it wouldn't be one who had been left to the tender mercies of Somerville and Curley. No amount of self-reassessment was going to bring you back from that dark pit.

'If you let her down at the end, then let her down gently, Jack,' Kate said. 'I'm not sure if she's in love with you, or thinks she is in love with you. I don't think she knows herself.'

This gave me enough to think about as we turned off the main road and skirted the mudflats and salty bents of Mill

Bay, before taking the Greencastle turn. As we drove down the Greencastle road, Kate surprised me.

'Have you got a gun?' she asked. I'd always thought of Kate as being, if not quite pacifist, then resolutely anti-violence.

'If Somerville wants to take me out, then he'll do it, gun or no,' I said.

'I wasn't talking about you, Jack, I was talking about me. I'm going to be on my own in the car when you're talking to him.'

I hadn't thought of that. I pulled off the fuse cover under the dash with my right hand and the little Beretta I kept there fell into my hand.

'Here you go,' I said, handing it to her. She turned it over in her hand, frowning a little at its miniature but efficient lines. I explained the workings of it quickly. She put it to her eye suddenly and aimed at a cow which was looking over a gate at us.

'You know, I think I could be a stone killer,' she said with comical seriousness. I started to laugh, but as we rounded the last corner, the laughter died in my throat. I could see Somerville standing by the pier, for all the world like a retired holidaymaker enjoying a walk on a mild autumn afternoon. I parked the car in the open.

'Don't forget to keep an eye out behind you as well as in front of you,' I said. Kate leaned over and kissed me on the cheek. The beach suddenly looked very bleak and windswept.

Somerville kept his eyes on the sea as I walked up beside him.

'It's a nice spot, Jack,' he said. 'Took us a while to find you.'

'Forget the pleasantries, Somerville,' I said.

'Let's walk,' he said. We started along the beach away from Kate. I walked slowly. I wanted to keep the car in sight.

'How is Mr Mellows?' Somerville asked.

'Seems to be all right,' I said.

'Curley would give a lot to get his hands on him,' Somerville said. Liam had crippled him and put him in a wheelchair.

'I'm sure he would,' I said, 'but we're not here to talk about Curley.'

'It's a good thing he has protection in America,' Somerville said, ignoring me. 'Do let me know if the American government loses interest in guaranteeing his health and safety.' Part of the deal to get us out of the fix at that time had been a US guarantee of Liam's safety.

'Donna McNeill,' I said.

'You always had an eye for a fine Irish girl,' Somerville said. I almost said that he always had an eye for a bald, crippled psycho – for Somerville and Curley were lovers – but I bit my tongue.

'Where is she?' I said.

'Safe,' Somerville said. 'Or safeish, I should say. Curley was never particularly an admirer of yours, Jack.'

'I want her back, Somerville.'

'Then all you have to do is give me the phial of blood.'

'What are you up to, Somerville?' I said, trying to avoid giving him a direct answer.

'What do you think I'm up to?' Somerville said, turning to look me in the eye for the first time. There was an amused expression on his face that I didn't like.

'Well,' I said, still playing for time, 'we have a dead pilot, poisoned with chemical agents. We have an aircraft being pulled up from the seabed bit by bit along with its cargo, which seems to be Iraqi military vehicles and laboratory equipment.'

'Very good, Jack,' Somerville said. 'So that was you that night in Warrenpoint dock. I couldn't be sure. And what do you think is behind all this rather lurid scenario?'

'Well . . .' I said, 'in the war in Iraq only one thing was missing.'

'A reason for it?' Somerville was positively twinkling.

'Exactly. They failed to find a programme of weapons of mass destruction, putting everybody under pressure – governments, intelligence services etc.'

'Go on,' Somerville said.

'So somebody decided to manufacture a solution. They created an Iraqi base complete with transport, laboratory and of course chemical and biological agents.'

'Precisely,' Somerville said, looking delighted.

'But then something goes wrong. The plane carrying this fake lab crashes on its way to Iraq, where were they going to put it – somewhere remote anyway, where you'd be able to come up with a positive reason as to why it wasn't found before.'

'A brilliantly informed speculation,' Somerville said.

'Now that the plane has crashed, who do they call in to recover it? The discreet Somerville and his technically accomplished sidekick Curley.'

'The resources the government has made available are practically unlimited,' Somerville said, rubbing his hands together.

'You gather up all the proof. All the bits and pieces. There's only one snag. A pilot gets washed up and a forensic pathologist just happens to take a blood sample.'

'If you give me the sample, I'll give you the girl,' Somerville said, turning serious. 'That's all there is to it, Jack. Her testimony is no good without the blood. Who would believe her? So just hand it over, Jack.'

'Why should I?' I said, making my voice and my face hard.

'Well, the girl is one of your more recent conquests, isn't she? By the way, what did happen to the beautiful and virtuous Deirdre Mellows?' There was an odd smirk on Somerville's face as he said this. I ignored it.

'I want something else as well,' I said.

'What?'

'I want my old job back.' Somerville laughed out loud.

'Out of the question, absolutely out of the question,' he said.

'This isn't a negotiation,' I said. 'If you want the blood, then I get my job back.' He looked out to sea for a moment, then turned back to me. When he spoke his voice was low and savage.

'I don't believe you, Jack. I don't believe you want your job back. I know you want your bedmate back. You always were a sentimentalist and a fool. Don't try to play me for time. I want that blood by noon tomorrow or I'll have Curley slaughter the girl like you slaughter a beast in an abattoir.'

He turned and walked away from me up the beach. I realised there was a black Pajero parked on the margin of the beach.

'By the way,' he said, turning, 'did you get the reference? Black dog? Churchill and Iraq? I thought that would amuse you.'

I didn't answer him. An image of Donna came unbidden into my head. I turned and walked up the beach. The wind had got up, and now that it was blowing into my face, tears started from my eyes.

THIRTEEN

I got into the Impreza. Kate knew from the look on my face that things weren't good. I told her what had happened.

'Give him the blood, for God's sake,' Kate said.

'That's the problem. I don't have it.'

'Then who does?'

'I don't know.'

'This is not good, Jack.'

'I know. Even if I did have the blood, and I gave it to him, there's no guarantee that he'll release her. By the way, he knew I was here all the time.'

'What are we going to do?' she asked. I knew there was only one way out of it. And there was only one person who could help. I reached for my phone and dialled a number, a number with a District of Columbia code. Not very many people had this number. It was a weighty business, having the access which the number commanded, but I needed Liam Mellows before morning, and only the man at the other end of the line could get him here before then.

'Stone,' the voice at the other end said. The voice was deep, authoritative, as befits a man who had been at the heart of the American intelligence and defence apparatus for many years.

'John,' I said, 'it's Jack Valentine.'

'Jack Valentine,' Stone said slowly, as if it was a name he had long consigned to the past and wasn't sure if he wanted to hear it again. I waited for him to speak again, but he didn't.

'Fair enough, John,' I said. 'Let's skip the pleasantries. Let me just tell you a little story.' I spoke for fifteen minutes, then Stone stopped me and made me start from the beginning again. This time I knew that others were listening, and what I was saying was being recorded. Every few minutes Stone interrupted me with shrewd, penetrating questions. I spoke for almost an hour, and when I had finished the muscles on my neck were stretched and taut, and the hand that held the phone was damp with perspiration.

'If this is true, then it is very serious. Very serious indeed,' Stone said.

'It's true, as far as I can verify the details.'

'Well, they chime with some of our own observations. It has all of the hallmarks of a damn fool mission if you ask me.' I could hear the anger in his voice. 'What the hell was your government thinking of?'

'Not my government,' I said. 'I'm Scottish.' Stone laughed unexpectedly.

'"The sea, the sea, *o gra geal mo chroi*. Long may she roll between England and me. The poor old Scotsman will never be free. But we're entirely surrounded by water,"' he quoted.

'Brendan Behan would be delighted to be quoted by such an august personage as yourself,' I said.

'I doubt it,' he said dryly. 'So, Jack Valentine, I assume I'm not being given this information through philanthropy and your love of the free world. What do you want?'

'I want Liam Mellows in Ireland.'

'That can be arranged, I suppose,' he said.

'I want him here before dawn tomorrow.' There was a long pause. I assumed Stone had gone on to another line to consult. It occurred to me, somewhat hysterically in the context of what we were talking about, that my next mobile phone bill would be astronomical. I hadn't any worries about it being tapped – calls to Stone's line were automatically scrambled. In the end he came back.

'There is a deal available here, Jack, but it's not just as simple as that.'

'I didn't think it would be.'

'We'll expect you to make yourself available for a thorough debrief about all aspects of this.'

'Of course.'

'You are aware, Jack, that as it stands, this has a major impact on transatlantic relations?'

'It's the reason I went to you.'

'Yes, well. If it gets out . . .'

'It won't get out through me.'

'If I thought for a moment that it would, we wouldn't be having this conversation, but you are not operating on your own. Without that phial of blood the public may not believe it, but there are more discerning palates than the public.'

'I appreciate that.'

'Are your colleagues discreet?'

'I guarantee it.'

'You had better, Jack. A colleague will speak to you later regarding Liam Mellows. Are you sure he will agree to come?'

'Loyalty was always paramount with Liam.'

'I think I remember,' Stone said, with a grim chuckle. 'I think I remember. Good day to you, Jack.'

'Good day,' I said, in unconscious imitation of his old-world Yankee manners. He broke the connection. I realised that somewhere in the middle of the conversation Kate had got out of the car and gone walking on the beach. I got out of the car. The air inside seemed fetid, rank with conspiracy. Kate linked my arm and we walked in silence back along the beach, the mountains opposite silhouetted in black against the dusk sky. When we were back in the car I sat for a moment before turning on the engine.

'What is it, Jack?' she said.

'We're going in for Donna,' I said. 'We're going in and Liam's coming home.' Kate nodded, carefully not showing her feelings, but a tiny pulse beat at her temple, small and birdlike.

'I think I need to be on my own for a while,' Kate said. 'I hate it when these things happen, Jack. I hate you going out and me thinking that you're not going to come back again. You can't be lucky for ever.'

'The same thought has occurred to me,' I said.

'Don't try to be funny, Jack. You know I could do with an hour or two on my own. I think I'm starting to miss my croft. I think I'll go for a long walk, maybe go along the beach to Kilkeel and get a bus to Newry.'

I started to protest, but she was having none of it, and I sat in the car watching her walk away, her stride easy and graceful. Wearily I climbed out of the car. I pushed the skiff down the beach and jumped in. The Seagull started first pull, and the fresh salt breeze did me good as I motored across to the *Castledawn*. It was almost dark and there was a lot to do before the morning. I moored the skiff at the stern and unlocked the wheelhouse. There was a lot to do, but something drew me to the big navigator's chair I had installed in the wheelhouse – not for practical purposes, if I was to be honest, but for moments like this. I had stowed a bottle of Redbreast and a classic 1960s Colleen-cut Waterford whiskey tumbler in the locker under the wheel assembly, and I fished them out now and poured a small one and sipped it and watched the night steal over the mountains and the lough, the mountains sheer black and the water glittering and quivering. When the light had gone I felt as if I had just been present at a great drama. I sighed and put the bottle and glass back in their locker.

As I stood up the mobile rang. A man with a brisk manner and an American accent told me to 'be advised' that Mr Mellows was on his way to an unnamed US Air Force base, and where did I want him delivered? I didn't ask him his name. I wouldn't get it anyway. I got a number off him and said I'd ring back when details were finalised. He hung up without saying goodbye. I decided against being hurt and went down below.

Normally I am fairly security-conscious and I had an instinctive routine of checks that I do, things that I look for, when I go back on board the *Castledawn*. It's amazing the things you start to notice when you train your eye. The bright thread of a fresh scratch on a brass lock which shows that it has been picked. An alien piece of mud or vegetation from someone's shoe. Even the way a boat will ride in the water with the additional weight of an adult male on board. But this time I was meant to notice nothing. It wasn't until I turned on the light, halfway across the stateroom and too far from the door for escape, that I realised that I wasn't alone. That there was a gun pointed at me, and that the hand holding the gun belonged to Sasha.

There was a long, frozen moment and then Sasha jerked the gun towards the banquette.

'Sit,' he said curtly. I sat down.

'Maybe I shoot you right now,' he said.

'Why would you do that?' I said. He looked tired. He lay back in his chair and rubbed his left hand over his face. The gun in his right hand remained fixed on my solar plexus.

'Did I ever tell you about brother? Brother that died?'

'You mentioned him.'

'He was a soldier too. Fight in Afghanistan. But he was lucky. Got wounded. Got sent home. In hospital he meet a nurse. Pretty girl. She came from small town in Ukraine, on the bank of Prypiat river.'

I had heard of the River Prypiat before, but I couldn't remember why.

'So he marries, leaves army, goes to work as a fireman in a nice town on bank of river.'

Suddenly I remembered why I had heard of the River Prypiat before.

'Chernobyl was on the banks of the River Prypiat.' Sasha nodded wearily.

'They sent my brother to build *sarcophag*.' The sarcophagus, I thought. The aptly named structure that suicidally brave men threw up around the crumbling reactor in order to contain the radioactivity in the days following the explosion.

'After three weeks he dies of cancer.' Sasha was looking at me very intently now. I met his eye. I didn't know where this was heading, but I didn't much like it.

'He has a wife and little boy. I help. I send money. But the little boy gets sick. I send more money but not enough. He needs a good doctor. So I arrange something.' He was speaking very slowly now.

'I arrange for a smuggler to get them to Germany. I arrange another smuggler to get them to Warrenpoint.' He smiled, but there was no humour in the smile. 'But Sasha wasn't there when they come. Sasha was in police station because his friend get him arrested. I wasn't there for a woman and a scared boy.' Almost casually, but with lightning speed, Sasha leaned across and whipped the barrel of the gun across my face. Searing pain blazed through my head and I reeled back in the chair.

'Your cop friend Whitcroft. I think he is a good man. I tell my story, he lets me go. He says he is looking for woman and boy. They came in a container. Maybe they are still in container. The two men you see me with. They took my money but they say they not know where the woman and boy are.' I remembered the stories of forced prostitution. I also remembered news reports of people dying in unventilated containers.

'Whitcroft said not to kill you. He said you will help me.'

With the pain in my head came clarity, and a sudden blinding realisation of where I had gone wrong, of what had really happened. I groaned inwardly as it unfolded. How stupid I had been.

'You were talking to them to arrange to have your sister-in-law and her little boy brought into the country,' I said flatly. He nodded.

'Listen, Sasha,' I said. 'I will help you find them. And I'm better equipped to do it. I'll do it anyway, to make up for what happened. But if you want to help me tonight . . . I know I have no right to ask, but it does involve you . . .'

'Tell me,' he said, in a noncommittal way.

I started to talk.

I dropped Kate back to Edentubber. She protested that she could get a taxi, but I told her I needed to talk to McCrink. When we pulled up at the house it was dark. The door had been fixed, and when we went in there was a fire in the grate and delicious smells coming from the kitchen. I went in. I couldn't see Deirdre but there was a chilli coconut chicken soup on the hob. I helped myself to a spoonful, realising I was starving. The door opened and Deirdre came in with a couple of handfuls of fresh herbs. Her hair had fallen down and her cheeks were pink from the cold, and for a moment she looked like the teenage girl I had met here many years ago. Her look back at me was open enough, but I thought I detected a wariness there that I'd never seen before.

'Good soup,' I said.

'You're welcome to a bowl,' she said.

'Thanks. Where's McCrink?'

'He had to go into Newry to get some things. He'll be back in a minute or two.'

Deirdre put a bowl of soup on the table, along with a loaf of tomato and fennel bread fresh from the oven. I realised I hadn't eaten all day. She sat down at the other side of the table, something she used to do when we had been together, watching me eat with an old-fashioned proprietorial expression on her face. I don't think she was aware that she was doing it, for when I looked up and met her eye, she seemed to shake herself, then she got up quickly from the table. She stood with her back to me for a moment, leaning on the sink. Then she swung around, eyes flashing.

'How can you just sit there and eat when . . .' she burst out.

'When Somerville is holding Donna?' I gave a harsh laugh. 'Compartmentalising, I suppose, Deirdre. Isn't that what you used to say I did? But look at it this way, if I can't eat I can't function, and if I can't function, then who else is going to help Donna?'

'You're going to go in, aren't you?'

'In the morning.'

'Is Davy going too?'

'I can't make him go, Deirdre, but he will want to.' She looked at me with that direct, intuitive gaze both Liam and she possessed. But this time I put all I had into masking my thoughts, into making my face and eyes a blank. I could almost feel her searching, but this was one time I couldn't afford to let Deirdre Mellows read my thoughts. For if she had, she would have seen nothing but pain ahead.

The door opened and the moment was lost. McCrink came in carrying a bag of groceries. He kissed Deirdre lightly and put the bag on the table.

'Any news?' he said, turning to me.

'Somerville has Donna,' I said, 'and he wants something I can't give him in return for her.'

'So what do we do?' he said, sitting down opposite me. For some reason he looked young and eager, his worry for Donna flickering momentarily across his face.

'We go in,' I said. 'In the morning.'

'Right,' he said slowly, 'I can see that. I like Donna, Jack, and I'm no professional like you are, but I'm going with you.'

'Davy . . .' Deirdre began, and there was a kind of despair in her voice.

'I know, pet,' he said, taking her face tenderly in his hands. 'I know. But I've spent too much of my life sitting on bar stools talking about things. Now I have a chance to do something positive.'

'Jesus,' Deirdre said, and this time she sounded angry. 'Do you two not know the way the world works? Davy, your lobbying and activism and picketing and pamphleteering, that's what makes the world a better place! That's what get things done. Nothing comes out of the barrel of a gun except misery.'

She didn't look at me when she was saying this. She didn't have to. I had led her into danger a few years before and she had been shot. She had recovered but the injury had left her unable to have children. As always, others seemed to carry the burden for me.

'Tell me how it works,' McCrink said. He looked scared but excited.

'Simple enough,' I said. 'We tail the ferry in, as close as we can get to it. They won't see us until the last moment. We try and take them out or pin them down while one of us looks for Donna. Preferably we get our hands on one of them. He can tell us where Donna is. One way or another.' I could see Deirdre look at me and shiver. I didn't care. As far as I was concerned, kidnapping Donna meant that their lives were forfeit, and it was a matter of indifference to me whether they died screaming or died easy.

'Just the two of us?' McCrink asked.

'I got some help coming,' I said.

'I could come,' Deirdre said. 'I don't want to, but I could drive the boat.'

'No!' I slammed my hand on the table. There was no way I could afford to have Deirdre on this expedition. She gave me a look as if to say that there was no point in feeling guilty about the past. It was a look I couldn't bear, because that wasn't the reason I didn't want her there.

'I want you to stay here tonight,' I said to McCrink. 'Get some sleep. I want you at Greencastle at five tomorrow morning. I'll give you a firearm.' Davy nodded nervously. Deirdre turned away from both of us and went out of the room.

'Do you think we can do it?' Davy asked. His voice was nervous.

'We can do it, Davy,' I said. 'You have to remember that they are in a public space. They're protected from on high, but they can't do any cops and robbers stuff.'

'How do we get out?'

'I'm working on that. Try to get some sleep.'

Kate was in the kitchen when I came through. I signalled to her to follow me outside. We stood at the gate looking down at the lights of houses in the valley below. Wind stirred the branches of the sycamore trees above our heads. I talked for ten minutes, fast and low. She asked questions at first and then grew quiet. As I drove away she was still standing under the trees and I could see her face, pale and worried.

Back on board the *Castledawn* I cleaned and oiled the Glock, put out some clothes for the morning and ran through several times in my mind what we had to do. Then I rang Alva.

'This is not about the situation we discussed,' I said as soon as she picked up. 'I need something else.' There was a sleepy remoteness in her voice as she answered my questions, a druggy obliqueness – I realised how late it was, and knew that Alva tried to wait until evening before indulging her habit to the full. I hoped she was registering everything I was saying.

That still left six hours to go. I needed something to take my mind off things, so I did what I always do at times like this. I cooked. It was almost two a.m. before I finished. I set the table properly with a white Irish linen tablecloth, lit candles and dined in what passed for splendour when you were on board a converted trawler. I put all thoughts of last meals from my head and finished off with Ben and Jerry's chocolate mocha from the freezer, reasoning that I was going to be burning off the calories in the early dawn. I read Noam Chomsky for an hour in order to reassure myself that the world was as mad and as venal a place as I thought it was, then I got ready, putting the Glock into a holdall which looked like a workman's bag. I put on an old donkey jacket, stuffing its pockets with spare ammunition clips. I slipped a new semi-automatic Beretta into my pocket, remembering that I had told McCrink I was going to bring a weapon for him. Sasha had told me that he would organise his own weapon, and I had told the Americans to make sure that Liam didn't arrive empty-handed. At five-thirty a.m. I was ready to go.

It was freezing out on deck. Above my head the stars glittered, cold and dead, and an icy wind blew up the lough. There was frost on the ratlines. I swung myself down into the skiff and headed towards shore. McCrink was the first to arrive, Deirdre's Alfa coming up the little road with its distinctive growl. Must be serious, I thought sourly, if she lets him drive her car. He pulled up alongside the Impreza and got out, his breath pluming in the cold air.

'We're waiting for Sasha,' I said.

'You said you had a weapon for me,' he said. I gave him the Beretta and showed him how to use it. When I was satisfied that he wouldn't kill either of us by accident, I gave him some ammunition. While he was loading it, I saw the headlights of Sasha's Land Cruiser coming up the road. It came to a halt beside the other two cars. He got out and shook McCrink's hand. I got a curt nod.

'You got your weapon?' I asked. He took a bag similar to my own out of the back of the Land Cruiser and opened it. I looked in and saw an AKS 74U machine-gun. It was a stubby weapon, designed for ease of use when getting in and out of tanks and APCs. It wasn't particularly accurate, but I doubted if sharpshooting was going to be required in any case. The two men clambered into the skiff and I turned the bow towards the *Castledawn*. Both of them sat silently, wrapped in their thoughts. Once we were on board I went below and fired up the engines. The whole boat shuddered and seemed to come alive.

'Make some coffee,' I yelled to McCrink and went to cast off.

It was high tide, but I stuck to the channel on the southern side of the lough, so that we would look like a fishing boat coming in early with a hold full of prawns. I told McCrink to stay on deck and keep an eye out for the ferry, so that we could tuck in behind it and follow it in. Sasha came into the wheelhouse and placed a steaming cup of coffee on the map table.

'I'm working on getting some help,' I said, without looking at him. 'I hope to have some results tonight.' He didn't reply, and I heard the wheelhouse door swing shut behind him. I blanked it out and turned my mind to the present. The bulk of the castle had disappeared into the night and I thought I could make out the shallow curve of Mill Bay, and the lights of Carlingford on the port side. Warrenpoint dock was opposite Omeath, just where the lough started to narrow. I eased off on the throttle slightly. Timing was everything now.

We steamed like that for twenty-five minutes, then I eased the wheel to starboard so that we were sailing across the lough rather than up it. I cleared the channel and eased the throttle again, though for different reasons. There were rocks and shallows here and I couldn't afford to run aground. I aimed the boat for the lights of the garage in Rostrevor. McCrink came into the wheelhouse, looking worried.

'No sign of the ferry yet,' he said.

'Not to worry,' I said. 'There's been a change of plan. We're docking at the pier in Rostrevor.'

'How come?'

'I'll explain it to you when we get there.'

I could see the light at the pierhead now. It was more of a stone jetty than a pier, with a few old buildings attached, but it was a secure anchorage, and more importantly it was on the road between Rostrevor and Warrenpoint four miles away. As I approached the pier I eased back on the throttle. I slid open the window and shouted to Sasha to secure the bow line. As he went into the bow and lifted the end of the line, a figure detached itself from the shadows under the pier wall and stood by one of the bollards. Sasha hesitated, then threw the line. The man caught the line and expertly made it fast to the bollard. He did the same with the stern line as I swung the stern in. I cut the engines. Suddenly the night-time quiet came flooding back, broken only by the noise of small waves on the shingle. I jumped on to the pier. The man didn't move.

'You look well, Jack Valentine,' said Liam Mellows. 'You look well.'

'You too, Liam,' I said, meaning it. The skin around the eyes was a little more lined, and there was a little steel-grey in the hair as well, but America had treated Liam Mellows well.

'Sorry about the speed of the summons,' I said.

'I nearly shot my way out of it,' Liam said with a grin. 'They had to get Stone on the phone to persuade me it was really you looking for me. After that it was fine. I got to see the insides of some pretty quick aircraft.'

'You didn't mind?'

'Mind? The construction industry is grand, but there's not a lot of excitement. No, I don't mind, Jack.' As he spoke he was watching me with the penetrating look he shared with his sister, the look that seemed to see right into your soul. I'd first seen it twenty-five years ago in a small town in Namibia, and I'd wondered many times since if I was still capable of living up to whatever standards he applied.

I was suddenly aware of McCrink standing beside me.

'Better do the introductions,' I said. 'This is Davy McCrink. Liam Mellows.'

'Liam Mellows, Jesus,' McCrink said, shaking his hand warmly. 'I've heard a lot about you.'

'Deirdre told me about you as well,' Liam said with a grin. He turned to the boat then. Sasha was standing on the rail, holding a stanchion. The two men sized each other up for a moment, and I could see that they read each other as fighting men. Liam granted him a wary smile. Sasha waved laconically in return. In other circumstances I would have bet on them being friends. But now I wasn't sure.

'Come on board and get warmed up,' I said. 'We're not going anywhere for about half an hour.'

Sasha stayed on deck while I fed hot coffee to Liam. I would have liked to talk more but McCrink bombarded me with questions about the operation. I told him to wait, that things would become clear shortly. I transferred the efficient-looking machine pistol that Liam had been provided with into my grubby bag, and got him to swap his smart, American-casual clothes for a grimy boiler suit. While he was changing I went up to the wheelhouse. Sasha sat on the rail, looking moody and watching the group of men who had materialised out of the early morning dark. I looked at my watch. It was time.

'Come on, Jack,' McCrink said as we walked down the pier. 'What are we doing?'

'Well,' I said, 'you see those men? They're all foreign workers going on shift at the docks. There is a bus which takes them there. It goes right to the place we want, and the security people don't check it. We just mingle with them and we're right where we want to go.'

Sasha thought about it for a while and nodded. Liam merely shrugged. I had told him it was a rescue operation, but not much more. He didn't seem to care. McCrink looked worried.

The men barely glanced at us when we joined them. It was a group of men you could have met in any pre-dawn in any part of Europe. Migrant workers doing the jobs that no one else wanted to do. They didn't talk. Some of them stamped their feet against the cold and smoke rose in the air from half a dozen cigarettes. They were a poignant group, I thought, that you could have mistaken for refugees. After a few minutes I heard the bus coming down the road. Simultaneously I felt rather than heard the deep thrum of the ferry engines and looked up to see the big ship coming slowly down the channel, lit up from bow to stern, men getting busy to berth.

Heads down, we paid our fare and shuffled on board the bus with the other men. We went to the back of the vehicle and others moved aside to let us sit down. There was a warm, companionable fug of cigarette smoke. It felt like the bus my father used to take to work at the shipyard in Glasgow, and for a moment I was transported back there, but then the deadly heft of the bag in my hand dragged me back to the present. Liam was sitting next to me, and he leaned into me.

'What in the name of God is going on here?' he whispered.

'I'll explain it all to you later,' I whispered back. 'First let's get Donna back.'

'You know where she is?'

'There are offices and storerooms at the back of this big hangar. She has to be in one of those. Somerville likes to keep his assets close.'

The bus rumbled along the Victorian promenade and turned into the town. Sasha looked relaxed – almost too relaxed, I thought, as though in the grip of a Slav fatalism. I hoped not. McCrink looked tense. My own mouth was dry, but I knew to expect that. McCrink had never really been tested in combat before.

The bus went out on to the dual carriageway, passing small factories on the left, and then we reached the harbour entrance. The bus rolled to a stop at the gates. A security man stepped out with a clipboard. The door opened and he came on board. I froze. He looked as if he was about to count heads, but at the last minute he grinned and said something to the bus driver and withdrew. I gave a sigh of relief as the doors closed again and the bus jolted into motion. In groups of three or four the men started to get off, walking off to their work, shoulders hunched against the cold. As we approached the hangar, there were only three men left on the bus. As the vehicle pulled up to drop them off at a small works entrance, a hundred yards short of the entrance I wanted, I motioned to the others to get off with them. Liam went first, and we found ourselves standing at the edge of the road beside a chain link fence. The three other men walked off, with a curious glance back at us. The bus disappeared around a corner in the distance. Suddenly I started to feel exposed.

'They have a lot of security, lot of men at hangar,' Sasha said.

'I think the front door might not be all that well guarded at the moment,' I said. We started to walk as if we were going to work. As we did so, I was able to scan the fence surrounding the hangar. I couldn't see any of the hard-faced men. There were cameras at intervals, but my eye followed the coaxial wires, which had obviously been put in hurriedly, for they were exposed and ran along the ground when they got to the bottom of the fence. I saw that they all ran into the security kiosk at the front gate.

'Act lost,' I hissed as we reached the gate. I turned and pretended to remonstrate with Liam. As I did so, I could see that there was only one man at the security desk, a hard-faced, blocky man who scowled out at us. I threw my hands in the air as though I was despairing of what Liam was saying and I walked towards the kiosk. The man watched me coming, but didn't open the glass. I held the bag at thigh level where he couldn't see it and pulled back the zip. I rapped on the glass and he opened it with exaggerated exasperation.

'Excuse me . . .' I said, and stuck the first gun my hand had lit upon in his face. Fortunately it was Sasha's ugly, functional Soviet machine pistol.

'Back, back, back!' I shouted. He backed away, hands in the air, as Sasha swarmed athletically through the opened window. I tossed the AK to Sasha, who caught it and made a brisk motion with the barrel. The man understood and lowered himself slowly to the floor. I took a packet of PVC hand ties from the bag and set about securing him. Sasha hit the gate button and it swung open. Moments later, McCrink and Liam were in the kiosk. As I worked on the guard, Liam took over the camera console.

'All the cameras are controlled from here,' he said. He flicked quickly from camera to camera.

'Wait,' I said. 'Hold it there.' Parked around the side of the hangar, but with its nose clearly visible, was a black S Class Mercedes. Scribner, I thought.

'Go on,' I said. From what we could see, much of the hangar was deserted.

'Where are all the men?' Sasha said, puzzled. I didn't answer. I was pretty sure I knew where they would be found.

I looked out over the buildings in front of us and could just see the radar dome on top of the ferry as it glided towards its docking place. We didn't have much time. I finished tying up the guard. I quickly gagged him with one of the ties, retaining the rag stuffed into his mouth. Then indicating to Liam to help me, I lifted him into a large corner cupboard and closed the door. Health and safety wouldn't exactly approve, but the alternative would have been a bullet between the eyes.

'Hold on,' Liam said. 'I have them now.' The camera was focused on the quayside. There were men in concealed positions behind crates and crouched behind the hangar doors. They were barely visible in the grey dawn light, but they were there and looked as if they were expecting an attack. Crane engines began to start up on the quays. From the big timber importers further on down a buzz saw joined in. World War Three could break out in the docks now, and no one would hear it. And from the look of things, the men on the dock were expecting some kind of minor conflagration.

'See if you can see a sniper,' I told Liam urgently. The bow of the ferry was visible in the channel now. The men were obviously expecting something from that direction, and would be suspicious if nothing appeared.

'Easy,' Liam said. 'On top of that little crane.' He pointed to a crouching shape.

'At least he isn't looking this way,' I said. 'What about . . .'

'There!' he said, swivelling one of the cameras. We were focusing on a solid-looking lean-to store against the back wall of the hangar. It was an undistinguished structure, but one thing made it stand out: the man carrying a machine pistol who leaned against the wall outside.

'That's it,' I said. 'Come on!'

We raced out of the kiosk, Sasha and Liam falling instinctively into a crouched, defensive run, guns constantly moving, McCrink running behind, with me taking up the rear. We hit the side wall of the hangar and crouched low. Once again it was Sasha and Liam who took the lead, moving us forward and giving instructions in brusque military hand signals. We got to the corner of the building and peered round. The man was less than twenty yards away. Liam beckoned to McCrink and me to stay put. He moved forward around the corner with Sasha. I watched them go, fast and silent and deadly. Suddenly McCrink was beside me. I could feel how buzzed up he was. Sasha and Liam got to within five yards of the guard before he sensed movement and turned. I'm not sure if he meant to fire. I'm not sure if the movement of the gun was involuntary. In any case he would not have got a shot away with Liam and Sasha both covering him. But it was McCrink who fired – the long, deadly rattle of a gunman who doesn't know to fire in bursts. The guard jerked, his face wearing a look of terrible surprise. He seemed to move backwards in a series of jerky steps, and you could see long filaments of thread from his clothes shimmering in the grey light as the nickel-tipped bullets exited his back and carried pieces of fabric with them. I grabbed the barrel of McCrink's gun and thrust it skyward. Too late for the guard, but at least it prevented him from shooting Sasha and Liam. With my other hand I disengaged his finger from the trigger.

'Shit,' he gasped. 'Jesus, Jack . . .'

'Don't worry about it,' I said brutally. 'He would have done it to you in a second.'

Sasha was already on his knees fishing through the dead man's pockets for a key to the heavy brass lock. Liam was covering the approaches from the dockside.

'Hurry up,' he said urgently. 'We're exposed here.'

Sasha found the key and threw the door open just as I drew level. I ran in. Donna was sitting in the corner with her back against the wall. Her hair was tangled and matted, but otherwise she seemed unharmed. She looked up in dumb fear and surprise. I went to her and touched her face gently, then lifted her into my arms. She covered her eyes when we went outside – even the early morning light was too much for her. McCrink was looking down at the dead man with a look of wonderment on his face.

'Two casualties,' Liam said quietly, looking at McCrink and Donna. I could see a flash of anger cross his face when he saw how Donna looked.

'No mercy for these boys, then – is that the way of it, Jack?'

'That's the way of it, Liam,' I agreed.

'Shit, Jack,' Sasha cried out. I looked. The black Pajero was sitting at the gates. As we looked a man got out. He looked into the kiosk, then he turned and saw us. He shouted out and reached into the passenger seat of the jeep. An SLR appeared in his hands and he knelt in an unhurried way and put the rifle to his shoulder. The SLR had a good range, but this man wasn't the sniper. A bullet pinged off the wall behind me and then I was running in the best crouch I could manage, urged on by Sasha, while Liam emptied a magazine at the Pajero. The chain link fence was coming up fast and then we were running along it, going in the wrong direction. Above us, and on the other side of the fence, towered stacks of containers. I held up my hand to call a halt. We were running right into the arms of the men on the dockside. The ferry must be close to docking, and they would have seen there was no threat. At any rate the men in the Pajero would be in touch with them. I looked desperately for a way over the fence, knowing in my heart there wasn't one, when I heard the whine of an electric motor. I looked around to see Liam descending on us on an ancient fork lift truck. Without stopping he rammed the forks under the fence and lifted. The truck groaned and shuddered and the smell of burning magneto filled the air, but the fence lifted.

'Under!' Liam shouted. We hit the ground and rolled as bullets rattled off the engine casing of the fork lift truck like deadly hail. Even Donna seemed to rouse herself, rolling through and getting unsteadily to her feet. Sasha stood and looked down the rows of stacked containers as if he had seen them for the first time, wondering, I knew, if one of them contained his sister-in-law and nephew.

'You know, Jack,' he said quietly, oblivious to the shots and the gunfire, 'after your friend the policeman released me, I come down here. I knocked on the side of containers and wait for an answer. Then another container. Then another. Always quiet like grave.'

He turned to look at me and I could not meet his gaze. Then a bullet struck the container beside us and a metal fragment hit me on the cheek, stinging me into action. I swung the Glock around and fired an aimed burst at the group of men who had just appeared from the direction of the docks. Then I turned and ran. Liam was supporting Donna, who was just about managing to stay on her feet. We were in a long corridor between stacked containers, metal walls soaring on every side. A killing zone if ever I saw one, I thought, my breath burning in my lungs, looking frantically on either side for a way out. I could see that Sasha was out in front – he was the man who knew the docks area best. I hoped he had something in mind.

'Come,' he shouted, shepherding us off into what looked like a dead end.

'Stay,' he shouted to the others. 'Jack, with me!' We ran around the corner and suddenly found ourselves surrounded by pens full of cattle. As soon as they saw us, they began to low. Sasha started to bang loudly on the metal rails. Then he raised his gun and fired into the air. The tone of the lowing changed. I realised what he was doing, and began to bang on the railings as well. Sasha fired another volley of shots. The lowing had changed to a terrified bellowing and cattle were flinging themselves at the railings, trying to escape.

'Stand back!' Sasha shouted. He flung the steel gates open and a couple of hundred frightened cattle streamed out of the gate. I barely got out of the way as the heaving, bawling mass thundered past me. The noise was deafening. The air filled with animal noises and stench. The cattle funnelled down between the containers, emptying the pen in what seemed like a matter of seconds. Sasha and I followed them. As we turned the corner a scene of chaos met our eyes. The Pajero had tried to drive down between the containers, but now it almost entirely blocked the way, and the frightened animals first milled around, then tried to scramble past and over the obstacle. The Pajero rocked from side to side as they tried to force their way between the vehicle and the containers, then one maddened animal took the more direct route, scrambling over the bonnet of the jeep, slipping on the polished surface as its hooves fought for purchase, then falling sideways and starring the windscreen before slipping off. Another followed suit and the windscreen shattered. Whoever was driving the jeep panicked and tried to drive forward instead of reverse, which only served to compact the cattle as the beasts at the back tried to force their way forward. The jeep slewed sideways, its engine roaring, then, as the cattle lunged forward, the Pajero went up on two wheels. Calmly Sasha raised his gun and emptied a magazine into the metal of the containers above the cattle's heads. The noise, amplified by the canyon, was deafening and the animals lunged forward again, desperate to get away from the source of the noise. The jeep went over. I saw somebody desperately try to scramble from the passenger window, then the whole vehicle seemed to be buried under a sea of cattle.

Liam led Donna and McCrink from the cul-de-sac in which they had been sheltering. Once again, as we limped towards the main dock area Sasha went on ahead, coming back with an ancient Datsun pick-up.

'Belongs to a friend,' he said. 'We borrow it.' I grabbed everyone's gun and stuffed them all into my bag. Sasha and Liam and Donna got into the cabin. I sat in the open back with McCrink. As we drove around the other side of the container park and out of the docks he kept looking at his hands as if he could see a stain there.

'I shot him, Jack,' he said to me. 'I shot him.'

'If you hadn't shot him, somebody else would have had to do it,' I said. My mobile started to vibrate inside my jacket. It was Deirdre.

'Did you get her?' she said urgently, and then: 'Is Davy all right?'

'Yes and yes,' I said, 'but some of us are a bit shook.'

'Can I talk to Davy?' she asked. I looked at McCrink. He shook his head.

'Can't,' I said. 'I can't get to him at the moment.'

'He is okay, though?' There was a tremor in her voice.

'Yes,' I said, 'he is all right.'

'Sorry, Jack,' she said.

'Don't say sorry, Deirdre,' I said. McCrink was still staring at his hands and I thought my heart would break. There was a click and a soft buzz, and the connection was broken. I looked through the little window at the rear of the pick-up's cab. Donna's head was down and her shoulders were shaking. Liam's head was close to hers, and it seemed he was talking hard and urgently. At least something was falling together, I thought. I still didn't know what had been done to Donna, but if there was one man who could dispense unsentimental wisdom and healing to her, then it was Liam Mellows. He would admit to it, I thought, and then with a twisted grin would acknowledge that it was at the price of his own blasted soul.

We drove up through the town, attracting the odd curious glance, black diesel fumes belching out of the back of the pick-up. I kept my eyes peeled for curious traffic policeman, as the Datsun didn't look as if it had any right to be on the public road. I was relieved when we reached the turn-off to the pier at Rostrevor. Sasha swung the Datsun in behind the outbuildings and I jumped out. I opened the door of the pick-up. Donna slipped from the seat and into my arms.

'Don't say anything,' she said. 'Don't say anything.' Her grip was fierce and I held her tightly, and kept on holding her as we walked down the pier. When we reached the *Castledawn* she looked up at me.

'Who dealt with you?' I said, feeling the anger well up inside me.

'The man in the wheelchair.' I looked at Liam. I didn't have to say it. When Liam had the opportunity to kill Curley, he should have taken it.

'He said it didn't matter if the goods got damaged a bit. He said I was dead anyway.' She shuddered.

'Did they do anything to you?' I said, trying to keep my voice even. She shook her head.

'That man Somerville, he'd say stuff like we're a civilised country and all that kind of thing. To be honest, I'd prefer Curley. But they didn't hurt me any more . . . I don't know . . . I shouldn't . . .' I put my arms around her again. I knew what was happening. When you're under the control of somebody who is truly indifferent to whether you live or die, your whole perception of yourself and your relationship to the world changes. It takes a while to come to terms with that. Liam and McCrink helped Donna on board while I went back to Sasha.

'The search is on, Sasha,' I said. 'I'll ring you this evening.'

'You owe now,' Sasha said. 'You owe.'

'I owed before this morning, but thank you for it.' He looked me in the eye and then his face broke into a grin.

'Was a good trick with cows?' he said.

'It was a hell of a trick,' I said. 'A hell of a trick.'

*

Sasha stood on the pier and watched us steam off into the early morning light. I know it wasn't intended that way, but the silent figure on the dock would remain in my head as a reminder of the pledge I had given him. I went into the wheelhouse and gave McCrink the wheel with instructions to keep dead ahead. We couldn't go back to Greencastle, so I thought I'd cross the lough to Carlingford. It might give us a little breathing space. Somerville would be after us, and I needed to find a way to get him off our backs. If only I could find that blood, I thought.

'Is everything all right?' I asked him. 'You want to talk?'

'You know I never killed anyone before.' There was an odd expression on his face.

'I'm not a psychoanalyst,' I said, 'but some things do bear being brought out into the open.'

'Is that right, Jack?' he said, with an odd, cracked laugh. 'To be honest, I'm better on my own. Maybe I'll talk about it later – is that okay?' I nodded. I'd tried anyway, I thought. I went out of the wheelhouse and closed the door behind me.

My thoughts were interrupted by the mobile. I looked at it. It was Jimmy Kerr. I almost didn't answer it. An image came into my head of a selfish old man brooding about long ago. I thrust the thought away as unworthy and answered the phone.

'Sorry to disturb you, Jack,' he said, and his voice was weak and tremulous enough to make me feel ashamed of my thoughts.

'It's okay, Jimmy,' I said. 'I'm still working on . . .'

'I know you are, Jack,' he said. 'It's just that I learned something.'

'What is it?' I said.

'On the back of the dog tag,' he said. 'I never looked at it before. There's something written.' This time I could hear the excitement in his voice.

'What is it?' I asked, starting to feel curious myself.

'Looks like it was done in a hurry, scratched out with something,' Jimmy said. 'It's the name of a ship. HMS *Opal*, it looks like.'

As I went down to the galley I turned the name HMS *Opal* over in my head. More clues from the grave, I thought. I called Davy Wilson, who glumly reported that he'd reached a dead end. He brightened when I told him about HMS *Opal* and went off happily to research it. Finally I got to the galley. Donna was having a shower and Liam was lying on the banquette reading a battered paperback he'd pulled from his pocket.

'We need to talk, Jack,' he said. I sat down and talked, quickly and quietly filling him in. His face grew grave.

'This is not good, Jack,' he said. 'Not good at all. The bastard.'

'We need to do something about it. Today.' I spoke under my breath as Donna came in, drying her hair.

'What's the big secret?' she said lightly.

'Not a thing, darling,' Liam said lightly, getting to his feet. 'Sit yourself down there. I believe Jack is going to cook breakfast.'

I was indeed going to cook, and I set to it with a kind of savagery. I dug a selection of things out of the freezer and while they were defrosting in the microwave I made a hollandaise. I put O'Dohertys free-range sausages in the pan along with

Clonakilty black pudding, chopped mushrooms in butter and pepper in one saucepan, and chopped tomatoes in another. I defrosted a batch of potato bread and put thick slices of ham on the grill. Liam set the table while I cooked. When everything was almost ready I poached eggs and toasted muffins, put the eggs on the muffins, the grilled ham on the eggs and the hollandaise on top. Sausages, black pudding and tomato on a platter finished it off.

'Read my mind, Jack,' Liam said, his eyes roaming greedily over the plate. 'The only thing I miss about the States is the fact you can get eggs Benedict for breakfast every morning if you want.'

I called McCrink and brought a plate and a mug of tea up to the wheelhouse. We were getting near Carlingford and I wanted to bring her in myself. As we crossed the channel we went under the stern of the superannuated minesweeper that patrolled the lough. One of her semi-rigid patrol boats sped in our direction and for a moment I thought we would be stopped and boarded, but the fast boat kept on going.

I pulled up at the pier and moored. The harbour was quiet. Many of the small fishing boats were out of the water for the winter, and there were few pleasure craft about mid-week. The town itself had an off-season feel to it. Carlingford had a Norman castle as well, dominating the harbour. Normally I had fond memories of it, but this time it seemed beset with ancient glooms. Today was not going to be a good day, I thought. After a while, Liam and Donna joined me on deck. I could hear McCrink talking on his mobile below decks. Deirdre, I thought. After a while he came up as well. We sat on deck for a while, drinking coffee, then McCrink said he needed to go into the town. Donna went down for a sleep. When I was sure she had lain down, I exchanged glances with Liam. There was no need to speak. I got the Beretta and stuck it in my pocket.

We combed the town first. There were only a few grocery shops and pubs open. The good restaurants and many of the bars wouldn't open till the evening, so it didn't take long. When we had finished, Liam nodded towards the castle. It was the only place we hadn't tried. We approached it from the landward side and once again I had the sense of an ancient malice lurking in its old stones. We found nothing at the first level. Instead we found him on the second level, sitting in the ruins of a window overlooking the harbour, mobile phone to his ear. It was still only early afternoon and yet the evening darkness already seemed to be creeping in, so that it was difficult to make out McCrink's features. As we approached he ended his call and slipped the mobile under his jacket.

'Jack . . . Liam,' he said. 'Were you looking for me? Is something wrong?' He looked down at the Beretta in my hand and faltered.

'Who were you talking to, McCrink?' I asked. 'Somerville maybe?'

'I don't know what you're talking about,' he said.

'Maybe Somerville isn't your handler,' I said. 'I suppose that's a possibility, Liam?'

Liam walked over to McCrink. He put his hand inside McCrink's jacket and pulled out the phone. McCrink flinched but didn't move. Liam brought up the last number and gave it to me.

'Jesus, Liam,' I said, 'that's not very spylike. You call the switchboard at MI6 and the number comes up on your phone. Would never happen with Mossad.'

'What's going on here, Jack?' McCrink said weakly.

'What I'm most annoyed about is that I blamed Sasha,' I said. 'Somerville always seemed to know what we were doing before we did it, and I couldn't figure out how. I put the finger on Sasha because he was talking to people smugglers at the docks, but it turns out he was just trying to sneak relatives into the country. Never thought of you. The idealist. But a little suspicion began to creep in. You were the only person who knew everything, including things I'd only said to Deirdre. Today was the test, McCrink. I told you we were going in after the ferry, and there was a reception party waiting for us. You didn't shoot that guard by accident. You shot him because he recognised you. I saw it in his face. You thought he was about to blurt out your name.'

McCrink hadn't moved, but his face looked ghastly in the evening light.

'Was it going on the first time I met you? In the miners' bar? The *agents provocateur* weren't there to stir the miners. They were there to give you a little light kicking, to give you credibility with the miners. Jesus, McCrink, you must have been useful. All those environmental organisations, all those political groupings, and all the time you were the security services' eyes and ears. What was it? Money?'

The minute it was out of my mouth, however, I knew that it wasn't money. I'd seen agents turn men before. The bad handler scares the subject, makes him afraid. The fear weakens the subject, leads to mistakes. The best handlers appealed to someone's pride, built them up to imagine themselves as superior to those around them, to possess special qualities that only the handler really recognised and appreciated.

'They were always so fucking smug, you know that, Jack? Smug and pathetic.' There was scorn in McCrink's voice now.

'They thought they had all the answers. But tell me this now, Jack, what happened to them all? They grew up and cut their hair and took the place of the people they thought they were fighting against.'

'I never wanted to be all that radical when I was young because I didn't want to be conservative when I was old – is that it then, McCrink?'

'You're a fucking hypocrite yourself, Valentine. What was the old gag about the Labour Party? The Labour Party always struggles with its conscience, and the Labour Party always wins. Well, you always win against your conscience, Jack, for all your show of struggling with it.'

'What about my sister?' Liam said, his voice neutral.

'Ah, the beautiful Deirdre. At least she puts herself on the line for what she believes in, even if she is a bit naïve.'

'And we don't?' Liam said, sounding puzzled.

'You used to, Mellows, but our friend Valentine here, he doesn't put himself on the line. He puts his friends on the line. On which subject, that's quite a hole Deirdre's got in her stomach. Proud of getting her shot, are you, Jack?'

Nothing I've ever felt in my life could match the palpable sense of malice towards another human being emanating from Liam. I could feel the hairs on the back of my neck stand up. I couldn't believe that McCrink was still talking, that he didn't notice. I knew that if Liam went for McCrink I wouldn't be able to stop him. Not with my fists, not with the Beretta.

'One more thing, Jack,' McCrink said, filled, it seemed, with his own cleverness. 'You know you've been played for a fool all along? Somerville's been ten steps ahead of you – you've been doing exactly what he wanted you to do.'

'How's that, McCrink?' I said, taking a step closer. McCrink seemed to swell with the delight of seeing Somerville make a fool of me. He was going to enjoy telling me about it. Except that he never got a chance. There was a loud and venomous boom, a sound I had heard too often in the past week, and a red rose bloomed in the middle of McCrink's forehead. Instinctively I hit the deck, but not fast enough to avoid the hot, sticky liquid spraying into my face.

'What was that?' Liam said, through gritted teeth.

'The sniper,' I said bitterly. 'The damn sniper.' I crawled over to McCrink. His unseeing eyes stared upwards. There was a neat hole in the middle of his forehead. I turned him over. The back of his skull was missing. Moving cautiously, I went over to the empty window space and eased myself up into a position from where I could see out. The shot could only have come from the direction of the sea, and there was only one platform that would have been suitable in terms of position and stability. As I looked, diesel smoke started to pour from the funnel of the naval minesweeper, and she began to gather way. I slumped down against the wall. Obviously Somerville had decided that McCrink was surplus to requirements. I wasn't sure what that signified. And what had McCrink meant when he said that Somerville had been using me all along? Too many unanswered questions. I looked down at McCrink's unseeing eyes. Had he always been corrupt? Somehow I didn't think so. I remembered sitting in the Rotterdam bar with him after he had come back from a globalisation protest in Geneva, his eyes flashing as he described what had happened, the roll-up in his hand being waved around in his enthusiasm. Was it possible to be both? To be both a spy and an activist? I thought that in some strange, prideful way McCrink probably thought that he could. I stood up.

'Come on,' I said.

'What about him?' Liam asked.

'He's their mess, let them clean it up.'

'He might be their mess,' Liam said, 'but he left behind another mess.'

'Deirdre,' I said.

'She thought a lot of him,' he said. 'This is going to break her heart. That stuff he said . . .'

'No, Liam,' I said, 'I won't tell her. Ever.'

'You'll do better than that,' Liam said. 'He died bravely, am I clear? We don't mention this spy stuff.'

'If you think so, Liam.'

'I do, Jack. Remember it.'

I walked slowly back to the *Castledawn*, leaving Liam to take a taxi to Edentubber. Donna came out on to the deck when she saw me coming.

'What happened?' she said. I brought her into the wheelhouse. I poured myself a Redbreast. I sat her down in the captain's chair and told her what had happened.

'Christ, Jack,' she said when I had finished, 'what sort of a world do you live in?'

'I don't know, Donna,' I said, 'but it doesn't stop turning, not ever.' A sudden weariness swept over me, more than just physical tiredness. I felt weary in my soul. I got to my feet.

'Where are you going?' she said.

'To keep a promise,' I said.

FOURTEEN

I went down to the office. I had to ring Alva, but first I checked my email. There was one which simply read 'Stone,' with an attachment. I opened the attachment. It showed a series of satellite photographs of a small oil exploration rig. The cloud cover had cleared, I thought. There was a crane on the platform and the photographs showed a sequence of a small truck being lifted from the water. There was also a blow-up of the door of the truck. The decal of the Iraqi star was clearly visible. There was also a series of shots of the Warrenpoint dock area. I wondered why Stone was sending me these things. What did he want me to do with them? I put the question out of my head and rang Alva.

'The two names you gave me, Kovitch and Stanovitch, are very well known to police forces across Europe,' Alva said. 'Involved in trafficking, prostitution, child trafficking, drugs.'

'Pleasant people.'

'Very. They are closely associated with the lap-dancing industry. They are also considered very dangerous – but then, so are you, Jack.'

'Am I?' I didn't like to think of myself in the same terms as Kovitch and Stanovitch.

'Certain men acquire the smell of death.'

'That's not really the kind of answer I wanted to hear.' She laughed a harsh laugh.

'Don't worry, Jack, it is also the case that certain women like that . . . aura . . . in a man. Anyway,' she went on, 'they have a club in Drogheda, a lap-dancing club called One-Eyed Jacks.'

'Original,' I said.

'Hardly. They take people in containers through the Hook of Holland and then move them by ship to Warrenpoint. The containers are opened at a distribution centre downriver from Drogheda.'

'Any idea where they go from there?'

'They have property all over the place. To be honest, Jack, I don't know what they would do with a mother and a little boy. The mother would be no good to them, I would expect. The little boy would have a . . . certain value.'

She wasn't telling me anything that I hadn't suspected, but the coldness of it made my heart sink.

'How long have they been in the country?' she asked.

'Not long – three or four days.'

'Then the chances are they are still there.'

'I would need to get moving.'

'That would be good, Jack. I hope you find them.'

'So do I.'

'By the way, Jack, I found out that the lawyer Scribner is a member of several exclusive gun clubs. Not for hunting, which you would expect from a person of his class. I looked into it.'

'And?'

'He represented Britain at several European and world championships. He is an expert marksman, Jack, a sharpshooter.'

The sniper, I realised – the lawyer was the sniper.

I called Sasha and told him quickly what I had learned.

'I see you, twenty minutes,' he said. 'We need to move quick, I think.' I thought so too. I didn't reckon on the reception committee waiting for me on the quay. At first I thought that Whitcroft was on a friendly visit, then I saw the two men in blue boiler suits and bullet-proof vests aiming guns at me from behind the pier wall.

'What's going on, Whitcroft?' I demanded.

'I'm taking you in, Jack.'

'Why?'

'We found Kovitch and Stanovitch.'

'That's good, isn't it?'

'They had their hands tied behind their backs. Each had a single gunshot wound behind the ear.'

'That's not exactly the worst news you ever heard, is it?'

'The bullets came from a Glock.' I was beginning to see where this was leading.

'They can't match mine, Whitcroft.'

'I'm afraid they do, Jack. And there's another thing. There's a container full of people out there, and Kovitch and Stanovitch were the only two who knew which container.'

'Shit.'

'Exactly.'

'It wasn't me, Whitcroft. I'm going to try to find Sasha's sister-in-law and her child. You'll have to shoot me to stop me.'

'Oh, I wouldn't shoot you, Jack. But these two gentlemen certainly would.'

I heard Donna come out on to the deck behind me, and her despairing words.

'For God's sake, Jack, what is happening now?'

'It's all right, Donna, these gentlemen are the police.'

'That's enough of the sarcasm, Valentine,' Whitcroft said.

'Fair enough,' I said pleasantly. 'I'll try another tack. There's a gun pointed at you from behind.'

Whitcroft looked around cautiously to see Sasha standing behind them with the stubby AK in his hands. I saw one of the blue boiler suits tense as if he was about to turn.

'Don't,' I warned. 'Sasha is former special forces. You'll die before you get a round off.' Whitcroft waved his hand and the two men raised their guns.

'Whatever about Valentine,' Whitcroft said to Sasha, 'you are now officially in very serious trouble.' Sasha shrugged.

'Listen,' I said, 'apart from the fact that we all look ludicrous standing here pointing guns at each other, the fact is that there are people out there who might be dying in those bloody containers, and I have an idea where they might be.'

'What are you suggesting?' Whitcroft said.

'That we all go together and sort this out afterwards.'

'I can't allow that,' he said.

'Listen, Whitcroft,' I said angrily, 'you're the one who gave me the big lecture on trafficking and prostitution, and all of that. Now you're in a position to do something, why the hell are you not doing it? I'll hand myself over to you straight afterwards, but there could be women and children dying while we stand here.' Whitcroft sighed, then turned to look at his two men. The older of the two shrugged.

'If you say we saw nothing, we saw nothing, sir.'

'All right,' Whitcroft said, 'but consider yourself in custody, Jack, to surrender yourself to me when we finish this thing. And perhaps your friend will put that doubtless illegal firearm away.'

'You are close to retirement, aren't you?' I said, unable to suppress a grin.

'You better thank your lucky stars I am,' he said. 'Let's go.'

Whitcroft and his two men went with Sasha in the Land Cruiser. As I started the Impreza, Donna got into the front seat beside me. I opened my mouth to object, but she glared at me and I shut it again.

It was a thirty-minute drive to Drogheda, then a long, unrewarding slog through far-flung industrial estates and semi-derelict factories along the banks of the river, getting further and further from the town. Just as dusk was falling we drove into a yard which seemed derelict. There were tottering piles of rotten pallets, skips of scrap metal and several asbestos-roofed outbuildings. We pulled up. I got out of the car and walked over to the other car. With the engines turned off the place seemed eerily quiet.

'It's not looking good,' Whitcroft said. 'We'll go a bit further down the river, then pack it in for the night. Your information wasn't exact enough, Jack. We need to go back and see if there is anybody we can talk to in the lap-dancing club.'

I hadn't noticed Sasha getting out of the car, but now he stood very still. Then he reached into the car and in a single rapid movement grabbed and cocked the AK.

'That smell,' he said quietly. 'I smell it before.' He started to move and we followed him, not aware of the odour at first but suddenly becoming conscious of a sweetish and sickly smell with something foul about it. I looked at Donna.

'I'm a forensic pathologist, Jack,' she said. 'I know what that is.'

Around the back of one of the derelict sheds we found an articulated trailer. There was mud on its wheels which had not quite dried, meaning it hadn't been there for long. The double doors at the back were padlocked. The smell was terrible, and I suddenly realised what Sasha had been talking about: the container of prisoners in Afghanistan. One of the two policemen, grim-faced, grabbed a crowbar and with one huge effort ripped the lock from the door.

The smell hit me, a cloying blanket of rot and death that made me gag and choke. The policeman swung the door wide. There were perhaps ten or twelve figures in the container, figures that looked like bundles of rags slumped on the floor. I heard Donna choking beside me. The walls of the container were caked in human waste, and one part of it was dented and scratched where someone had tried in their desperation to get through the metal wall. A few empty water bottles lay on the floor. The two policemen had backed away, choking. Whitcroft looked on, pale-faced and grim. Sasha was the first to move. He vaulted into the container. I don't know if he had seen a tiny movement, or if instinct led him, but he went straight to the back of the container and scooped a small bundle from the floor. He came back without pausing at any of the other figures. I held out my arms and he passed down the feather-light body of a fair-haired little boy. I stared at the closed eyes, then put the sensitive skin of my cheek next to his nostrils to see if I could feel a breath. There did not seem to be anything.

'All dead, except maybe him,' Sasha said harshly.

'Get me water, quickly!' Donna said. 'Put him down here.'

She laid out her coat on the ground. One of the policemen ran to Sasha's jeep and came back with a bottle of water. Donna took a handkerchief from her pocket, wet the end of it, then held the wet end to the boy's lips. She wet it again, and this time the boy's lips opened slightly and she was able to get some moisture into his mouth. He stirred and made a faint noise.

'Call an ambulance, quick!' Donna said. There was a note of command in her voice I hadn't noticed before. Sasha bent down and brushed back a strand of the boy's hair which had fallen forward on to his brow. Then he went back into the container. This time he carried out the body of a woman. She was pretty in a dark-haired, Russian way. Young too, I thought, though death had not erased the signs of a hard life from her face. He laid her down as well, though far enough away so that, if the boy awoke, he would not have to look upon his mother's body.

The boy stirred again and moaned. I moved over to Whitcroft. His face was white with suppressed anger.

'I know those two bastards are dead . . .' he said.

'I didn't kill them,' I said quietly. 'But I think I know who did. I think Somerville killed them. And that means that Somerville is responsible for this. If they hadn't been dead, they would have been here, and he wouldn't have let his assets die. Look . . .' I led him by the arm to the container. All of the dead, apart from the boy and his mother, were young women.

'They were bringing these girls in to work – lap dancing or prostitution. They had invested in them, and they weren't going to let their investment die.'

'What are you trying to say to me, Valentine?'

'I'm saying let me go after Somerville.'

'Listen, Valentine, your weapon killed those two men. Believe me, bullets from that damn thing have been identified on the database before now – referred to your spook bosses, no further action, but you're not above the law now . . .'

'McCrink was working for Somerville,' I said. 'He must have got the gun off the *Castledawn* and given it to Somerville or Curley. They used it on Kovitch and Stanovitch and put it back.'

'Why?'

'I don't know. To frame me, I suppose.'

'Maybe you have an exaggerated sense of your own importance.'

'Maybe, maybe not. But McCrink told me that Somerville was using me. But I haven't been able to figure out how or why. Maybe that usefulness has come to an end and he has found a way of taking me out of circulation.'

'Then why did he not put a bullet into you? That seems to be the way you people operate.'

Because, I thought, Somerville never burns an asset. I would be tried and convicted behind closed doors, put away for life. But how long would it be before somebody from MRU would be in the visiting room offering inducements if I would help them? Put in a cell with a subversive with orders to gain his confidence and find out what I could from him? I could still be very useful to Somerville, even inside. There was another aspect to the thing too, and that was the one I gave Whitcroft.

'Somerville would like the idea of me rotting in prison. It would appeal to his sense of symmetry. Along with Liam, I put Curley into a wheelchair. A life sentence, if you like. It would be sweet revenge.'

In the distance I could hear an ambulance. The two policemen had their attention fixed on the little boy, who was starting to writhe and mutter as Donna bathed his face and dribbled water into his mouth. I started to move towards the Impreza. Whitcroft watched me go. I think that he still did not know what to do. Then the little boy started to scream. The scream went on and on, and seemed to join with the siren of the approaching ambulance in an eerie and heart-wrenching symphony. Whitcroft stood with his hands in his pockets, his gaze fixed on me. I started the engine of the Impreza. The two policemen straightened up, guns suddenly appearing in their hands. They looked to Whitcroft for a signal. The signal never came. Gravel skidded out from the Impreza's tyres. Neither Donna nor Sasha looked up as I gunned the car along the rough gravel road.

The door of the cottage at Edentubber was open. I knocked and went on. Liam was sitting at the kitchen table. There was a whiskey glass in front of him and an open bottle of Paddy on the dresser.

'Where's Deirdre?' I asked.

'Gone,' he said.

'Where?'

'I don't know. Kate is out looking for her.'

'How did she take it?'

'Badly,' Liam said. 'Very badly.' He went to the dresser and returned with a glass. He put it down in front of me and poured a large one, then topped up his own glass.

'Sometimes things happen to a person that – what's the word I'm looking for? – distort, that's it, things happen that distort a person's character, Jack. Sometimes it springs back, sometimes it doesn't.' He looked up at me. 'I'm worried about her,' he said. 'Really worried.'

'I don't know what to do here, Liam, what to say . . .' I said, a feeling of helplessness washing over me.

'You'll do the only thing you can do now,' he said, 'which is to play this thing out to the end. Now bring me up to speed.'

I told him what had happened. McCrink's treachery over the Glock. The container and its human cargo. I couldn't tell what he was thinking. You never could with Liam. There was a long silence. He picked up his glass and walked to the window. He stood looking out for a while and then he turned.

'There is something wrong here,' he said, 'something very wrong. I can't put my finger on it . . .'

'I had the same feeling,' I said, 'but once I discovered what McCrink was up to, I thought that was what was troubling me.'

'No, there's something more, something deeper,' Liam said. I listened to him with a growing feeling of unease. I trusted Liam's intuition.

'You need to talk to Stone,' he said, 'and after that you need to talk with Somerville.'

'How am I going to talk to Somerville?' I said. 'Do I just walk in and ask to see him?'

'It might just come to that,' Liam said. 'But for now we're

going to the *Castledawn*. Stone didn't send you classified satellite photographs for nothing. I'd be surprised if he isn't looking for you already.'

The first thing I did when I got to the *Castledawn* was check the Glock. It was safely in its place under the binnacle. What I should do now, I thought, is sling it overboard. But then I wouldn't have a weapon. I put it back in its place.

Liam had been right. There was an email from Stone telling me to go to the reception in McKevitt's Hotel at nine o'clock and wait there. I looked at my watch.

'You hungry?' I asked Liam.

While I was cooking, Liam studied the satellite photographs. It only took fifteen minutes to come up with crab toes with garlic aioli served with wheaten bread. We wolfed it down and five minutes later we were walking down the quay. We went into the small hotel and sat down in the foyer. We didn't have long to wait. At exactly nine o'clock two men came in. You knew they were Agency immediately. They wore identical slate-grey suits with white shirts and restrained blue ties. I always thought of CIA men as looking like some kind of deadly Jehovah's Witnesses, convinced beyond argument of their own rectitude. We were politely and firmly invited to go upstairs into the small conference room. We waited in front of a large video screen for several minutes while the two men moved quietly and efficiently about the room. The video screen flickered into life and we had a mike pinned on to us. I was aware of the two men leaving the room, dimming the lights as they did so. After a moment the screen flickered and the face of John Stone appeared.

'Good evening, Jack,' he said. 'Good evening, Liam.' The

voice was as ever measured. Stone hadn't changed much. Perhaps a little more grey around the temples, but we all had that. He was a man in his late fifties or early sixties, tall and well built, but not necessarily a man who would stand out in a crowd. Not until you looked into his shrewd eyes and found yourself wondering what terrible knowledge was concealed behind them.

'I suppose you're going to tell us what is going on here?' I said.

'I will certainly give you my interpretation of it as far as I can, Jack,' he said, 'and ordain a course of action in relation to it. But first perhaps you could fill me in on events.' The American always chose his words with care, and I didn't like the suggestion that a course of action would be ordained. I told him what had happened since I had last spoken to him. He listened without interruption, and when I had finished talking he sat, his head bowed in thought, for several minutes. You could hear the faint oceanic hiss of the satellite signal coming in through the ether. It was Liam who broke the silence.

'What we have to do,' he said, 'is destroy the plane. That's obvious.'

'It may be what Somerville wants us to do,' Stone said.

'All the same, even if we are doing what he wants, we should destroy the plane,' Liam replied.

I had the feeling of some esoteric conversation being conducted over my head, as if they understood what was going on, not on the level of logic, but on some deeper plane. Perhaps they did understand it on a deeper level. Liam had an instinct for the game that I had never possessed.

'What did McCrink mean,' I said, 'about Somerville using me?'

'Well,' Stone said, steepling his fingers, 'you would hardly seem to be involved in all of this by accident.'

'I was involved because body parts belonging to my neighbour's brother were washed up on a beach,' I said. 'Somerville's reach is long, but even he can't go back fifty years.'

'No,' Stone agreed, 'of course he can't, but he can get hold of a situation and exploit it. But I agree that your role, unwitting as it may be, goes to the core of this whole affair. I think Liam is right. The next move on the chessboard is to destroy that aircraft, in fact the entire contents of the hangar. It would be nice to get our hands on that phial of blood, but since it has been mislaid . . .' The tone was mild but the rebuke hung in the air. I wasn't really in the mood for it.

'Can I remind you that I don't work for the government any more?' I said. 'I can walk away any time.' This sounded unconvincing, even to me.

'Can I remind you, Jack,' Stone said, in a faintly amused tone, 'that *you* contacted *me*?'

'Hang on a second,' I said, suddenly suspicious. 'You knew about this *before* I rang you. In fact . . .' I thought about it, trying to work my mind around the implications, '. . . this plane, the whole scheme . . . it has your fingerprints all over it . . . that plane is one of yours, isn't it?'

It was getting to be a familiar feeling. As soon as I thought I was getting a grip on what was going on, it seemed to slip away.

'The situation was a little more complicated than that, Jack,' Stone said patiently, 'but that is hardly relevant now.

Where, and with whom, the mission originated hardly matters any more. What does matter is what happens to it, and as Liam rightly says, it has to be destroyed. And the only people who can do that are you and Liam and your friend Guydarov, if he can be persuaded. And if it can be done.'

'I know how to do it,' Liam said quietly.

'Usual conditions, Jack,' Stone said. 'You go in as completely deniable operatives. Conclude the mission successfully and I will give you cover within reason.'

'Within reason?'

'This is a major operation in the middle of a town. One civilian casualty and all bets are off.'

'And why do you think I'll do it?' I asked.

'Because that's what you do,' he said. 'You and Liam and your Russian friend. That is the kind of men you are. Liam has another incentive. His immigration status in the United States is shaky. Equally, his status in Ireland is uncertain – let's say there are certain unresolved political issues from the past. I will make both things go away.'

'And Sasha?' I asked.

'I don't think that he will back out, considering that you cleverly got him to blame Somerville for the death of his sister-in-law. However, if he needs more persuasion, you can tell him that I will have him sent home. And that his period of reflection in the Afghan mountains is referred to as desertion by his former superior officers.'

'And the little boy?' I said. He smiled mirthlessly.

'Apparently Russia is a democracy these days. I'm sure there are social services to look after him. Don't say it, Jack. You were going to say that I used to act in the greater interest of humanity, that I had a heart, that I thought that the thing I was fighting for wasn't worth having unless we protected the innocent. That's all changed now, Jack. I'm an outpost of a garrison under siege. Ethics are a luxury I can't afford.' Stone's face set in an expression I hadn't seen before. Arrogant, prideful even. He settled back in his chair with a look which could only be described as smug. I remembered the little boy in the back of the container and I felt anger well up inside me. I opened my mouth, but Liam slid his foot across the carpet and kicked me hard. I turned to him, angry at first, but then I read his look. Once again, that ability to grasp what was going on under the surface. I don't know how he conveyed it, but I understood immediately. *There are other people in the room with Stone,* Liam's look said. *He's talking like this for their benefit. You think he would have survived in Washington if they had scented weakness?*

I nodded. I understood. There might be concessions that I could extract from Stone in private, but on this conference call, he might as well have been standing on the floor of the Senate.

'Remember this, Jack,' Stone said, leaning into the camera so that his face filled the screen. 'You and your friends are foot soldiers, infinitely expendable. Do what you are told and your chances of survival are enhanced. Disobey and you are terminated.' Stone's hard gaze filled the screen for a moment and then without warning, the screen went dead.

Enhanced and terminated, I thought. Hard words. The two CIA men moved swiftly and silently into the room, as Liam and I sat in silence.

'You'd better get moving,' one of them said. 'You haven't

much time.' Once again anger welled up in me – who was this youngster to order me around? But Liam didn't even seem to notice him, and once again the Irishman's equilibrium brought me back to earth. I got up and followed Liam outside.

'Give me a minute,' he said. 'I need to think about this.' He walked off along the pier, disappearing into the evening gloom. As if on cue, my mobile rang. It was Deirdre.

'Hi, Jack,' she said. There was something utterly desolate in her voice.

'Hello, Deirdre,' I said, and paused. The connection between us seemed slender, liable to snap at any minute.

'I needed somebody to talk to,' she said, then, with a broken laugh: 'What am I saying? I need to talk to you. Nearly everything good I had in my life, I lost around you, and yet you're the only person I can talk to. Isn't that funny?'

'It's not funny, Deirdre. It's not funny at all. And I am sorry about McCrink, desperately sorry.'

'Funny the way you always called him by his second name. Kind of a male intimacy thing, I suppose. He always used your first name. See, I'm talking in the past tense about him, that means I'm coming to terms with it.'

'Where are you, Deirdre?' I said, injecting urgency into my voice. I had never heard her talk like this before.

'Doesn't matter, Jack. Did he say anything? Before he died?'

'No,' I said. The word sounded blunt and unforgiving.

'How come the person standing next to you always dies,' she said, 'and never you? Never you, Jack.' I heard the receiver being replaced in its cradle with a soft click. I put the phone back into my pocket. I found that I was breathing hard and my palms were sticky. I felt as if I'd had a phone call from someone who had crossed over into death. I heard Liam calling me and made my way towards the sound, groping along the pier like a blind man.

FIFTEEN

We rendezvoused later that night in Edentubber. Kate was there when we arrived. She would not tell us anything about her pursuit of Deirdre, except that she did not know where she was. When Liam went out of the room I told her about the phone call. She shook her head wearily.

'There's nothing I can say, Jack,' she said. 'This has completely devastated her.'

Our conversation was interrupted by the arrival first of Sasha and then of Donna. Sasha said that the little boy was in hospital and doing well. Everyone else in the container was dead.

'Whitcroft, he say that girls save their water for boy. That is why he live. But he sit up and talk. There are Russian girls, nurses who work in hospital. He feel safe.'

'And his mother?' Kate asked.

'In morgue,' he said shortly.

'What was her name?' Kate said.

'Katya.'

'Katya,' Kate said, rolling the word around on her tongue as though she was thinking about somebody who might be a friend in the future. For some reason it seemed to bring alive a person we had never met. It was, I suppose, part of Kate's gift of healing, and it made the meal that followed a sad, but companionable thing, Kate cooking *soupe de poisson*. While she was cooking, helped by Donna, Liam and I sat with Sasha and explained what Stone had told us. I expected anger, but Sasha grinned, showing his teeth.

'I happy to kill them for nothing. Only need to ask. What is plan?'

On our way to Edentubber we had stopped to reconnoitre the docks area. We pulled into a side road and drove up the side of the golf course to a hill overlooking the docks. It was immediately apparent that the security had been stepped up, and extended to take in the entire docks area. A Portakabin had been installed at the gate and was staffed by hard-looking men. Uniformed guards patrolled the boundary fences and the water's edge. But they weren't some half-trained, half-baked security men hired from an agency. These men were alert and professional, and once again you could see the outlines of concealed firearms under their crisply pressed uniforms.

'Either they are very stupid or very confident,' Liam said. He took out one of the satellite photographs.

'The whole boundary of the docks is secure, but it seems that the actual hangar has little security. They've made it really hard to get into the docks area, but once you get in, you can operate with impunity.'

'Fair enough,' I said, 'but how *do* you get in?'

'I'm sorry that it had to be so,' Liam said, 'but the terrible happening in Drogheda and Sasha's story about Afghanistan gave me an idea. We go into the docks inside a container, with whatever weapons we need. Sasha – you can operate a crane?' Sasha nodded.

'We get Sasha to lift the container to here.' He pointed to a spot beside the hangar fence. 'He lets us out, we cut the fence and in.'

I suppressed a shiver. Something about the idea of using a container to get in seemed like tempting fate.

'What then?' I asked.

'Bring plenty weapons,' Sasha said, looking wolfish this time. 'Kill all. Destroy damn plane.' Looking at him, I was glad I was on his side.

'I got special stuff,' he said. 'Good weapons I bring from Russia.'

We decided that we would go in after the morning shift had started. That the best option would be to burn the hangar if we could. That we would retreat through the hole in the fence, lose the weapons and mingle with the workers who would, in the event of a major fire, be evacuated from the other factories and businesses in the dock area.

'We can't make any specific plan about getting into the hangar until we get there.' Liam said. 'There is marine fuel stored there – Jack saw it the time he was there – but whether we can get it to light up enough to get it going . . .'

'I have some weapons,' Sasha said again. 'We meet at my house, okay?'

'At ten o'clock,' I said. 'Then we go in.' Liam looked down at his hands.

'It'll be a bloody fight,' he said. No one answered. We were all lost in our own thoughts for a minute. Then Sasha stood up to go.

'Ten in morning, then,' he said. There was a lightness in his step as he left which I recognised. It was the gait of a fighting man who has been lost in moral complexities and recognises with gratitude the simple bounty of a fight where you either killed your opponent or got killed. I went to the kitchen for the Paddy bottle. Donna was there, washing up.

'Look,' she said, directing my gaze out of the kitchen window. I could see Sasha standing at his jeep. Kate was with him. I realised that they were facing each other and were holding each other's hands lightly, like teenagers. Kate laughed lightly and as she threw her head back she was suddenly very beautiful in the dim light. Then they kissed and I turned away.

'I missed that,' I said.

'Did you, Jack?' Donna said, with a soft smile. 'You miss a fair bit here and there, don't you?' She pecked me on the cheek and went out of the room. I reached for the Paddy bottle, poured myself one and swallowed it down. The back door opened and Kate came in. She looked at me, and realised at once that I had seen her and Sasha together. She reddened and looked flustered, then I grinned and we both burst out laughing.

'I'm sorry,' I said, 'I wasn't spying . . .'

'It's all right,' she said, touching her warm cheek. 'I wasn't embarrassed about you seeing me and Sasha.' She smiled self-deprecatingly. 'I suppose I didn't want you to see me . . . or me to think of myself . . . as only bringing solace to injured men. I think I'm a bit more than that.'

She had spent some time with Liam a few years ago, when much of what he defined himself by had fallen apart. And with me before that.

'I wasn't injured,' I said, faking hurt.

'That's true,' she said, touching my face affectionately. 'You were very young and very sweet.' She laughed at the expression on my face.

'And very virile,' she added, laughing.

'Thank God for that,' I said. But her expression had turned serious.

'You could all be dead by this time tomorrow.'

'Well,' I said, affecting levity, 'we're all dinosaurs from the twentieth century anyway.'

'Veterans of wars that everyone else has forgotten,' she said softly. 'Sasha said that. But it's all one war, Jack, and it never ends. So don't get killed tomorrow and don't kill my lover, okay?' She kissed me softly and left me.

I went back into the house. Liam had a stripped-down Beretta on the table, oiling and working the slide. I went through the kitchen and down the corridor to Donna's bedroom. I knocked lightly on the door. When I went in Donna was lying on the bed reading a magazine. She turned around when I came in and sat up. Her expression was grave and sad.

'I'm leaving tomorrow, Jack,' she said. She bit her lip, and I saw that her eyes were bright.

'I'll have to take my chances with what happened at the lab, and with the pilot's blood.'

'If we succeed tomorrow, then you won't have to worry. Apart from everything else, I have the full intention of making sure that Somerville won't bother anybody again.'

'And if you don't succeed?' she said softly. I told her what we had in mind.

‘It sounds as if you’ll all be killed,’ she said, her eyes wide in alarm.

‘Don’t underestimate me, or Liam and Sasha,’ I said.

‘Oh Jack,’ she said, ‘how the hell did I get into all of this?’ She stood up and leaned her head against my chest. I lifted her face to mine and kissed her. There was a question in the kiss. She pushed me away gently. There were tears in her eyes.

‘You’d better go now, Jack Valentine,’ she said. I held her hands as long as I could. She backed away, her gaze still meeting mine, and then suddenly my hands were holding nothing. I turned away and fumbled my way out of the door. I had nothing to say to Liam. Our arrangements were made. I slipped out of the kitchen door, but as I opened the door of the Impreza, I looked up to see Liam standing in the living-room window, a dark figure with the light behind him, his expression impossible to divine.

I hadn’t expected to sleep that night, and I didn’t. When I got back on board the *Castledawn*, I cast a longing glance at the Redbreast bottle, but thought better of it. I put Django Reinhardt on the CD player. Django measured out his gypsy melancholy precisely and with wry good humour, exactly what I needed. I made myself an espresso and took it up to the wheelhouse, switching over to the speakers up there. It was a clear, cold night, the lough waters still and surrounded by lights. On nights like this, the place always seemed to resemble a frozen, northern latitude Bay of Naples. Above my head the constellations spiralled off into infinity. I should move here, I thought, if I lived through tomorrow. Something in it felt like home now, and my far-off Scottish croft seemed a shabby thing. I thought about Jimmy waiting night after night for news of the dead. I could end up like that, I thought, I could end up waiting on the dead.

I turned up Django and went out on the deck, letting the cold night air drive away dark thoughts. I could see the lights of Warrenpoint docks less than a mile away. I could see the lights of cranes moving cargo, the line of lights along the front of the hangar. There was going to be a fight in the morning and something in me welcomed it. I took a deep draught of the cold night air. It was a fine night, and there was the clarity emerging out of the conspiratorial murk of the whole affair, the clarity of a fight where some would live and some would die.

SIXTEEN

'Jesus,' Liam said, 'a few of these . . .' We were standing in the small garage behind Sasha's house, looking at the array of weaponry that he had laid out on the floor.

'It's quite an arsenal, Sasha,' I said.

'You think so?' he said, almost beaming with pride. 'I've been collecting.'

I didn't ask how he got them into the country, but he had the capacity in that garage to start a small war. There was the whole AK range of Kalashnikovs, there was the legendary AN 90. But the weapon that caught my eye – and made me think that I might yet survive the morning – was the GP25.

'Ah, you like that?' Sasha said, seeing me look at it. 'A pity I only have two. But,' he continued brightly, 'I got plenty of ammo.'

'How do you use that thing?' Liam asked, picking one up. It was a chunky cylinder about ten inches long with a large aperture at one end and a trigger mechanism at the other.

'It's an under-barrel grenade launcher,' I said. 'I've heard of them but I've never seen one.'

Sasha picked up an AK47 and showed us how the device fitted underneath the barrel of the otherwise conventional weapon.

'It shoots a grenade,' Sasha said. He showed us the grenade, which looked more like a stubby rocket. He pushed it into the aperture and twisted it into place.

'When you arm the grenade you have fourteen seconds exactly before grenade go off. Make sure to put the safety on. GP 25 has a big recoil. Also, see this.' He picked up another grenade. This time it was in two halves, connected in the middle by hard black rubber.

'This is good,' Sasha said. 'Anti-personnel. Hits the ground and bounces. Goes off at waist level. Plenty of shrapnel. It is called the frog.'

'Some weapon,' Liam said.

'There is also a good trick,' Sasha said. 'You fire grenade in the air on a curve trajectory like a mortar. Reload and count to nine while grenade is in the air, then fire another grenade at the target. Target gets hit from above and from straight ahead. Target thinks there are two of you, maybe more.' Sasha laughed out loud at the plight of the imaginary attacker. I was starting to feel sorry for the poor bastard, particularly if Sasha was the man holding the GP 25.

In the end Sasha and Liam took GP 25s and I armed myself with the AN 90, which was capable of firing two shots almost simultaneously. The impact of the second bullet on the same spot as the first one would penetrate body armour.

Sasha brought us outside. We crossed the street to a small freight yard. There was a Scania in the middle of the yard, its engine running. I felt a small stab of fear as I looked at the container on the back. I could almost smell the stench from the container in Drogheda. But there would be no backing out now. A young man with a cigarette between his lips jumped from the cab. He gave us a grin and a thumbs-up and said something in Russian to Sasha. Sasha spoke back, then took us around the back of the truck. He unlocked the container. Liam looked at me, then swung himself in.

'Look,' he said, 'I fix so you can open from inside.' He showed us where a small hole had been cut in the rear door, too high up to see out, but big enough to enable you to reach the handle and open the door.

'In case you get fright,' Sasha said, laughing. That's all very well for you, I thought, but I had already heard one tale of death in a container in Afghanistan, and then seen it with my own eyes, and I found the empty interior of the container distinctly unappealing. Liam reached down his hand. I grabbed it and pulled myself up. The container was old. You could see pinholes of daylight through the roof, and the walls were rusty and scarred and damp. It smelt of decay. Like a mausoleum, I thought, then told myself to stop being melodramatic. Sasha handed up the weapons.

'Okay,' he said, 'see you in fifteen minutes.' And with that the door swung shut with a clang. I flinched. I hadn't reckoned on the pitch darkness, the only light being a small gleam from where Sasha had cut the hole. I couldn't even see Liam.

'Dark, isn't it?' he said – rather unnecessarily, I thought. I stretched out a hand and fumbled towards the metal wall. Sasha shot the bolts on the door with a sound of finality. I could feel the trailer lurch as he climbed into the passenger seat of the cab. The lorry lurched into motion and suddenly I went flying into the wall, striking it with an impact that left me dazed.

'Right,' Liam said, 'I'm out of here.'

'What?' I said.

'You heard me.' I could see Liam's face now, caught in the square of light from the cut-out in the trailer door. Then the light was dimmed as he pushed his arm through the gap. He gasped with effort and then I heard the bolt sliding back. The door opened and light flooded in once more.

'Where are you going, Liam?' There was a tremor in my voice I wasn't used to hearing. We were going into combat and you expected the tense, dry-mouthed companionship that went with it. You didn't expect your comrade-in-arms suddenly to announce that he wasn't going to be there.

'Something I have to do.' Liam turned in the doorway. He was holding one of the GP 25s, and as I made a move towards him, he lowered it so that it was pointing at my chest.

'Back off, Jack,' he said, his voice uninflected, almost casual. I stopped in my tracks. I had heard that curiously neutral tone in Liam's voice before and I knew that it denoted the hair-trigger moment, the interval where Liam could explode into violence in a way that seemed a surprise, even to him.

'We've known each other a long time, Liam,' I said.

'We have, Jack,' he replied, 'and that's why you'll go through with what we've agreed. In the meantime, there is something I have to find out.' The truck stopped at the yard entrance. In one swift movement he dropped off the back of the trailer and slammed the door shut. I dived towards the door but the bolt was shot from outside with a decisive sound. I heard a rattle as he wrapped chain around it. I was trapped.

I pounded on the side of the container with the butt of the AN 90, but Sasha couldn't hear me over the noise of the engine. As the truck moved forward again I pushed my hand through the gap and felt for the lock, but it was tightly wound in chain. The lorry struck a bump and threw me off my feet. I fell backwards, and the rifle fell from my grasp and slid away from me into the darkness. Frantically I scrambled after it, feeling blindly for it as if somehow it would provide protection against the darkness and the sudden dragging uncertainty caused by Liam's actions. What did he have to find out that would necessitate leaving Sasha and me to fight against what seemed like impossible odds?

My fingers found the rifle, and I grasped it to my chest as the truck struck another bump. I wedged myself uncomfortably into the corner to stop myself being flung around, as I thought what hell it would be for a small child to make a long journey in such a way. The noise was tremendous, every sound magnified by the walls of the container. It smelled as if diesel fumes were somehow finding their way from the exhaust into the container. I tried to interpret the motion of the lorry in order to work out what progress we made, but it was difficult, and soon I was completely disorientated. There was one long halt, which I realised was probably the dock gates, then the lorry started again, throwing me back against the wall. It struck me how crude and violent the process of travelling in a vehicle was when you took away powerful suspension and comfortable seats.

Finally the lorry came to a halt. The engine was switched off and I could hear the sound of an approaching crane. Then there were several loud clangs as chains were attached to the container. I waited in the darkness. The crane engine started to rev and as it did so, the container swung loose from the trailer and, with a sickening feeling of vertigo, I was hoisted high into the air. The container swayed alarmingly as the crane lurched into motion, travelling down the quay. Once the initial vertigo had passed, the gentle swaying motion made a pleasant change from the violent movement of the lorry.

I don't know when I realised that something was wrong, but I had a growing sense that the crane had travelled much further than it was supposed to. I tried to reassure myself that my sense of time had become distorted in the darkness of the container. It didn't work. Then suddenly and ominously the crane stopped. The container swayed gently in the air, and I had the feeling that it was being lifted upwards. Then, with a sudden, sickening, vertiginous jolt, the container plunged towards the ground.

There is no word to describe the terrible bone-jolting impact as the container struck the ground. No word to describe the awful tormented clang that reverberated in the interior of the container, or the clouds of filthy, choking dust dislodged from its floor. And no word to describe the fear, or the shout that burst from my mouth, as I realised that the container was travelling upwards again. Again and again the container hurtled towards the ground until it seemed that every inch of my body had been beaten by hammers. I desperately tried to protect my head. I had never felt so helpless, deafened by the noise, unable to see, hardly able to breathe through the dust. It seemed that I had always lived in this hellish tumult.

It did end, though. With one final plunge to the concrete dock it stopped and left me crawling in the dust like a helpless mewling baby, numb fingers feeling for the rifle, hardly knowing where I was. And then the doors opened. Screwing up my eyes against the light, I crawled towards the door, my only thought now to escape my metal prison. I'm sure it was a moment that Somerville enjoyed. The first thing I saw as I reached the lip of the container was a pair of well-polished brown brogues. I lifted my eyes. Somerville was smiling pleasantly at me. Beyond him I could see four or five armed men. Sasha was on the ground in front of one of them. There was an ugly gash behind his ear, but his eyes were open. Curley sat to one side in his wheelchair. He held the GP25 and was looking at it with interest. Somerville stepped past me and peered into the dusty black interior of the container.

'Where is he, Jack? Where is Mellows?'

'Go to hell, Somerville,' I hissed through my dust-parched lips. Through accident or design, Somerville chose the hand with the missing finger to stamp on with his polished brogue. The pain was excruciating and I felt tears of rage and hate spring to my eyes. I moved weakly forward, and he brought his foot down again.

'I intend for you to die in there, Jack. I intended Mellows to perish as well, but no matter, without you we'll catch him quickly enough.'

Behind Somerville I could see the plane. It seemed that it had been almost completely reassembled. Somerville followed my gaze.

'Impressive, isn't it?'

'McCrink said you were using me.'

'Of course I was. You were my conduit to Stone. I knew you would go to him.'

'What had Stone got to do with it?'

'I think Mr Scribner could tell you more about that.' I hadn't seen the lawyer. He was leaning against the nose cone of the plane. He held a sniper's rifle loosely in one hand. He looked comfortable with it. My suspicions were confirmed. He was the man who shot Fiona and McCrink. He strode forward at Somerville's invitation.

'You're looking a little shook up, Valentine,' he said, an unpleasant smile on his face.

'Who are you working for?' I said. 'You have the look of MI6 about you. A murdering thug acting sophisticated.'

'Nothing as banal as that, I assure you,' he said. He casually lifted the barrel of the rifle until it was pointed at my head.

'You will of course be terminated, Valentine, but first I want you to know how stupid you have been. The whole operation was set up by Stone, or so he thought. It was his idea to provide a *post facto* reason for invading Iraq by putting a chemical weapons lab in place. Unfortunately for him we were aware of it. We fed him everything: the Russian plane, the laboratory, the Iraqi vehicles, even the remote area where the plane was to land.'

'But it never got there,' I said.

'No,' Somerville said, 'a small microwave-controlled bomb brought it down. We were lucky. It almost went into the Beaufort Dyke. Fortunately it crashed in shallow waters and we were ready with the platform to fish it out again.'

'How was I used?' I could hear the desperation to know in my voice, but I didn't care. 'How, Somerville?' I asked. But it was the lawyer who answered.

'A brilliant piece of improvisation by Mr Somerville, I have to say.' Somerville inclined his head modestly. 'When he saw you at the inquest he knew you could be relied upon to do the obvious thing and go to Stone. We needed a reliable conduit who would tell Stone that we had the evidence implicating him directly in a plot to plant a chemical weapons factory in Iraq. You were that conduit, Jack.'

'Now he knows that, we have . . . that word the Americans use . . . leverage. We have as much leverage as we can use in this administration,' Scribner added.

'Stone is obviously desperate enough to send in three second-rate adventurers to try to destroy the evidence. But of course we knew every move before you made it,' Somerville said.

It was true. They had always been ahead of us. But how? Even after McCrink's death, they had still anticipated everything. Somerville was watching me closely.

'Work it out, Jack,' he said softly. 'Black Cat and Black Dog were mission names, of course, but you know me, Jack. There's always a little more to things. Black Dog was also the name of an agent. Amusing, I thought. What deceased agent could be Black Dog, do you think?'

I stared at him, starting to see a little light in the darkness, piecing it together and feeling my blood freeze.

'Yes, good, isn't it? McCrink was Black Dog. And if there was a Black Dog . . .'

'There also has to be a Black Cat . . .' I said in a hoarse whisper. 'McCrink was killed . . .'

'Remember one of the golden rules, Jack,' Somerville said, 'you don't burn an agent . . .'

'. . . unless you're protecting another, more highly placed agent,' I said, appalled to my very soul. Somerville was laughing out loud now, but the sound seemed to be coming from a great distance. I looked up, knowing what I would see, as

Donna McNeill stepped out from behind one of the ailerons of the wrecked plane.

'Hi, Jack,' she said, smiling. As she smiled I thought I could see a cruel curve to her mouth that I hadn't noticed before, but perhaps that was just my imagination.

'My God,' I said, suddenly feeling more weary than I had ever felt in my life before, 'the whole thing . . . the pilot . . . the fishermen . . . the phial of blood . . .'

'There was no pilot, Jack,' she said briskly. 'No pilot, no fishermen. I thought you might have been a little suspicious . . .' No, I thought bitterly, I swallowed it hook line and sinker.

'The blood?' I said.

'Ah yes, the famous phial of blood,' Somerville said with a smirk.

'It was of course a fake,' Donna said, 'although it did contain sarin. You were supposed to give it to Stone, who would then know that we had the plane.'

'But you couldn't even get that right,' Somerville said.

'Yes, Jack,' Donna said, 'what the fuck did you do with the phial?' I watched as those beautiful lips framed the obscene word with a terrible deliberation.

'How long?' I said, my voice sounding weak.

'Donna is one of the new breed,' Scribner said, 'recruited straight out of college. The best and the brightest are going into the service now. We don't recruit out of the slums any more, Valentine.'

The insult barely registered. I was too busy trying to assimilate the new information, and too tired and bruised even to start thinking of a way out. Half of me, stunned and betrayed, felt like telling them to put a gun to my head and get it over with. Donna stepped forward until she was standing over me, smiling. Yes, I thought, that cruel line was there all right. I remembered the first night, the night in the little cottage and the passion, and then after that, how she had always managed to slip away from me when I reached for her. She had done just enough to ensnare me. I let my face rest on the concrete and shut my eyes. When I opened them again I realised that I was staring directly into Sasha's eyes. He was also face down on the concrete, and there was an intensity in the way he was staring at me that sent a small surge of adrenaline through my exhausted body. Sasha was trying to tell me something, almost trying to communicate by sheer force of will. Something was on, I realised. And then I remembered that Liam was still out there. As I felt myself tense for action there was a curious noise, somewhere between a pop and a bang. Somerville looked around, frowning. The GP 25, I thought, and then recalled how Sasha had described how to use it to fake a multiple attack. One of its grenades was in the air now. Sasha's lips were moving, counting.

'. . . two, three, four . . .'

Scribner picked up Somerville's unease and his grip tightened on the sniping rifle as he scanned the rooftops behind us. I turned my head slightly. I could see my own gun a few feet behind me.

'. . . five, six, seven . . .'

I lay there with my face pressed to the concrete. The seconds passed like years. Scribner turned back to me. Whatever happened, I was not to escape. He placed the muzzle of the rifle against my temple

'. . . eight, nine . . .'

There was another bang and I saw a projectile streak across the hangar. I looked up and saw one of the grenades seeming to hang in the air. Somerville saw it as well and spun towards the corner of the hangar where it had come from, but before he could open fire, both projectiles reached their target, exploding with eardrum-shattering reverberations. A jet of flame lanced out from the fuel tank of a Transit van parked beside the wall of the hangar. The other grenade struck the fuselage of the plane and within seconds flames and oily black smoke had started to pour from the stricken aircraft. As the grenades struck, I forced my screaming muscles into action, swivelling around to sweep Scribner's feet out from under him, toppling him into Somerville. I squirmed sideways and grabbed the AN 90. Out of the corner of my eye I saw the man that had been guarding Sasha holding his face in evident agony, and Sasha grabbing the GP25 from Curley, sending the crippled man sprawling backwards out of his wheelchair so that he lay on the ground, arms moving feebly like some malicious beetle. Donna was looking around her in alarm.

'What's the matter, college girl?' I said, as I whirled the butt of the AN 90 into Somerville's jaw. 'Never seen a little fight before?' Her mouth tightened in fury and suddenly she was no longer beautiful. With one swift movement she brought her hand up to face level. She was holding a can of mace. It was a swift movement but I had the momentum. Just as she pressed the button I caught her hand with the butt of the AN 90. The impact was enough to turn the nozzle of the spray back on to her own face. With a scream of pain she dropped the can and reeled away, her hands covering her eyes. As Scribner attempted to get up I kicked the rifle away from him. Liam was in the open now, raining automatic fire on Somerville's men.

'Cover Sasha,' he yelled. 'Let him do the demolition.' One of the armed men ran towards me. I brought the AN90 to bear on him and felt the peculiar double kick as two bullets were fired almost simultaneously. The front of the man's flak jacket exploded and he flew backwards. I saw Sasha working his way down the fuselage, firing grenade after grenade into it. In seconds it seemed the choking black smoke had filled the entire hangar, and I found myself firing at shapes that emerged from the blackness. The entire shoreside wall of the hangar was a mass of flames. If we were to get out of here, it would have to be by sea. There was an eruption of flame as Sasha targeted the mobile chemical lab, and then a man ran past me, his torso a mass of flame, his head seemingly untouched but wreathed in blue chemical flame, his mouth open in a wordless scream.

'Pull back!' I yelled. 'Pull back!' I didn't think I would be heard over the roar of the flames and the muffled explosions coming from the fuselage of the aircraft, but suddenly Sasha and Liam were either side of me, their faces smoke-blackened, Liam firing from the hip and Sasha pumping his remaining grenades into the smoke. And then suddenly a sharp gust of icy wind from the lough parted the smoke like a curtain and a hellish tableau unfolded in front of us. It seemed that flames billowed from every corner of the hangar. Three or four men lay dead in various parts of the building. I saw Curley crawling frantically away from his upturned wheelchair. A plume of dark smoke rose high in the air above the building. Of Somerville and Scribner there was no sign. Then Liam touched my arm.

'Look,' he said softly, pointing. Fifty yards away I saw Donna. She was running along the dock, her hands still pressed to eyes rendered sightless by the mace. She could not have been more than two feet from the edge, and the sixty-foot drop to the bare concrete exposed by the ebb tide, but she ran straight and true, unaware of the danger, and it seemed for a few moments that she might make it. Then I saw the mooring bollard in front of her. I couldn't help it. I called out her name and it seemed as if she might even have heard me, for her hands dropped from her face and she lifted her swollen eyes to the cold wind. Then her foot struck the hard metal of the bollard and she veered one foot, two feet to her left and suddenly the ground disappeared from under her. I watched as she plummeted soundlessly from the dock, her hair billowing out behind her, almost graceful, and I thought for a moment of the girl who flung herself from the dark tower to join her lover in eternity. But no welcoming hands rose from the dark tide to catch Donna McNeill. I stared at the spot where her crumpled body lay upon the concrete, until the wind died away again and a veil of dirty smoke hid the scene from our eyes.

'Come on,' Liam said urgently. 'We're done here.' We followed Liam as he turned and raced towards the water's edge.

'There aren't any boats,' I said dully.

'There are now,' Liam said. In front of us I saw one of the elderly ferries that used to carry throngs of day-trippers the short distance across the lough to Omeath. The day-tripper trade had died away, but the ferries still creaked across the lough at the weekends. The one Liam had commandeered was a thirty-foot deep-bellied skiff with a clinker-built hull and wide bench seats which were completely open to the elements. Her ancient diesel engine was running and we leapt on board as Liam eased her into reverse, then swung her round towards the far shore.

It was a short trip but the tide was running hard against her and her pace could be described as stately at best. We were halfway across when I heard a noise like heavy raindrops falling in the water alongside us. I looked up and saw men firing from the shore. Sasha braced the GP25 against the bench and fired off a curved trajectory round.

'Last one,' he said.

'More in my rucksack,' Liam said.

'Trouble astern,' I said. The minesweeper had launched one of its semi-rigids and the fast little boat was speeding towards us, packed to the gunwales, it seemed, with armed marines. The AN90 was a better weapon for this. I leaned it across the seat and switched to single shot. A plume of water rose beside the semi-rigid, and she seemed to slow. Meanwhile Sasha's first round had landed close enough to the men on shore to spoil their aim, and another one was on its way. Liam had the throttle cranked up as high as it would go and smoke belched from the exhaust.

'Don't blow her engine!' I shouted to him. He grinned and shook his head. A bullet gashed the gunwale beside my hand and I fired off another couple of rounds at the marines. I didn't particularly want to hit them. Killing a covert operative was one thing. The risk was part of the job – after a decent interval a death notice would appear, noting your tragic death in a car crash or something equally banal. But the military didn't like their people getting killed in what seemed to them like spook vendettas, and they would demand their pound of flesh if one of their men went down. But I needn't have worried. The semi-rigid slowed, then, with a roar of its engine, it turned towards the far shore. The message was clear. It would take Somerville's men across the lough and let them carry the fight to us. The marines weren't going to risk their lives.

It gave us a breathing space, and Liam feathered the straining engine down slightly.

'What's the plan?' I asked.

'A hike over the mountain to Edentubber is the only option,' he said. 'About seven miles. It could be rough with them boys behind us.'

'We'll manage,' I said. 'Thanks for back there.' An image of Donna's body plummeting from the dock seemed imprinted on my retina. I rubbed my eyes, suddenly becoming aware of every bruised fibre.

'You all right?' Liam asked, concern in his voice.

'I suppose,' I said wearily. 'What made you suspect?'

'Donna? It was the way she was watching last night when we were talking about the details of the operation. Like she was memorising everything. There was more to it than that, though. I can't explain it. Something rotten in her . . . I'm sorry, Jack.'

I shook my head. I knew better than to go against the almost psychic ability Liam had to see to the core of a person. Perhaps it was something I should have seen myself.

'It wasn't just that, though. I caught her going through my rucksack later. She said she thought it was yours, and I nearly swallowed it, but along with the rest . . .'

'That was the reason she looked surprised when we rescued

her,' I said. 'We weren't meant to be there. Somerville hadn't captured her. He was taking her out. Her job was done.'

Liam killed the engine and the boat slowed as it approached the shore, the bow burying itself in the mud with a soft sound. I looked back. The semi-rigid was wheeling away from the shore.

'Time to get out of here,' I said. We scrambled up the bank and into the scrubby trees that lined the lough. Behind me I heard fire engines screaming down the dual carriageway towards the docks, where a great plume of smoke drifted seawards. No doubt it would be described as an industrial accident. I wondered silently if I had fulfilled my promise of justice for the young girl who had died in my arms at Newcastle. No, I thought. There was no such thing as perfect justice in this work, anyway. I turned and started to haul my tired bones up the mountain.

SEVENTEEN

We crossed the small road which led along the side of the lough and ducked into the trees at the other side. Just as the other shore of the lough was industrial, this shore was mountainous, partly covered with pine trees and relatively uninhabited. Liam and Sasha were moving fast, but I quickly realised I couldn't keep up. It felt as if I had torn the muscle between my ribs, and when I looked at my ankle I realised that it was badly swollen. I had to lean on Liam's shoulder to climb and even then every step sent a jolt of pain through my body.

Halfway up the hill I told them to stop. I took my old Leicas from my rucksack and steadied myself against a tree. The pursuit was closer than I thought. I counted the men as they came up through the trees, fast and silent, sure of where they were going. Seven, I made out, and then, striding effortlessly along at the rear, came the lawyer Scribner. As I focused on his face, he stopped and seemed almost to sniff the air, as though he sensed my presence. The eyes were hooded, feral, a predator in his element. Then I saw what he had in his hand. It was a microwave receiver. Somehow they had got a bug on either Liam or Sasha so that they could track the two men. Curley had held Sasha's GP25 for a while, and perhaps he had jarked it. But that didn't seem likely. I remembered Liam had said that he had seen Donna at his rucksack. She had slipped a bug into it somewhere. As I watched, one of the men turned to Scribner. He glanced at the receiver in his hand, then urged them up the hill with a curt gesture. After one final look around he followed them. I grabbed Liam's rucksack and went through it quickly. I couldn't find anything. There wasn't time to start a proper search. We either had to stand and fight or make for Edentubber and the border.

'They can always bring in more men,' Liam said. 'We have to get out of here.'

I can't remember much of the next four hours. By the time we got to the top of the hill the pain was so bad that I could barely put my foot on the ground. But worse than that was a kind of weakness which seemed to seep into my bones. Liam and Sasha were hunted men, but at least they looked alive, alert to every noise and nuance of their situation. To me it seemed as if the whole world was dull and grey and featureless, and I think that if Liam and Sasha hadn't been there I would have sat down and waited for the pursuers to catch up. There is probably a name for what I was feeling, a way of describing it in terms of psychological stress, but I don't think a psychologist would have done me any good. Deirdre would have suggested a priest, and she would have been closer. I had been betrayed by a close friend, then by my lover, and I had just seen her die violently. I was sick and weary down to my very soul, as close to broken as I had ever been. Sasha and Liam both knew what was happening to me. They had seen it on the battlefield before.

Sasha unslung the GP 25 and fitted one of the frog anti-personnel grenades. We watched it arc into the sky and drop into the forest. He fitted another.

'We have to find some transport,' Liam said urgently. He put my arm over his shoulder and we started to struggle down the other side of the hill. It took all of Liam's considerable fieldcraft to keep us out of range of Scribner's sniper's rifle. We moved along the line of ditches, or of dry stone walls. We used small plantations of fir trees and scrubby riverbank margins. But this meant we weren't following a straight line, and the pursuit was getting closer. At one stage they were actually between us and the house at Edentubber, until Liam used the railway line to lead them away. I could hear traffic in the middle distance and wondered, vaguely, at people going about their ordinary lives while we played out this desperate game.

'That's what we need,' Liam said suddenly, pointing at a farmyard on a hill above us. I couldn't see what he was talking about, but I hobbled along in a daze of pain as he set out for the farm.

We skirted the boundary wall of the farm. I could hear a machine working in the yard. Liam let me slip to the ground and motioned to Sasha. They disappeared into the yard. I got to my feet and looked after them. There was a JCB Farm Master in the yard – a large earthmoving machine converted for farm use. I could see Liam gesticulating with his gun, telling the driver to get down. The young man climbed down from the cab, and went with Liam and Sasha. There was a heavy metal plate covering an open drain in the yard, and they struggled to lift it. It took me a moment to work out what they were doing as they manipulated it on to the cab and propped it against the rear windscreen. Rudimentary armour, I realised, to protect the driver from bullets. I glanced behind me and to my horror saw Scribner's men only fifty yards away. I was hidden from them by a fold in the land, but not for long. I ducked inside the farm wall and gesticulated urgently to Liam. He seemed to understand. He got behind the controls with Sasha standing on the footrest beside him, like some modern-day bandit. He gunned the powerful diesel and swung the Farm Master around, and I realised that there was a large round bale of silage, wrapped in black plastic, impaled on the two forks which replaced the digger bucket.

Liam powered the machine through the farm gates, and gunfire broke out from down the hill. I could hear bullets thudding into the silage bale, which shielded the driver. Liam sped towards the downward slope at full revs, then suddenly rammed on the brakes while simultaneously dropping the massive bale. The bale hit the slope at speed and picked up momentum. I saw Scribner and his men scramble to get out of the way. One man was standing on a small patch of shale. As he tried to move, the shale gave way beneath him. The silage bale hit a small rise and bounced high in the air. It seemed to hang there for ever. You could see that the man on the ground knew what was coming. He stared transfixed as the bale plummeted towards him. Then it hit him, slamming him into the ground with a sickening thud.

Sasha grabbed me and swung me up into the cab, and the vehicle lurched forward. In the middle distance I could see the clump of trees surrounding the house at Edentubber, half a mile away through the small fields. Liam swung the machine towards the first field, aiming not at the gate but at the dry-stone wall. With an almighty crash and an impact that threw me forward into Liam's back, the machine demolished the wall, and we were in the first field. Halfway across there was a loud clang at my back and then another, as bullets struck the metal plate which Liam and Sasha had manoeuvred into the cab. Sasha answered with a hail of bullets, but it was impossible for him to aim properly as the machine bounced and swayed across the field. We hit another wall hard and broke through. More bullets struck the metal plate. The machine yawed wildly as Liam gunned it over an earth mound, then through a small stand of pine trees, which sent huge shards of timber high into the air.

Bullets were striking the machine again, but this time they were aimed at the radiator of the rear-engined JCB. As we tore up the hill towards the house, the engine note became ragged and there was a smell of burning. I risked a glance back. Black smoke was billowing from the engine. We crashed through a thick hawthorn hedge and on to the lane leading to the house. The engine stopped, then caught again. There was a stone horse-trough to the side of the lane. Liam swerved to try to avoid it, but the front wheel caught it and turned it on its end, so that it speared into the rear suspension, wrecking it. The whole machine began to slew sideways. But still it went on, flames coming from under the engine cover now. We were at the house. Liam tried to brake but the brake lines had gone. We narrowly missed the end of the house and hit the slope behind it sideways. It was too much. The machine reared up on two wheels, then toppled over. I was thrown on top of Liam and my full weight fell on my injured foot. I heard the snap before I passed out.

*

When I came to I was lying on the floor in the kitchen, the place wreathed in gun smoke. Afterwards I found out that Liam and Sasha had carried me in, and had found Kate waiting anxiously in the kitchen. There was no sign of Deirdre. They told Kate about the pursuit. She said nothing, but started moving furniture against the windows and barricading doors. The pursuit had only been five minutes behind, and they barely had time to fortify the place. Liam saw the first of the pursuers flitting across the bottom of the garden in the twilight, then the gunfire began. It was like a western for a while, Liam said, with Kate reloading weapons and handing them to the two men while they kept up a continuous barrage of fire.

We would have been lost had not Sasha produced two old but serviceable night scopes for the two weapons. They weren't able to calibrate them, but at least they could see. I couldn't tell how long this lasted. I was drifting in and out of consciousness, but more than that, a terrible lethargy seemed to have come over me. I watched my friends fight with a terrible lack of interest. The windows of the cottage were shot in, lumps of plaster had been lifted from the walls and ceiling. There were gaping holes in the timber doors and still the fire kept coming. When it seemed that they were exhausted and could fire no more, I saw Sasha hand his gun to Kate. Keep firing, he told her, you don't have to hit anything. He took a long-bladed knife from his pack, rolled out of the bedroom window and was gone.

Liam and Kate kept firing, and then, over the noise of combat, there rose a man's scream, a scream which reached an unearthly pitch, dying away into an eerie moan. I could feel the hairs on the back of my neck stand up, as if some ancient beast had come marauding out of the thick pine woods near by and had taken prey. The firing outside stopped, as if there was some uncertainty among the attackers. Moments later Sasha slipped back through the window. His face was sprayed with fresh arterial blood. I thought that the gentle Kate would be appalled. Instead she reached for a towel and, almost tenderly, wiped the blood from his face.

After that, the tactics of the men outside changed. They seemed content to sit back, firing the occasional aimed shot at the windows if they thought they detected movement inside. Enough to keep the nerves of those inside frayed, until at last, tired out, Liam moved too close to a window. The shot that came through the window narrowly missed him, but it struck the heavy old mirror behind him, shattering it. I turned my head to see Liam sitting on the ground, a heavy shard of glass buried deep in his shoulder, his face pale.

The best thing would have been to leave the glass in the shoulder, immobilise the patient and take him to hospital. None of these options were available. While Sasha held Liam still, Kate grasped the glass and wrenched it from his shoulder. Liam gasped in pain as Kate stood ready to stanch the blood from whatever main blood vessel had been punctured. They were lucky. Blood oozed from the wound, but there was no arterial spurt. Kate bandaged him up as best she could, but he still only had the use of his left arm. The night stretched on.

'What are they doing?' Kate had asked.

'Waiting for first light,' I said. They all turned to look at me as if they had forgotten that I was there. 'They have no night vision gear and they know that the dark gives us an advantage.' Kate went to the sink and fetched me a glass of water. I moved to take it, but the pain from my foot swept through me again.

'Don't move,' she said gently and put the glass to my lips.

'I think he has a fever,' I heard her say, as if from a long distance. I let my head fall back against the wall and slept.

They came in the first grey light of dawn, a withering fire raining down on the house, the front door kicked off its hinges and a stun grenade rolled in. I half-woke from a fever dream to see Sasha kick it back out again and follow it with a grenade of his own from the GP25. But he hadn't noticed that the stun grenade had caught on the door jamb. It went off, half in and half out of the house. Sasha reeled back, half deafened and disorientated. Someone was trying to push through the window blocked by the wardrobe, and Liam aimed a burst of fire through it. Followed by another burst of fire into the roof where he heard footsteps. But still they kept coming, filling the doorway with a hail of lethal fire that none could survive. I saw Liam's AK clicking on an empty cylinder. He reached for a new magazine but there was none. He pulled the Beretta from his pocket and fired aimed shots. A bullet struck Sasha's GP 25, wrecking the mechanism. He flung it aside and grabbed his knife from his belt. Kate crouched on the floor, eyes wide, in a house wreathed in gun smoke. I tried to get to my feet, but I was too weak, the broken foot too painful.

That was when we heard the first shot outside. A shot that sounded different from the deadly, high-pitched crack of the attacker's guns. More of a boom, a sound that echoed through the empty valley below the house. Then another, then another. The attackers' guns had fallen silent, and a familiar voice rang out, shouting words of hatred and pity. I crept to the door and peered out. Through the gun smoke, in the grey morning light, I saw a figure striding down the path that led from the mountain, a figure totally exposed yet seemingly invulnerable, a pump-action shotgun – a Remington Wingmaster – grasped in both hands. As we heard the voice again, we saw Deirdre's face, anguished but resolute beyond anything we had ever seen, as she lifted the gun to her shoulder and fired again.

'This is my house, you bastards!' she cried out. 'This is my house, I was born here!'

With a yell Liam charged out of the door. A man rose from the bushes by the gate, seemingly confused, and Liam cut him down with the pistol. Then Liam fell to the ground, blood pumping from his shoulder. I looked behind me. Sasha's head had been cut and blood was streaming down into his eyes. Kate was vainly trying to stanch it. I looked up. The attackers had regrouped. I could see three men moving cautiously through the gun smoke.

'Get up,' Deirdre yelled at me, tears streaming down her face. 'Get up and fight, you bastard!' Somehow I managed to get to my feet, the door jamb supporting me. She grabbed a sub-machine-gun that one of the attackers had dropped and thrust it into my hand.

'Wait,' I said. I called to Sasha to come out. He fumbled towards me, almost blinded. I put my arm over his shoulder.

'I'll be your eyes,' I said, 'if you can keep me upright.'

Together the three of us drove forward through the smallholding as though eradicating vermin, driving the attackers back to the narrow roadway. They kept up a hail of fire, but we burned with a fury that seemed invincible, indifferent to the lead-filled air around us, and somehow this communicated to the attackers, so that you could see their resolve weaken as they backed away, carrying their dead as they went, with at least two others injured. The lawyer Scribner took up the rear, firing from the hip as he went, his face a mask of anger and frustration, until at last he slipped in the mud and the rifle fell from his hand – and he found himself staring up into my eyes and into the muzzle of my gun.

'Do it, Valentine,' he growled. 'Damn you, pull the trigger.' I moved the muzzle to the right a little, the better to train on the lawyer's head, but at the last minute Deirdre's hand touched the barrel and moved it gently aside.

'No more,' she murmured gently. 'I couldn't stand any more.' I stared into the lawyer's eyes for a moment more, then lifted the gun away from him. Scribner scrambled back away from us, then turned, his tall figure hunched over, and fled, casting hate-filled glances behind him as he ran. Sasha leaned back against a tree and watched him run. I put my arms around Deirdre and she buried her face in my chest. As we stood there the sun rose, pale and defiant, over the hills to the east. Kate walked slowly down the garden with Liam, his wound stanched for the moment. She put her hand in Sasha's hand and together we stood in silence as winter sunlight began to flood the valley.

EIGHTEEN

The first thing I saw when I woke up was a bunch of artificial flowers. They reminded me of graveyards, and I swiftly looked away. The next prospect wasn't much better. It was a young man in a blue suit. The sort of young man wearing the sort of blue suit you might meet in any American embassy anywhere in the world. I decided that I'd better try again. I knew that in the end I would have to look at the young American, but I wasn't in any hurry. I gazed around the room. It was a plain, clean hospital room. My view was partially obscured by the metal cage that kept the bedclothes off my newly pinned-together ankle.

It wasn't the first time I had woken, but it was the first time that I'd done so without being in a haze of drugs and pain. I vaguely remembered being found on the mountain by Deirdre and Sasha, and being carried to the car. After that was a blur of white coats and antiseptic smells. I did remember that Deirdre told me I was safe. And I remembered that she had bent and kissed me on the cheek before I had slipped out of consciousness again.

I was suddenly aware of being ravenously hungry, and realised that, before I could see to the hunger, I would have to see to my guest. Reluctantly I looked back in his direction. He wore the same expression, managing to combine patience and superiority.

'I take it Stone sent you?' I said.

'Mr Stone did indeed instruct me,' he said.

'To lavish praise on me for the service I did for your country?' I said.

'Mr Stone didn't go that far,' he said.

'What? No pension for life?'

'His instructions were to assure you that the arrangements agreed would be adhered to,' he said stiffly. Arrangements? I thought. I suppose the lifting of his threat would amount to an arrangement.

'What about Somerville?' I said. 'He's not going to take this lying down.' Particularly, I thought, since this was the second time I had done this to him.

'By the time Mr Somerville has explained his conduct,' he said smoothly, 'he will not have the time to bother you, even if he did have the inclination.'

'He had no approval for this job?' I said. The young man smiled slightly, the way you do when a child says something naïve. Even if Somerville had tacit approval, it would be denied when the job went wrong. A fiasco like this would be the end of the line for Somerville, I suspected. Although he had wriggled out of things before.

'A fascinating operation,' the young man said. 'Almost baroque in its complexity.'

Baroque? I thought sourly, thinking of the trail of death the whole thing had left behind.

'Is that it?' I said.

'More or less,' he said. 'The evidence has been destroyed.

Apart, of course, from the phial of blood.'

'The phial of blood was a fake,' I said.

'Nevertheless it is still a phial of blood contaminated with tabun and cyclo-sarin,' he said. 'It could still point to the existence of the Black Cat Black Dog operation.'

'Is that what you're calling it now?'

'It seems apt. The blood, Mr Valentine?'

'If you didn't take it, and Somerville didn't take it, then I don't know where it is,' I said.

'Stone thought you would deny it. He also said that holding on to it for insurance purposes would be most unwise.'

'I don't have it.'

'Well, I suppose in your position I would say the same.' I kept my mouth shut. Was it better to be a well-dressed, well-spoken, amoral thug like him, or a man with pretensions to conscience like myself, who seemed to leave nothing but destruction in his wake?

'By the way,' he said as he reached the door, 'you'll find something welcome in your bedside locker.'

'What did you do?' I asked. 'Search the room when I was sleeping?'

'Yes,' he said, smiling, 'as a matter of fact I did.'

He left. I resisted looking in the locker until I was sure that he was gone. There was a basket inside. When I opened it, there was one of Kate's macrobiotic meals. I couldn't have told you what was in it, apart from brown rice and soy sauce, but it was simple and delicious and I wolfed it down, knowing that she had probably put it together specifically for the healing of fractured bones. As I put the plate down, the door opened and Kate came in.

'Is he gone?' she asked.

'The CIA man? Gone about ten minutes.'

'Good. I'm sorry, I couldn't stay in the room with him any more.'

'Bad karma?'

'Something like that,' she said. 'How are you feeling?'

'Better after the food,' I said. 'What about Liam and Deirdre?'

'Liam's shoulder is stiff and sore, but not too bad. Deirdre – I don't know. She doesn't talk much, but they're fixing up Edentubber, which is helping, I think. I don't think she really believes she went bursting into the place with a shotgun in her hand.'

'And Sasha?' I think she blushed when I said that, but she turned away quickly so I couldn't be sure.

'We – he has the little boy with him. That part of it is good. The bad part is that we have to bury his sister-in-law tomorrow.'

'So the little boy is on his own,' I said.

'No, Jack,' she said, 'not on his own.' I put my hand on her arm.

'Neither is his mother, I suppose,' she continued.

'What do you mean?'

'They found Sasha's friend Dimitri. The body washed up. He'll be buried in the next grave. The little boy knows his mother is in heaven. It gives him comfort to think that she'll have some company.'

'Dimitri . . .?'

'Sasha saw the body. There was a clear bullet hole in the skull. But the cause of death was put down as drowning. Your lot always cover their tracks, don't they, Jack?'

'Most of the time.'

'I forgot. Sasha said to tell you – I have to remember this – that it was a copper-jacketed .303 round, I think, that killed Dimitri . . . then something about hollow point?' I nodded. A sniper's bullet.

The next day was raw and sleety. I insisted on discharging myself. The reassuringly old-fashioned ward sister refused to let me go, to the point of locking away my clothes, so I started off down the hallway in a hospital gown. My ankle was held together by a medieval-looking cage contraption which made it almost impossible to walk without crutches. We compromised in the end. She would get me clothes and crutches and I would wait for the ward rounds. After the consultant had inspected his handiwork and advised me to get back into bed, I started to get dressed. The sister, who I was starting to like, accused me of immaturity, but softened when I told her where I was going. She helped me to get dressed and sent me off in a wheelchair. At the front door of the hospital I hailed a taxi.

I can't ever remember a funeral where the sun shone, and this one was no exception. The small graveyard was on a hillside to the north of Drogheda, exposed to the bitter north-west wind, and you could see sheets of hailstones marching in across the Meath plain. The taxi dropped me in the car park. The first person I saw was Whitcroft.

'Well,' he said wryly, 'I hear you created your usual quota of mayhem.'

'What about you?' I asked. 'Was your investigation successful?'

'How can you call it successful when you have this?' He nodded towards the church.

'Those two boys are dead, the people traffickers,' he went on, 'but there are plenty more like them. As a matter of interest, do you know who killed them?'

'Somerville. He must have been working with them, then they outlived their usefulness.'

'Those people in the container would be alive now if it wasn't for him, then?'

'You're a good cop, Whitcroft,' I said, 'but your jurisdiction only extends so far.'

I looked up and saw Liam and Deirdre coming towards us. Liam had his arm in a sling and Deirdre was pale, with dark shadows under her eyes. Deirdre greeted Whitcroft warmly, and the policeman and Liam exchanged wary handshakes. Then Sasha arrived, looking sad and handsome in a dark suit. We followed him into the church.

It seemed a poor turnout, I thought. The priest rattled through the mass and the wind whistled through the old church, and Sasha looked pinched and far away. As the coffins were wheeled from the church, Sasha put his hand on his friend's coffin and walked beside it. Then I realised that someone was singing. I looked around and saw that it was Deirdre singing 'Ave Maria', the pure and inflected sound rising in the ancient building and seeming to fill it.

Outside, the coffins were loaded into two hearses. Deirdre linked my arm as we walked behind. After we had covered a little distance I realised that more people had joined the cortège. And then, as we reached the cemetery gate, the crowd swelled again. I couldn't figure out where they had come from.

As we gathered around the freshly dug graves, I scanned the faces in the crowd and realised they were the fruit-pickers, the stevedores, the factory workers, the deckhands – the immigrant poor who had flooded the country to do the jobs that no one else wanted, coming legally on bonded labour contracts or illegally in the backs of trucks. Some of the women were still wearing their chambermaid uniforms from the rash of new hotels, others – the lap dancers and allied trades – were shivering in short skirts and high heels. The wind carried the priest's words away, but it didn't matter, I thought. It mattered that two displaced people were not allowed to pass alone into the far country. Sasha was standing ramrod straight, as if he were on some far-off parade ground, and when the priest stopped he saluted, and held it. I looked up towards the hillside and saw Kate standing there, her hand on the shoulder of a little boy.

The mourners seemed reluctant to go, and we stood there in silence for what seemed like an hour. Then they dispersed, reluctantly it seemed, to their cheap flats and shabby workplaces. I walked back with Deirdre.

'I wish I could understand what it was all about,' she said.

'As far as I can see,' I said, 'there was an operation to put a chemical lab into Iraq to provide evidence of WMD. It was an American operation, but Somerville knew about it all along, even provided them with material. Then he sabotaged the flight.'

'Why?'

'To understand that, Deirdre, you have to know how people like Somerville think. He wanted, I suppose, control over other people who think the way he does. He would be able to spring a scandal that would be bigger than Iran Contra, bigger than Watergate. The administration wouldn't be able to survive it if it got out. That gives you immense power in the spook world. In any world.'

'But now it's over.'

'Yes, except for one detail. That phial of blood.' We walked along in silence for a moment, then she turned to me.

'Did you love her?' she said abruptly.

'Donna?' I said slowly, 'No . . . no, I don't think I did. I liked her. But I suppose . . . if you did love somebody that much, then the shock of that betrayal . . . No . . . I didn't love her. And you?'

I looked at her. Her eyes were bright with tears, which I suppose was answer enough.

'Yes . . . yes, I did. If . . . well, let's say if I applied your test . . . if he had betrayed me the way she betrayed you, I would have died, I think. At least this way I have some memories.' She turned to me and there was a kind of pleading in her eyes. She was too intuitive not to know there was something wrong about McCrink's death.

'He was a good man,' I said. 'I'll miss him.' Looking back, I wonder if he had ever been a good man, but when a friend is lying to himself, sometimes there is a duty to go along with the lie. Besides, I didn't think I was necessarily in a position to pass judgement on my treacherous, dead friend.

'What are you going to do now?' she said.

'I don't know,' I admitted. 'Get back to the *Castledawn* and sail her back to Scotland, I suppose.'

'Not like that,' she said, looking at my ankle.

'It might be tough,' I admitted. In truth I felt pretty weak. Not just the surgery, but the battering my body had taken in the container, had left me feeling that it was going to take a long time to recover.

'Come and stay in Edentubber for a while,' she said. 'No strings, no attachments, no hand-holding . . . well, maybe hand-holding.'

So I went back to Edentubber. I stayed for a week. The weather was fine and clear. Liam worked on the roof and windows, and I painted, and when I got too tired to hold a paint-brush I cooked, and then the three of us talked long into the night. Sometimes Deirdre would ask me something about McCrink and the times we had spent together, and I would tell long, glorious lies while Liam watched me with a wry, patient smile. She also questioned me about Donna in a dogged, feminine way which seemed to amuse Liam.

'Was she really a forensic pathologist?' she asked one night.

'I think so,' I said. 'She was able to test the DNA in the finger bone. And it would have been good cover.' Good cover for a covert operative, I thought, and appropriate. Down among the gruesome bits.

And then one night, when we had eaten well and polished off a few bottles of Château Beauséjour, Liam went to bed. Deirdre was sitting by the fire, and I was in an armchair with my leg propped up, when she asked me another, blunter question.

'Did you sleep with her?'

'No,' I lied.

'Don't lie,' she said, smiling. From where I was sitting the smell of her perfume reached me. She turned her head towards mine and held my gaze. The years seemed for a moment to drop away to the first time we had met, and had stayed in Edentubber. Then my mobile went off. I tried not to curse.

'Answer it,' she said. I looked at the number. It was a Larne code. I pressed the green button. It was Davy Wilson.

'Mr Wilson,' I said, 'you picked a fairly late time to call.'

'The old don't need as much sleep,' he said impatiently. 'So do you want to hear my news about your friend's brother and his ship?'

'I do,' I said, sitting up. 'Sorry, Mr Wilson . . .'

'That's all right,' he said. 'Now listen to this.' I listened intently for a long time. When I hung up I rang Jimmy and told him to take the one-thirty flight to Aldergrove the next day.

'At least I can solve one small mystery,' I said. I told her what Davy Wilson had said.

'Does your past always catch up with you?' Deirdre asked.

'I don't know,' I said. 'Sometimes, sometimes not.' She stood up.

'Well, maybe I should keep running from ours,' she said, kissing me fondly on the forehead as she passed, and then I heard the living-room door close behind her.

Jimmy was waiting apprehensively at the airport when we arrived. Deirdre was driving, and Davy Wilson was sitting in the back. I needed the extra foot-room in the front for my ankle.

'Who's he?' Jimmy said gruffly, nodding his head towards Wilson. I explained that Wilson had helped track the captain of HMS *Opal*.

'HMS what?' Jimmy said.

'Honestly, I think it's better if the captain tells you himself, Jimmy.' Jimmy sat stiffly in the back beside Wilson, who maintained an injured silence. That was a good start, I thought to myself. Deirdre grinned at me. She gunned the Alfa GTA down the airport road, and left rubber on the series of roundabouts leading towards Craigavon. Soon the two old men seemed to have forgotten their wounded pride and were virtually clinging to each other. My ankle was stiff and sore, and I had to stop every hour or so to stretch it. So I asked Deirdre to pull in. We screeched to a halt in the car park of a small wayside bar. While I stumped about, Deirdre brought the two men inside and, without asking, ordered small bottles of Guinness each with whiskey chasers. Within minutes she had charmed the two of them into wartime reminiscences, reminiscences which continued in the back of the car until we reached the gates of the small nursing home behind the area hospital.

We found Captain Elliot in a small sunroom to the rear of the nursing home. He was sitting in a wing-back chair, his legs covered with a blanket. He must have been in his late eighties, but there was an authority about the long, aquiline face and the deep-set blue eyes that made the two seamen look as if they were about to snap to attention. Wilson took over the job of the introductions. With a wave of his hand, Elliot indicated that we should sit. He closed his eyes as though gathering his thoughts, then he sat up. He looked as if he was about to speak, then he hesitated.

'May I see your brother's dog tags, Mr Kerr?' Silently Jimmy handed them over to him. Captain Elliot ran his fingers over the sea-corroded surface of the tags, then gave them back.

'So many men,' he said.

'Thirty-five, sir,' Wilson said.

'That many? I'm sorry. I had forgotten. I forget quite a lot these days. But I don't forget the *Jane Goode*.'

After the war, he explained, his ageing destroyer had been assigned to various dogsbody tasks before being turned over to experiments involving chemical weapons. Without looking at her, Elliot read Deirdre's disapproving expression.

'They were different times, young lady. They had them, so we had to have them.'

'That's what they said too,' Deirdre said.

'Perhaps we'll have the ethics argument some other time,' I said.

'Tell me,' Jimmy said hoarsely. There was a pause, then Elliot began again. He explained how they had been dispatched to a bleak Hebridean island.

'The brief was to test methods of delivering chemical weapons. In other words, loading the damn stuff into shells and firing them at this island to see what happened.'

The *Jane Goode* had been the support ship in the exercise. She had carried supplies and scientific equipment. The island, Elliot explained, was long and low, but only five or six hundred yards across.

'The *Jane Goode* was told to hold position off the end of the island,' he said, 'and on no account to be in the fire zone, which was the middle of the island.'

I could see what was coming. The unravelling of what had seemed like a conspiracy. How many times does a simple mistake become an historic conspiracy through the desire of civil servants to cover up?

'We were firing in fog, which was a mistake. I can't remember what was in the shells – sarin, I think. Anyway, the *Jane Goode* had drifted down towards the centre of the island. We were firing shells at low trajectory. Not low enough. One shell missed the land altogether, flew across the centre of the island and struck the *Jane Goode* amidships.'

There was a long silence in the room. I could hear a clock ticking. Jimmy turned the dog tags over and over in his hands.

'We didn't even realise until the next morning,' Elliot went on. 'We found her drifting. All hands were dead.'

'How did she end up at the Beaufort Dyke?' I said.

'We got a line on board – a man in a chemical suit. The scientists thought that the compound might be inactive, but we couldn't be sure. We towed her to the Beaufort Dyke and put a high-explosive shell into her. She wouldn't sink. We fired on her again and again. By the time she did sink she had drifted a mile.'

'Enough to take her into shallow water.'

'Yes.' The old man's face was grey with the effort of talking, but he turned to Jimmy.

'I'm sorry,' he said.

'I just wanted to know,' Jimmy said. 'Do you understand? Before I died. I needed to know what happened to him.'

'Yes,' Elliot said, 'I know.'

We sat there for another few minutes. There didn't really seem to be anything more to say. Elliot's head slipped forward and his breathing became gentle and even,

'Come on,' Jimmy said. 'Let the man rest.'

We went out into the grounds of the nursing home. It was a fine, cold day and the trees stood stiff and bare, framing a path which led down to a small river. Jimmy muttered something and wandered off down the path. We let him go.

'How did you find Elliot?' I asked Wilson.

'He found me. He found out I was enquiring and rang me,' Wilson said. It seemed that Elliot's desire to tell the truth before he died was almost as strong as Jimmy's need to know that truth.

'I'll be a minute,' Wilson said. He followed Jimmy down the path and through the trees I saw him walking alongside my neighbour, their heads together in conversation. Deirdre linked my arm and helped me to walk slowly along the gravel path.

'What are you going to do now?' I asked.

'I don't know,' she said, 'I had thought of giving up the office job, coming to live in Edentubber and maybe doing field development work six months of the year. Now, I don't know. I'll stay at Edentubber for a while, but Sasha and Kate and the little boy seem to have taken over there for the time being. You?'

'Time I went home,' I said. 'I can come back for the *Castledawn*. Bill can take care of her in the meantime. In fact, I'll give him a ring.'

I dialled Bill's number on my mobile. He answered straight away. I could hear machinery in the background. I told him about my ankle, and asked if he would keep an eye on the *Castledawn*. He agreed. I started to say goodbye, but he interrupted me.

'Listen,' he said, 'you know them frozen fish you gave me to look after, the ones I put in the cold store.'

'Yes, yes, of course,' I said, trying to keep my voice from showing concern.

'Well,' he said, 'I started thinking that if I left them there, someone would lift them or drive a fork-lift over them, so I brought them home and put them in my own freezer. Do you still want them?'

I tried to hold back a wave of hysterical laughter, tried to think fast.

'Listen, Bill,' I said, 'I'd like to make a present of them to a friend of mine. He'll call to collect them.'

I hung up. Deirdre looked at me.

'What's wrong with you?' she said. 'Are you choking or something?'

'I'll be all right,' I said. 'It's just the phial of blood . . . in the package of fish . . .'

'What are you talking about?'

'Wait a minute,' I said. I dialled a number from the directory on the phone. It rang for a while and then answered.

'Stone,' the voice said.

'This is Valentine,' I said.

'Jack,' the voice said, sounding neither pleased nor displeased.

'I want one of your men to pick up a package at Bill Quinn's boatyard in Kilkeel, County Down. Tell him I sent you.'

'What's in the package, Jack?' Stone said, sounding puzzled.

'Fish,' I said. 'It's a package of fish.'

NINETEEN

It was springtime in London. I stepped out of the tube at Chancery Lane into pleasant late afternoon sunshine. The wind rustled through the leaves of the plane trees as I made my way along the street, squinting at the A-Z in my hands. The ankle had almost healed, but it wouldn't take too much stress, so I walked slowly. I was early for my appointment anyway. I liked to leave plenty of time for these things. I turned off the main thoroughfare into a side street and suddenly the noise and bustle died away, and I found myself in a narrow street lined with Tudor buildings with diamond-pane windows. It was very pleasant. Halfway along the street there was a narrow passage leading off to the right. I turned into it. There was an air of expensive services discreetly rendered about the whole street, and the impression continued to grow as the passageway opened out into a little square. There was a small railed park in the centre, the grass trimmed as if with a pair of nail scissors. The buildings around it were Georgian, each with a small brass plaque shining brightly, polished no doubt every morning. I put the A-Z into my pocket. I didn't need it any more. I knocked on one door. An intercom buzzed beside my ear. I gave my name, which for the purposes of this interview, was Black. I thought it appropriate, ironic even.

The office had the gleam of a Dutch interior, but whereas the Dutch masters understood how to fuse beauty and meaning, the effect here was bleak and loveless. As in the best and most expensive offices, I was ushered straight in. The room I entered was lined with legal tomes. There were legal certificates above the Edwardian desk. One wall held a case containing two Purdy shotguns with beautifully chased mechanisms. When Scribner turned from his desk and saw me, he smiled. It reminded me of the description of Sir Robert Peel's smile as being like the gleam of a brass plate on a coffin lid.

'Mr Valentine,' he said, 'how is the ankle?'

'The ankle is fine,' I said.

'Mr Black,' he said. 'I should have realised. Please take a seat.'

'I would rather stand,' I said. 'The ankle gets stiff.'

'Of course,' he said. 'You have some rather powerful friends. I wanted to go shooting in your part of the country – I often shoot in the Highlands. Sometimes a cull has to be carried out.'

'Who do you work for anyway?'

'Are you looking for a deathbed confession?'

'I have no intention of harming you,' I said.

'That's reassuring,' he said. 'As to your question, I act as a conduit for certain governmental interests.'

'Which government?' He laughed mirthlessly but did not reply.

'They found the girl, you know. Her body washed up.'

'Which girl?'

'Fiona Lawless.'

'Fiona . . . oh yes, the little reporter.'

'The little reporter. She was buried last week. Tell me, why did she have to be killed? She knew very little, and what she did know she couldn't really have used.'

'She was a threat,' he said. But as he spoke, his eyes darted to the Purdy shotguns on the wall. I don't think he was aware of it, but the look gave him away. He was the hunter and she was the prey. That was all I needed to know.

'You're a sentimentalist really, aren't you, Valentine? And do you know, the sentimentalist, the one who cries over dogs and little children, is really the deadliest of them all.'

'You might be right,' I said.

'On which count?' he said. 'The sentiment or the deadliness?' I didn't answer, and didn't look back as the door of his office closed behind me.

Later that evening I sat in a car in Eaton Square. It was a very exclusive address. Deirdre would have appreciated the cars, I thought, the Lamborghinis and Bentleys. Their paintwork gleamed softly in the streetlights, which seemed to emit a more refined kind of illumination than streetlights elsewhere in the town. In front of me and to my left a door opened and Sasha came out, closing it gently behind him. He was wearing an overcoat and scarf and looked as if he might be one of the wealthy Russian businessmen who owned property there.

He got into the passenger seat of my hire car. I looked at him with raised eyebrows. He muttered something in Russian.

'What?' I asked.

'Drive,' he said. 'Please drive.'

*

The following evening I was on the teatime London to Glasgow 737. I think I was the only person on the flight without a briefcase and a laptop. When the flight attendant came round I asked her for an evening newspaper and an Irish whiskey. I got the paper, but I had to settle for a Laphroaig instead of the Irish.

I opened the paper. The item I was looking for was on page five. Accidental death of prominent Queen's Counsel. Lord Chancellor expresses shock and regret. Bar Council states that he would be sadly missed. Police report that he was fatally wounded while cleaning a weapon at his home in Eaton Square. Scrivener was reported to be a keen collector of vintage firearms. Sources stated that the weapon he was cleaning was a vintage Kalashnikov, believed to have been one of the first batch ever produced. Nice touch, Sasha, I thought. I leaned back in my seat and sipped the Laphroaig. Beneath the plane the dark miles reeled away. I took another sip of the peaty whisky. Not bad, I thought, not bad at all.